CHAIN
REACTION

ALSO BY SIMONE ELKELES

Perfect Chemistry
Rules of Attraction

CHAIN REACTION

SIMONE ELKELES

SIMON AND SCHUSTER

First published in Great Britain in 2012 by Simon and Schuster UK Ltd
A CBS COMPANY

First published in the USA in 2011 by Walker Publishing Company Inc.,
a division of Bloomsbury Publishing Inc.

Copyright © 2011 Simone Elkeles
Book design by Nicole Gastonguay

This book is copyright under the Berne Convention.
No reproduction without permission.
All rights reserved.

The right of Simone Elkeles to be identified as the author and illustrator
of this work has been asserted by her in accordance with sections 77 and 78
of the Copyright, Designs and Patents Act, 1988.

1 3 5 7 9 10 8 6 4 2

Simon & Schuster UK Ltd
1st Floor, 222 Gray's Inn Road
London WC1X 8HB

Simon & Schuster Australia, Sydney
Simon & Schuster India, New Delhi

A CIP catalogue record for this book is available from the British Library.

PB ISBN 978-0-85707-747-9
eBook ISBN 978-0-85707-748-6

This book is a work of fiction. Names, characters, places and incidents
are either the product of the author's imagination or are used fictitiously.
Any resemblance to actual people living or dead,
events or locales is entirely coincidental.

Printed and bound by CPI Group (UK) Ltd, Croydon, CR0 4YY

www.simonandschuster.co.uk
www.simonandschuster.com.au

To my agent, Kristin Nelson, and my editor, Emily Easton,
for having faith in me and your unending support

CHAIN
REACTION

1
Luis

Being the youngest of three boys definitely has its advantages. I've watched my brothers get into some serious trouble when they were in high school. I was never expected to follow in their footsteps. I get straight As, I don't get into fights, and from age eleven I knew what I wanted to be when I grew up. I'm known as "the good kid" in *mi familia*—the one who's expected to never fuck up.

My friends know I have a crazy rebellious streak, but my family doesn't. I can't help it—I'm a Fuentes, and being rebellious is deeply rooted in my genes. The kid my family sees on the outside isn't necessarily what's on the inside, and I intend to keep it that way. I vowed never to stray from my ultimate goal of going to college and studying aeronautics, but taking a few physical risks every once in a while feeds that adrenaline rush I crave.

I'm standing at the bottom of a rock formation in Boulder Canyon with four of my friends. Jack Reyerson brought rock climbing gear, but I don't wait to strap on a harness. I grab one of the ropes and attach it with a carabiner on my belt loop so when I reach the summit I can anchor the rope for the rest of the group.

"It's not safe to go up without gear, Luis," Brooke says. "But you already know that, don't you?"

"Yep," I say.

I start a free solo ascent, making my way up the rock formation. This isn't the first free solo I've done at Boulder Canyon, and I've had enough training to know what the hell I'm doing. I'm not saying it's not a risk—it's just a calculated one.

"You're crazy, Luis," Jamie Bloomfield yells from below as I climb even higher. "If you fall, you'll die!"

"I just want everyone here to know that I'm not responsible if you break every bone in your body," Jack says. "I should have had you sign a liability waiver."

Jack's father is a lawyer, so he has an annoying habit of announcing his lack of responsibility about pretty much everything we do.

I don't tell them that climbing without a safety harness is an adrenaline rush. It actually makes me want to push myself harder and take more risks. Jamie called me an adrenaline junkie after I snowboarded down the black diamond slope in Vail on the winter break trip last year. I didn't tell her that fooling around with the girl I met in the lobby that night was also an adrenaline rush. Does that qualify me as a junkie?

When I'm halfway to the summit, I've got my right hand secured above me and one foot planted inside a small crevice. It's high enough to make me look down to see what I might be falling on if I do lose my grip.

"Don't look down!" Jack says in a panic. "You'll get vertigo and fall."

"And die!" Jamie adds.

Dios mío. My friends seriously need to chill. They're white, and haven't been brought up in a Mexican family full of guys who thrive on challenges and living on the edge. Even though I'm supposed to be the one Fuentes brother who's smart enough not to take risks, I feel most alive when I do.

The summit is a few feet away. I stop and look across the sky, getting a bird's-eye view of the landscape. It's fucking amazing. I used to live in Illinois, where the landscape was completely flat except for the skyscrapers. Looking out across the Colorado mountains makes me appreciate nature. The wind is at my back, the sun is high in the sky, and I feel invincible.

I reach up with my left hand and grab on to the edge of a crevice in the rock face about ten feet from the top. I'm almost there. As I scan the rock for a spot to place my foot, I feel something sharp pierce my hand.

Oh, hell. That wasn't good.

I just got bitten by something.

Instinctively, I quickly plant my foot as I snatch my hand back and glance at it. Two small puncture marks are on the back of my hand with my blood streaming out of them.

"Stop scratching your balls so we can get up there before the sun sets, Luis!" Eli Movitz screams from below.

"I hate to break the news to you guys," I call down to them as the tip of a snake's head appears above me, then sneaks back inside for cover, "but I just got bitten by a snake."

I didn't get a good look at the sucker, so I have no clue if it's venomous or not. Shit. I look down at my friends and vertigo hits almost immediately. This was not in the plan. My heart is racing and I squeeze my eyes shut, hoping to stop my head from spinning.

"Holy shit, man!" Eli yells to me. "Was it a rattler?"

"I don't know."

"What did it look like?" Jamie calls up to me. "Did it have stripes?"

"I only saw the tip of the head, and I'm not about to go back up there and get a closer look," I tell her, wondering if I should move sideways and continue the last ten feet of my ascent or attempt to go back down.

I'm a math guy, so I immediately consider the odds of surviving this situation. My hand definitely stings, but it's not numb. Surely if I was just pumped with a shitload of venom I'd start feeling numb and stiff right about now.

"I knew Luis shouldn't have free solo'd it," Jack's voice echoes from below. "I knew it! Nobody listened to me, and now he's stuck up there while venom is probably spreading throughout his body."

"Shut the fuck up, Jack!" I yell. "Snakes don't have fuckin' legs, so how was I supposed to think there'd be one hidin' in the face of a damn rock that's ten feet below the summit?"

"Do you feel, like, *normal*?" Brooke asks.

"A snake just punctured my skin with its fangs, Brooke," I say as I head back down slowly. It might be my imagination, but I think my hand is starting to get numb. "Of course I don't feel normal."

"Get a ranger with antivenom!" Jack yells to the rest of them. We'd have to drive to find one. None of us have our licenses yet, so we're screwed. Actually, I'm the only one who's screwed.

With all the talk of antivenom and rattlers, I can't think straight and lose traction.

My foot slips. Then my hand, the one without two puncture holes in it, starts sweating all of a sudden and I lose my grip. I slip down the side of the rock face and hear the gasps and screams of my friends below while I scramble to get a foothold or a hand on something solid. It's no use.

All I can think of before I hit the ground is *I'm not ready to die.*

2

"I love you, Marco."

I said it. I couldn't look into my boyfriend's deep, dark eyes as the words flowed seamlessly from my lips, because I'm also holding something back. I figured saying *I love you* as a conversation starter would be easier than saying *I might be pregnant*. It was cowardly not to look into his eyes and tell him everything, but saying those three words is a start. I feel more vulnerable than I've ever felt before.

I don't do vulnerable well.

I breathe out slowly and gather up the courage to look up at my boyfriend of a year. We lost our virginity to each other a month ago when his parents went to Mexico to visit his grandmother.

I can't even think about it now as I focus on him. *Okay, I said I love you. Your turn to say it back, like you whispered in my ear the first time we made love. Then I'll tell you I missed my period this month and I'm freaking out. Then you'll tell me everything will be okay and that we'll deal with it together.*

He's smiling. Well, kinda. The side of his mouth is quirked up, like he's amused. I wasn't going for amused. I was going for affection and adoration—signs that it was okay to tell him my secret. I look toward Lake Michigan, wishing we weren't outside and hoping nobody from our high school suddenly shows up. I wrap my arms around myself. It's not that warm in Illinois yet, and the wind off the lake is definitely making me shiver. Or maybe it's my nerves.

"You don't have to say it back to me," I say to fill the silence, but that's a complete lie. I do expect Marco to say it back to me. I don't want to hear it just on special occasions and when we're making love.

The first time he said it was after the homecoming dance back in September. Then on New Year's Eve. And on Valentine's Day. And my birthday. So many nights I lie alone in my bed and think about how our love will last forever.

We don't have the same friends because we live on different sides of Fairfield, but that's never mattered. We've made it work. After school, we usually go to my house and just . . . be with each other.

And now we might be having a baby. How is he going to take the news?

Today is the last day of our freshman year of high school before summer break. Marco suggested we go to the beach after school when I told him I needed to talk.

It makes sense, really. The beach is our special place.

We had our first kiss on the beach last summer. He asked me to be his official girlfriend there the second week of school. We made snow angels on that same beach back in January when we had a snow day. We come here to share all our private secrets, like once he told me where gang members stashed guns around town so the police wouldn't catch them carrying it. Marco has always known guys who were heavily connected.

He steps away from me, and immediately I get goose bumps as if my body knows something is up besides the wind coming off the lake. He combs his fingers through his jet-black hair. Then sighs. Twice.

"I think we should see other people," he murmurs.

I cock my head to the side. Obviously I didn't hear him right.

There are a few phrases that a girl expects to hear after she declares her love to her boyfriend. I can think of a few right off the top of my head, but *I think we should see other people* isn't one of them.

I'm stunned. And I can't stop shaking as I think about being pregnant without him at my side, smiling and telling me everything will be okay.

"W-w-why?"

"You always said you'd never date a gang member, and I'm gonna be one."

"Of course I won't date a gang member," I blurt out. "Just two days ago you told me you'd never join the gang, Marco. It was right before we made love. Remember?"

He winces. "I said a lot of things I probably shouldn't have. And could you please not call it *makin' love* . . . every time you say it like that you make me feel like shit."

"What do you want me to call it?"

"Sex."

"Just sex, huh?"

He rolls his eyes, and I swear my stomach lurches in response. "See, now you're makin' me feel like shit on purpose."

"I'm not doing it on purpose."

He opens his mouth to say something, then must think better of it, because he shuts it.

I scan his face, hoping he'll say *Just joking! Of course I pick you over the Latino Blood*, but he doesn't. My heart feels like someone is chipping away at it, piece by piece.

"We're just . . . so different."

"No we're not. We're *perfect* together. We go to the same school, we have the best time together . . . we're both Mexican."

He laughs. "You don't even speak a word of Spanish, Nikki. My parents and friends talk about you while you're in the room, and you're clueless. You're not *really* Mexican."

Is he kidding me?

My parents were born in Mexico, just like the rest of my ancestors. Nobody would mistake them for anything other than Latino. Spanish is their first language. My parents came to the United States after they got married. After that, my dad went to medical school and did his residency at Chicago Memorial.

"The gang doesn't make you more Mexican, Marco. Don't make the gang more important than our relationship."

He kicks up the sand with his toe. "*No hablas pinche español.*"

"I don't know what you said. Can you translate, please?"

He holds his hands up in frustration. "That's my point. To be honest, I've been hangin' with the Blood for a while now."

How can he say that? I put my hand over my stomach in a weak effort to protect any baby that might be growing inside me. I can't help tears from welling in my eyes. I know I look desperate and pathetic as a stream of tears runs down my cheeks. Everything I thought I had with Marco is blowing up in my face. I feel more alone than I ever have in my life.

"I can't believe this," I say in almost a whisper.

I should tell him my secret. Maybe it'll make him change his mind, knowing that we might have a baby. But if I'm not pregnant, am I just prolonging the inevitable?

"I just don't want you to give me shit for bein' a Blood," he blurts out. "All of my friends joined."

I look down at my nails. I'd painted them last night and drew a red heart design in the middle of each nail. On my thumbs, inside the little hearts, I put the initials MD—Marco Delgado. I thought he'd be flattered. Obviously I was delusional. I quickly hide my thumbs in my fists.

"I'm sorry," he says, then rubs my shoulder like a parent consoling a child. "Don't cry. We can still, you know, be friends . . . friends with benefits, even."

"I don't want to be friends with benefits, Marco. I want to be your *girlfriend*." The entire contents of my lunch threaten to come up on me.

What is the gang giving him that I can't?

He stays silent and kicks the sand again.

My hands fall limply at my sides as I realize I can't fix this. He's looking at me differently, as if I'm just one of the other girls at school and not the girl of his dreams or the future mother of his children.

He pulls his cell phone out of his pocket and glances at the time. "Um . . . about tonight."

"The end-of-year party at Malnatti's?" It's the "officially unofficial" pizza party for Fairfield High students. They put up a big tent outside their restaurant and have a DJ and an all-you-can-eat pizza party from six to eleven. Afterward, most of the students hang out at the Fairfield football field back forty until the police come to break it up.

"Yeah," he says. "So, uh, if you know of anyone who wants to be hooked up, let me know."

"You're selling drugs?" I ask him.

He shrugs. "It's money."

"It's dirty money, Marco. And illegal. Don't do it. You could get arrested and locked in jail."

"I don't need a fuckin' lecture from you."

He checks his phone again. Is he waiting for someone to call or text him? I feel like I've already lost everything we ever had.

The tears running silently down my cheeks are a clue that I am most definitely *not* okay, but he doesn't seem to care. I swipe them away and curse myself for being so weak.

I can handle this. I'm an independent girl who doesn't need a guy to figure out what to do. Obviously this is my problem, and my problem alone. If I'm pregnant, he'll figure it out when he sees my stomach swell up like a balloon. He'll know it's his. If he chooses to acknowledge us and clean up his life, then we'll talk.

I look up at Marco and give him a small smile. "I don't want to control you. I never wanted to be the girl who held you back."

"But you did . . . you have. I can't do it anymore."

I guess in reality I'm not independent. Our relationship *did* define me, and I liked it that way. I can't believe he wants me out of his life. It doesn't make sense.

He gets a text, but I can't see who it's from. He texts back. "Can you make it home on your own?" he asks me. His fingers move fast and furious as he continues texting.

"I guess."

"Cool." He leans down and kisses me on the cheek. "My friends thought you'd go all *loco* on me. They thought you'd punch me or somethin'."

Now there's a thought. But no, I couldn't punch him.

Before I can open my mouth to beg him to come back to me and lose any dignity I have left, he turns to leave. Then he's just *gone*. Out of sight, but definitely not out of mind.

He picked the gang over me.

My breath hitches. I look out at the lake and feel like jumping in—to swim away and pretend this isn't happening. Desperation washes over me like waves washing footprints off the shore, and I start to shake uncontrollably. My knees crumple to the sand, and I can feel my hot tears start to fall again. This time I don't swipe them away. I break down and cry while recalling every single moment Marco and I spent together, and praying that my period is just late and I'm not really pregnant.

Pregnant at fifteen was never my plan.

3

Luis

I guess my secret is out. If it wasn't for that damn snake, I wouldn't have fallen off the rock and *mi'amá* wouldn't be sitting in the hospital room continuously shooting me threatening stares that translate into *You are in so much trouble*.

Ends up I didn't have venom running through my body. One of the snake's fangs punctured a nerve in my hand, which is why it felt numb. After I fell, Brooke called her father in a panic. He picked us up and drove me to the hospital. Surviving the snake bite was the easy part. Getting continuously lectured by *mi'amá* has been torture.

During the fall down the face of the rock, I scratched up my legs pretty bad. I should be grateful for finally being able to grab part of the rock that jutted out with my good hand, even though in the process I ripped my skin open from palm to wrist and almost needed stitches. In the end, the doc decided the cuts weren't deep enough to require stitches and decided to have a nurse bandage me up instead.

Mi'amá crosses her arms on her chest as she watches me adjust the hospital bed so I'm not lying down flat. "You scared me half to death, Luis. Who told you to climb up a mountain without a safety harness?"

"Nobody."

"It was stupid," she tells me, stating the obvious as she watches the nurse bandage my hand.

"I know."

I look over at my brother Alex, leaning against the window watching me. He's shaking his head, probably wondering how he got stuck with two younger brothers who were destined to do reckless, stupid things. *Papá* died before I was born, so Alex has been the oldest male in our immediate family since he was six. Now he's twenty-two.

I've got to give Alex credit. He's always tried to keep us out of trouble. Carlos was a lost cause from the start. *Mi'amá* said our other brother was born kicking and screaming, and never stopped until he was a teenager. Then all that pent-up energy was used to start fights with anyone who was stupid enough to piss him off.

Alex was twenty when *mi'amá* sent Carlos to live with him so Alex could straighten Carlos out.

Now Carlos is in the military and Alex is about to get married to Brittany Ellis, the girl he's been dating since high school.

A nurse peeks her head into the room. "Mrs. Fuentes, we need you to sign a few papers."

The second *mi'amá* leaves the room, Alex steps toward me. "You are one lucky motherfucker," he says. "If I ever find out you free solo again, I'll personally kick your ass. Got it?"

"Alex, it wasn't my fault."

"Oh, hell," he says, covering his eyes with his hand as if he has a big headache. "You sound just like Carlos."

"I'm not Carlos," I say.

"So don't act like him. I'm gettin' married in two weeks. *Two weeks*, Luis. The last thing I need is one of my brothers fallin' off a fuckin' cliff and killin' himself."

"Technically it wasn't a cliff," I tell him. "And the odds of gettin' a snake bite on an ascent is like—"

"Give me a break," he says, cutting me off. "I don't need statistics, Luis. I need my brother at my weddin'."

Five girls, including Brooke, Jamie, and three of their friends, appear in the doorway. They're all carrying balloons that say *Get well soon!* on them. I give a short laugh as my brother glances at the parade of girls with shock as they tie their balloons to the side rail of my bed.

"How are you feeling?" Brooke asks.

"Like crap," I tell them, lifting up both of my bandaged hands—one with the snake bite and the other from being ripped open by the rocks.

"We came here to make you feel better," Jamie says.

I smile wide and immediately feel better. Now that I know I'm not about to die, it's all good. "What do you girls have in mind?"

I think I hear my brother snort as he steps back and the girls surround my bed.

"Want a back massage?" Angelica Muñoz asks with a flirty lilt to her voice.

"I brought some cookies from the Pearl Street Mall bakery," Brooke says. "I can feed you since you can't use your hands."

"You've *got* to be kiddin'," Alex mumbles from behind her.

Angelica settles behind me and starts massaging my back while Brooke takes one of the chocolate chip cookies she brought and lifts it to my mouth.

My future sister-in-law walks into the room, her high-heeled boots clicking on the hospital floor and her hair secured in a long blond pony-tail running down her back. She takes one look at my entourage and shakes her head in confusion.

"What's going on here?" she says to Alex.

"Don't ask," Alex says, coming up to her.

"Alex called me in a panic and said you'd had an accident," she tells me.

I hold up both of my bandaged hands again. "I did. Hurts like a bitch, but the doc says I'll survive."

"Obviously," she says. "But I don't think you'll be happy when your mother walks in the room and catches her fifteen-year-old son sur-rounded by his own harem. You know how protective she gets, Luis."

"If she's like my mom, she'll freak," Angelica says, then says to the other girls, "Maybe we should leave."

Angelica is a girl I've casually fooled around with a few times at parties. She's got Mexican parents, too, so she gets it. The other girls don't have a clue how protective Mexican mothers can be.

I tell the girls that I'll text them when I can use my hands, and they leave right before *mi'amá* walks back in the room.

"Who brought the balloons?" she asks. "Was it those girls I saw in the hallway?"

"Yeah," I tell her. "They're just friends from school." No use getting into detail about how I've made out with three out of the five of them at one point or another. That will bring on another lecture I definitely want to avoid.

The doc releases me a half hour later, after giving *mi'amá* instruc-tions on how to rewrap my wounds at home.

"You're not invincible," Alex tells me after Brittany and *mi'amá* walk out of the room. "None of us are. Remember that."

"I know."

He pokes a finger into my chest and blocks my path. "You listen to me, Luis, because I know all too well what was goin' through that head of yours when you decided to climb that rock without safety gear. You liked the rush of knowin' you were sayin' *fuck you* to danger. I've got one brother in the military, a best friend who's been six feet under for more than four years, and I'm not about to sit back while my baby brother gets *la tengo dura* by flirtin' with danger."

"You take life too seriously," I say, moving past him. "I'm not your baby brother anymore, Alex, and I'm not as innocent as you think. I'm almost sixteen. You know that girl Brooke who brought me cookies? She's not innocent, either. You want to know how I know that?"

I can't help but crack a grin as Alex puts his hands over his ears like earmuffs.

"Don't tell me," he says. "You're too fuckin' young, bro. I swear, if you get a girl pregnant you'll have more than just two bandaged hands to deal with."

4

Nikki

I don't know how much time has gone by. Every time I get a call on my cell and realize it's not Marco, I ignore it. Every time I get a text from one of my friends, I ignore it.

I don't know how long I've been sitting on the beach crying, but I don't care. I tell my baby to give me strength, but I feel as weak as ever.

Until I hear a familiar voice. "Nik!"

I look up. It's Kendall. Kendall and I have been best friends since preschool, when we both wore the same dress on picture day and told everyone we were twins even when Miss Trudy said that lying wasn't part of the school's "core principles." We didn't know what "core principles" were back when we were four, but when Miss Trudy talked about them in her stern voice we knew we were in trouble.

Before I say anything, she kneels down to me. "I heard."

She might have heard about the breakup, but she has no clue I might be pregnant. I bury my face in my hands. "I can't believe this."

"I know." She sits beside me.

"He picked the gang over me." I look up at my friend who has light hair and hazel eyes—the exact opposite of me. "He said I wasn't Mexican enough."

Kendall shakes her head and snorts. "He's an idiot."

I sniff a few times, then try to wipe the tears off my face. "How did you find out?"

She winces. "I tried to call you and text you, but you didn't answer. So I texted Marco and asked where you were. He told me."

"I told him I loved him. Then he said he wanted to see other people. Then he said he was already hanging out with the Blood and we could be friends. *Friends with benefits*, Kendall. Can you believe it? As if I could just turn my feelings off like a faucet."

Just saying the words *friends* and *benefits* in the same breath makes me cringe.

Kendall sighs. "I know it doesn't seem like it right now, but you'll find someone else."

"I can't do this without him."

"Do *what*?" she asks, confused.

I look up at her, the one friend I can trust more than anyone else. "I might . . . be pregnant."

Her look of shock mixed with a hefty amount of pity is enough to make me cry all over again.

She puts her hands on either side of my face and urges me to look at her. "You're going to be fine, Nikki. I'm here for you. You know that, right?"

I nod. I wish I'd heard those words come out of Marco's mouth.

"How late are you?" she asks.

"A week and a half."

"Did you take a pregnancy test?"

I shake my head. I guess I thought after I told Marco, we'd get one together at a drugstore a few towns over where nobody knew us.

Kendall urges me to get up. "First, I'm going to get a pregnancy test for you. Then we're going to figure it out. Listen, it is what it is and you can't change it. Let's find out so we know for sure. Cool?"

Truth is, at this point I don't know if I want to know for sure. Ignorance is bliss, right?

I'm silent as Kendall drives me to a drugstore and back to her house. I sit on the edge of her tub and bite my fingernails nervously while she reads the instructions and hands me the stick I'm supposed to pee on so I know if I'm carrying Marco's baby.

I look at the stick. "I can't," I tell Kendall. "I just . . . need to see Marco one more time. I need to talk to him face-to-face before I do this. He'll be at Malnatti's. If I can pull him away from the party and talk to him, maybe we can work things out."

"I . . . I don't know if that's a good idea."

"I have to see to him tonight, Kendall." I look down at the pregnancy test. "I can't do this without him."

I know I sound desperate. I just have to find out if there's anything I can do to change his mind about the Latino Blood . . . and me . . . and dealing drugs.

Kendall stands. "You sure you want to talk to him tonight?"

"Yeah." I feel like I have so much to say, and was too caught off guard to say it before. If he knows how much I truly care about him, he's got to change his mind. I can't imagine any girl loving him more than I do. I put the pregnancy test back in the package and shove it in my purse.

"Come on, let's get you ready then," she says, taking me to her room and scanning her closet to pick something for me to wear. "I think seeing Marco right now is a horrible idea, but if you're determined, I'm not going to stop you. First I'm going to make sure you look so hot, Marco will shit in his pants when he takes one look at you."

In the end, Kendall picks out tight skinny jeans and a designer top that her mom gave her after she decided she didn't want it anymore. At the party, I take a deep breath and hold my head high as I walk through the big white tent at Malnatti's with Kendall at my side.

I scan the main area. It seems like the entire school is here celebrating the beginning of summer break.

Music is playing.

Some people are eating.

Some people are dancing.

I scan the tent for the familiar face that makes my heart race every time I look at him.

I finally see him . . . making out with Mariana Castillo in the back corner. She's one of the tough, pretty Latino Blood homegirls that most girls at Fairfield steer clear of. He's kissing her in that familiar way I know all too well. And feeling her ass with hands that touched my naked body just two days ago.

No.

I close my eyes, wishing the image would disappear. But it doesn't.

I open my eyes, and now I notice that most of the freshmen and sophomores are staring at me. I get looks of pity from girls on the north side, but I notice most of the Latina girls from the south side are whispering to each other and laughing. They're gloating, happy that Marco dumped his rich north side girlfriend.

I tell Kendall not to follow me as I turn and run out of the tent, not stopping until I reach my house twenty minutes later. I bolt upstairs and lock myself in my room, feeling like a complete fool.

I pull out the pregnancy test from the zippered section of my purse and unwrap the stick. I let out a long, slow breath. This is it. *The moment of truth.*

I sneak off to the bathroom, glad the rest of my family is watching television in the family room.

After I follow the instructions, I hold the stick in my hand and wait impatiently for the results to show up. As I stare at the little plastic window that will tell me my fate, three things Marco taught me today race through my mind: boys will lie to your face just to have sex with you, don't trust any boy who says *I love you*, and never date a boy who lives on the south side of Fairfield.

5

Luis

Two weeks after my showdown with the snake, I'm in a tuxedo at my brother's wedding. I never thought I'd see Alex get married. Then again, I never thought I'd be back in Illinois again. This time, though, we're at a rented house on Sheridan Road in Winnetka. It's less than fifteen minutes from the south side of Fairfield where we used to live, but it feels like a whole other world.

"*¿Estás nervioso?*" I ask Alex as I watch him attempt to adjust the bowtie so it sits straight.

"*Estoy bien*, Luis. It's just that this damn thing won't go on right," Alex growls, then slides the strip of fabric from under his crisp white collar and whips it on the ground before running his hand through his hair. He sighs heavily, then glances at me. "How the hell did you get yours to tie without lookin' like a kid did it?"

I pull out a piece of folded-up paper from the back pocket of my rented tuxedo pants, ignoring the pain from my still-raw hand. "I printed instructions off the Internet," I tell him proudly as I hold out the piece of paper.

"You're such a geek, Luis," our brother Carlos chimes in as he moves from the opposite side of the room and rips the instructions out of my hand.

Carlos didn't have to worry about renting a tuxedo because he's wearing his dress uniform from the army. From the way he stands straight and tall when he wears it, I know he's proud he's in the service instead of being in the gang he was in when he lived in Mexico with me and *Mamá*.

"Here," Carlos says as he picks up the tie and shoves it and the instructions into Alex's empty hand. "You don't want to keep that bride of yours waitin' at the altar. She might decide to ditch you and marry a white dude with an investment portfolio instead."

"You tryin' to piss me off?" Alex says, shoving Carlos away when he laughs at the clear plastic container with the red rose boutonniere packed neatly inside.

Carlos nods. *"Estoy tratando.* I haven't had a chance to give you shit since I was deployed nine months ago, Alex. *No puedo parar."*

Just as I'm about to offer to tie Alex's bowtie for him, *mi'amá* comes into the room.

"What are you boys doing?" she asks, as if we're still little kids messing around.

"Arguin'," Carlos says matter-of-factly.

"There's no time for that."

Carlos kisses her on the cheek. "There's always time for arguin' when you're a Fuentes."

She glares at him, then looks up at the ceiling. *"Dios mío ayúdame."*

She grabs Alex's bowtie and wraps it around his neck. As if she's a pro, she has it tied in less than thirty seconds.

"Thanks, Ma," Alex says.

When she finishes, she looks up at Alex and cups his face in her hands. "My oldest *hijo* is getting married. Your father would be so proud of you, Alejandro. Graduating from college, and now getting married. Just . . . don't forget where you came from. *¿Me Entiendes?*"

"I won't," he assures her.

Mi'amá pins his boutonniere on his lapel, then steps back and looks at all three of us. Her hands press against her heart and her eyes get watery. "My boys are all grown up."

"Don't cry, Ma," Alex tells her.

"I'm not," she lies as a tear escapes the corner of her eye and runs down her face. She quickly brushes it away, then straightens and heads for the door. "Carlos and Luis, you should collect the rest of the groomsmen and tell them to line up soon." She glances at Alex. "Finish getting dressed, Alejandro. The procession is about to start."

She closes the door, leaving us alone.

I watch as Alex walks over to the window overlooking Lake Michigan. Chairs set up on the private beach are filled with guests waiting for him and his bride.

"I can't do this," he says.

I step closer, hoping to get a hint that he's joking.

He's not.

I glance at the clock on the wall. "Umm, Alex, you do realize that the weddin' is supposed to start in ten minutes, don't you?" I ask.

"I'll handle this," Carlos says, taking control. He braces his hands on Alex's shoulders. "Did'ja cheat on Brittany?"

Alex shakes his head.

"You in love with another chick?"

Another shake.

Carlos leans away from Alex and crosses his arms on his chest. "Then you're goin' through with it. I didn't get leave and fly all the way to Chicago for you to call it off, Alex. And besides, you love the *gringa* and promised you'd marry her after you both graduated college. This is a done deal. No backin' out now."

"What'd you do, Alex?" I ask, completely confused now.

He sighs heavily. "I haven't told her the news that at the end of the summer we're movin' back to Chicago."

Our entire family has lived in Colorado for almost three years. Moving back here isn't gonna fly with Brittany. "What do you mean, *you're movin' back to Chicago?*"

"It's a long story. Brit's parents are handin' over custody of her sister, Shelley, to the state of Illinois. She's twenty-one and can go on state fundin' for her care. That means she'll be pulled from Sunny Acres and moved back here. Brit doesn't know yet. She also doesn't know I got into Northwestern for grad school. I accepted."

"And you didn't tell her any of it?" Carlos asks. "Oh, man, you are screwed."

Alex rubs the back of his neck and winces. "I kinda never even told her I applied to Northwestern. She thinks we're stayin' in Boulder after the weddin'."

I know full well my brother's soon-to-be wife doesn't want to come back to Illinois. I've heard her talk about her fear of coming back to the place where Alex got shot, and beat up within an inch of his life to get jumped out of the Latino Blood. He's told her it's safe now, since the gang broke off into different factions and the new head of the gang, Chuy Soto, is in jail. We've all assured Brittany that Alex doesn't have a target on his back, but she's skeptical.

I know it took a lot for Alex to convince Brittany to have their wedding back here. I think she agreed for the sole reason that she hoped her parents would attend the ceremony—despite their hatred of my brother.

They hate him because he's Mexican.

And he's poor.

And he was in a gang.

He's still batting two out of three, which makes him an unacceptable match for their daughter. She comes from a rich, white, and stuck-up family. I have to give Mr. Ellis, her dad, some credit. He did try to get to know Alex. A while back when he came for a visit to Boulder, he invited Alex to play golf. That was a bad idea. My brother is not the golfing type. One look at his old gang tattoos should've been a clue.

Brittany's parents haven't shown up. Not yet, at least. Brittany hopes to have her parents at her side when she walks down the aisle, but plan B is to walk down with Carlos's girlfriend's dad, Dr. Westford. Either way, my brother will be waiting for her at the end of the aisle.

Alex shrugs into his black tuxedo jacket and heads for the door. "Just promise me one thing. If she kicks me out of our room tonight, let me sleep in one of yours."

"Sorry, bro," Carlos says. "I've been away from Kiara for nine months. I ain't sharin' my hotel room with anyone but her. Besides, your virgin bride'll want to consummate the marriage."

Alex rolls his eyes. I'm pretty sure they consummated their relationship years ago. I'm also pretty sure Carlos knows that fact.

"You've got to tell her," I say. "Before the weddin'."

"There's no time," Carlos chimes in, totally amused. "Nice to start your marriage with lies and deceit. You're a stellar role model, bro." He pats Alex's back.

"*Cállate*, Carlos. I'll tell her."

"Before the ceremony, or after?" I ask.

From the open windows, harp music starts flowing into the room.

The three of us look at one another.

We know our family will never be the same.

"Well, guys, this is it," Alex says as he opens the door. He stops suddenly and bows his head. He squeezes his eyes shut. "I wish Paco were here," he mumbles.

Paco was Alex's best friend. He died when he and Alex were seniors in high school. My brother has never gotten over it.

"Me too," I say, crossing myself as I think of the one guy who we treated like an honorary Fuentes.

"Yeah," Carlos says. "But he's here. You know he's watchin'."

Alex nods, then straightens. If it weren't for Paco, Alex wouldn't be here. He'd be in a coffin, too.

My brothers aren't aware that I know how Paco died. Hector Martinez, the head of the Latino Blood, shot Paco. Hector also killed my father, and even shot Alex. Hector was the enemy. My life would have been very different if the enemy weren't dead, because I would have dedicated my life to getting revenge.

I was eleven when I found out who shot *Papá* when Alex was six years old and *mi'amá* was pregnant with me. I held back the urge for revenge, but I felt it like a fire slowly burning inside me until Hector's death years ago made my family safe.

Just the thought of Hector Martinez can get me riled up. I take a deep breath and follow Alex and Carlos to the processional. We stand near the priest with the rest of the wedding party, and for the moment I forget about the past.

"Alex, you got the *arras*?" Carlos asks him.

The *arras* are the thirteen gold coins he'll give Brittany as a symbol of his trust and confidence in her. They've been passed down from my grandparents to my parents, which is a good thing, 'cause there's no way my brother would be able to afford the coins otherwise. They're not having a traditional Mexican wedding since Brittany isn't *Mexicana*, but they've put some Mexican traditions in the ceremony.

Alex pats his pockets. "Shit. I left the *arras* in the room."

"I'll go get 'em," I say, then head back to the makeshift dressing room.

"Hurry," I hear Carlos and Alex call out behind me.

I swing open the door to the dressing room and find I'm not alone. A girl about my age is in the room, looking out the window. Her white dress contrasts with her honey-colored skin, and just the sight of her makes me stop in my tracks. She's smokin' hot, with dark wavy hair running down her back and a face that reminds me of an angel. She's obviously a guest at the wedding, but I've never met her before. I'd definitely remember her if I had.

I flash her a smile. "*¡Hola! Yo soy Luis. ¿Quieres charlar conmigo?*"

She doesn't say anything.

I point to the door. "Umm . . . *la boda va a empezar*," I tell her, but it's clear by the way she rolls her eyes that she doesn't really care.

"Dude, speak English," she says. "This isn't Mexico."

Whoa. *Chica* with an attitude in the house. "Sorry," I say. "Thought you might be Mexican."

"I'm *American*," she says, then holds up a blinged-out cell phone and waves it in the air. "And I'm on the phone. It's a private conversation. Do you mind?"

The side of my mouth quirks up. She might claim she's a full-blooded American, but I'd bet my left nut she's got some Mexican blood running through her feisty veins.

I pick up the *arras* and give her a smile. "Save a dance at the reception for me, *mi chava*."

She hangs up with whoever she was talking with and sneers at me. "Ugh, you're one of those guys who flirt and smile to get with a girl, then they dump that poor girl on their ass when they least expect it."

"Oh, so you've heard about me," I say, then wink at her. She starts to walk out of the room in a huff, but I reach out to stop her. "I was just kiddin'. Don't take life too seriously, *mi chava*."

The angel gets in my face. She does it to intimidate me, but all it does is fire me up. "How dare you tell me not to take life too seriously! You don't even know me."

I don't usually mess around with girls with attitude. I've been around enough of 'em to know that *muy creídas* are more trouble than they're worth. They've always intrigued me, though. I can't help it. I think it's in the Fuentes blood to mess around with girls who most definitely don't want to get messed with.

"Luis, you're holding up the ceremony," *mi'amá* calls loudly from the hall. She walks into the room, then raises an eyebrow at the sight of me standing close enough to the angel that if I bent forward the slightest bit I'd be kissing her. "What's going *on* in here?" she demands, as if we were about to get it on and she got here just in time to break it up.

"Yeah, what's goin' on?" I ask the girl, deliberately putting her on the spot.

The girl holds up the cell. "I was in the middle of a call when *he* came in here and started to hit on me."

"That's my son. And you are . . ." *Mamá* says, her eyes narrowed into slits. Oh, man. She's in interrogation mode. You don't want to meet *mi'amá* when she's got her mind set on getting information out of you.

"Nikki Cruz," the girl says with pride. "My dad was Alex's surgeon."

Not Mexican, my ass. I was right. This angel has more than a little red, white, and green blood running through her veins. Dr. Cruz was the one who took the bullet out of Alex's shoulder at the hospital when he got shot years ago. The doctor has been in contact with Alex ever since, keeping tabs on him.

Mamá nods, then scans Nikki Cruz—the surgeon's daughter—from head to toe. "The wedding is about to start. *Ándale*, Luis."

Before I turn around and walk out of the room, I give Nikki a completely arrogant and secret wink/nod that's sure to once again bring out that Latina attitude in full force.

She flips me off. She doesn't do it to amuse me, but it does.

I can't wait for the reception. Like my two older brothers, I don't ever back down from a challenge, and Nikki Cruz is definitely not one that will surrender easily. By the end of the night I bet I could convince her to be my next girlfriend—well, at least until my flight back home to Colorado.

6

I watch as Luis follows his mom out of the room with his arrogant head held high. I was about to hang up with Kendall when he popped into the room and I froze. For a brief second I thought he was Marco. They're both about the same height, age, and physique.

When Luis smiled at me and I felt a flicker of attraction, panic swelled inside me. I can't let my guard down, and a guy like Luis is as dangerous as Marco. I can tell by that smile. He looks innocent enough, but I know better. He might be able to fool other girls, but not me.

It's been two weeks since Marco and I broke up, and the pain is still as raw as it was when he left me on the beach. I never want to feel as desperate and devastated as I did that night. If hatred and bitchiness will protect me, I'll use it.

I hold my head high as I walk back to the ceremony. The music starts, and I quickly grab the empty seat between my mom and my younger brother, Ben. Ben is slouched down in his chair, annoyed that Mom and Dad didn't let him play his handheld video game player. He has to sit here like all the other bored twelve-year-old boys at this wedding.

My parents and Ben have no clue Marco and I broke up. I didn't want to talk about it. I also didn't want my parents to gloat and say *We told you so.* Ben wouldn't care since he hardly said two words to Marco the entire time we were dating.

If my parents had it their way they'd probably want to set up an arranged marriage for me, because they want me with a *nice* boy who comes from a "good background." The last thing I want is my parents picking out my boyfriends or, heaven forbid, my future husband.

Ben hasn't had a girlfriend yet. He's been spared any parental input on his love life, because his love life is nonexistent—unless you count Princess Amotoka from the online game he plays. Needless to say, she's not real.

My eyes wander to the front, where Luis is standing next to the rest of the groomsmen. When our eyes meet for a split second, he winks while flashing me a killer smile. I look down, pretending to suddenly be very interested in a stray thread on the bottom of my dress. I feel nauseous.

Right behind me I hear a girl whisper loudly, "Omigod! Do you see that hottie with the spiked hair? Omigod, who is he?"

If she says *Omigod* again, I'm turning around and slapping her.

"It's Alex's brother Luis," someone explains to the Omigod girl.

"I think he just winked at me," I hear her squeal.

I don't mention that I have a good idea that his wink was meant for me. I force myself to ignore him and focus on the bride and groom. I just wish I wouldn't find it so hard not to stare at Luis, for the sole reason that I'm doing my best *not* to stare at him. I hate that.

The ceremony is just like every other beach wedding ceremony at twilight while the sun is going down. Okay, I admit the whole setting is super cool, but the beach has a negative vibe to me right now. I thought it was my special place with Marco, but it's not. Being here, staring at Lake Michigan in the background, only reminds me of our breakup.

The bride, Brittany, is about to walk down the aisle, but she hesitates and glances anxiously at the entrance before taking the arm of an older man about to escort her.

"Poor girl. Her parents didn't show," my mom whispers to me.

"Why not?" I ask.

Mom shrugs. "I'm not sure. I just overheard some of her bridesmaids talking about it before the ceremony started."

Brittany walks down the aisle and looks like she came right out of the pages of a designer bride magazine. The groom, Alex, can't take his eyes off her.

As soon as the priest opens his prayer book to start the ceremony, I can't help but glance at Luis. He's listening intently to the priest and suddenly has a serious, worried look on his face. I wonder why, until . . .

"You can't get married," Luis chimes in loudly.

More than a few gasps come from the crowd. Every guest is in shock.

This is getting good.

Alex slaps his hand over his eyes. "You didn't," he says to Luis.

Luis steps forward. "I just . . . Alex, tell her. You can't start your marriage on a lie."

Brittany, whose mouth has been wide open ever since Luis spoke up, lifts her veil and furrows her perfectly plucked eyebrows.

"Tell me what?" She's turning whiter than her wedding dress, if that's even possible. I hope the priest or maid of honor, who looks like she wants to murder Alex, is ready to catch her if she passes out.

"Nothin'," Alex says. "We'll talk later, *chica*. It's not a big deal."

"Don't *chica* me, Alex," his bride snaps.

"I think she's gonna deck him," Ben murmurs, amused.

The bride isn't buying it. Maybe they're about to come to the realization that happily-ever-after doesn't exist. "It's a big-enough deal for your brother to stop our wedding," Brittany argues.

"This is ridiculous," Alex growls. He mumbles something to the best man, who seems more amused than shocked.

I feel a sisterhood bond with Brittany, even if she's not aware of it.

Alex's mom, sitting in the front row, has her head bent as if she's watching an ant on the ground and it's the most interesting thing she's ever seen. I think I just saw her crossing herself. When she looks up again, she's got daggers in her eyes as she glares at Alex and Luis.

With nowhere to run except through the crowd or escape into the Lake Michigan water, Alex says, "We're movin' back here."

Brittany blinks a few times. She cocks her head to the side as if she didn't hear him right. "Here? As in *Chicago*?"

All I can think is, *Oh, Alex, you're clueless.* Looking around at the other guests watching this drama unfold, I notice a couple of girls two rows in front of me not too upset by the chain of events unfolding before our eyes. I think they've got the hots for Alex, and won't be disappointed if he's suddenly single. I'm sure the Omigod girl is available behind me, although Alex is probably too old for her.

Brittany backs away from Alex. "And you didn't tell me because . . ."

"Because you were busy plannin' this weddin', and studyin' for finals, and, to be honest, I didn't want you to start freakin' out."

"So my opinion doesn't matter? What about my sister?" Brittany points to the girl in the wheelchair next to the maid of honor. "I'm not leaving her in Colorado."

"Would you two like to take a break and discuss this privately?" the befuddled priest asks.

"No," Brittany snaps. "I don't want to go anywhere with *him*."

"It's your wedding," the priest reminds her. "Umm . . ." He looks at his Bible, as if that has the answers to help the couple mend their problems.

"Let's just get married and discuss this later," Alex tells her. "You'll agree once you hear me out."

"We're supposed to be a team and make decisions together, Alex. Lying is a deal-breaker."

Yes! She's finally getting it. He lied. Boys always lie. I want to scream *Break it off with him while you have the chance!* but I restrain myself.

"I didn't lie, *chica*. I just delayed mentionin' it for a little while. *This* is not a deal-breaker."

She crosses her arms on her chest. "Maybe it is for me."

"Marry me, Brittany, 'cause you know it's gonna happen anyway. Shelley will be with us, I promise. This is all about keepin' us together."

He closes the distance between them. Without another word, he pulls her to him and kisses her with lips, a peek of tongue, and . . . I think I hear some breathless sighs coming from the guests. Nobody can take their eyes off that sensual kiss full of passion.

Don't fall for it! I want to scream, but I can tell it's no use. Her bridal bouquet falls to the ground as she wraps her arms around his neck.

I glance at the girl behind me. The Omigod girl is all dreamy-eyed as she watches the make-out session. All the girls are looking like that. I can just imagine their minds racing, wondering if they'll have as much chemistry with their boyfriends/husbands one day. With that thought, I glance at Luis again.

He's looking right at me, and a shock wave runs through me. So what if we have chemistry. Chemistry doesn't miraculously turn bad boys into good ones.

"I'm mad at you for keeping something important from me," Brittany says to Alex, although her conviction has definitely been compromised after that kiss.

"I know," Alex says. "I promise I have no other secrets."

"But I do," she says. "As long as we're spilling secrets I might as well tell you mine." She looks down at her stomach and places her hand over her midsection. When she looks back up at him, her eyes are glassy. "Alex, I'm pregnant."

My stomach clenches in response.

7

Luis

When I objected to the wedding, I didn't know it would turn into the Fuentes Family Circus. I just wanted Alex to come clean to Brittany.

That's it.

I had no clue my soon-to-be sister-in-law is pregnant. Oh man, seeing our ma's face when Brittany announced the news was classic—her face turned bright red.

I'm glad it's over, though. Brittany said "I do" and my brother said "I do" and she didn't toss the *arras* back at him, and Brittany Ellis is now Brittany Fuentes.

My brother is going to be a father . . . man, I can't believe it. Neither can he. After the initial shock, he hasn't stopped smiling, and at one point he even knelt down and kissed Brittany's stomach over her wedding dress.

I look across the room at everyone dancing on the moonlit dance floor having fun.

Mi'amá comes up to me. She's still flushed, but I can't be sure if it's from the shocking news she's going to be a grandmother, the fact that I saw my cousin Jorge make her do shots of tequila, or if the realization hit that she just married off one of her three kids.

I've already danced with all of my female cousins at least twice. And Brittany's single friends who didn't bring a date. One girl was seriously on the prowl and grabbed my ass a few times while we were dancing. I think she's one of Brittany's sorority sisters. She has no clue I'm fifteen, because she asked me what frat I was in.

I look over at Nikki Cruz, the one person who's not having fun.

She's sitting at one of the tables by herself. I swear the chick looks like she'd be happier taking a final exam than being at this wedding.

I head over to her. "You might want to think of smilin' at some point tonight," I tell her. "It's a weddin', you know."

She looks up at me with big eyes that I swear are made of brown silk. It's dark out, but the lights make her eyes shine.

"Smiling is overrated," she says.

"How would you know if you haven't tried it?" I take the chair next to her and straddle it. "Come on, I dare you."

"Go away."

She's bitter, and trying her hardest to have a shitty time tonight.

I fold my arms on the back of the chair. "Did you know smilin' reduces the level of stress hormones in your body like epinephrine and dopamine? Seriously, even a fake smile'll help. Try it."

She ignores me, so I cup my hands over my mouth and do something I haven't done in years—barnyard sounds. I start with my imitation of a sheep and end with an impressive moo. Girls used to eat it up when I did them back in fifth grade. They'd hang around me for entertainment, which is just what I wanted at the time. Guys who didn't have any entertainment value were ignored. I was a kid who refused to be ignored.

I still refuse to be ignored.

I look at Nikki while I'm doing the sounds, but I get zero reaction from her. *Nada.*

Until she scans me up and down like I'm a creature from another planet. "Are you for real?"

"As real as they come, *mi chava.*" I stand and hold out my hand. "Dance with me."

She eyes my scabs and winces. "What happened to your hand?"

"Long story involving me and a snake. The snake won."

She obviously doesn't believe me. "Why don't you dance with that girl over there?" she says, pointing to this girl I was introduced to named Yvette. She's one of Brittany's aunts' cousin's kids or something like that. She's got dyed blond hair and a fake tan. Brittany said she's on the swim team at school, and last year won state in the two-hundred-yard free-style. Great body, but not my type.

"You want me to dance with someone besides you?"

"Yes," she says, sticking her cute nose in the air like a princess.

I shrug. "Suit yourself."

Whatever. If that's the way she wants it, she can sit here and be miserable. I look at the dance floor. My three-hundred-pound aunt Rosalita is waving me over. Last time I danced with her, she stepped on my foot and almost crushed my bones.

Just as I'm about to leave Nikki alone to drown in her own misery, Alex pats me on my shoulder. Standing next to him is Dr. Cruz, Nikki's father.

"Alex tells me you'll be applying to Purdue to study aeronautics engineering after graduating high school," Dr. Cruz says to me with the slightest hint of an accent.

I stand. "That's the plan, sir."

"Good for you. I really respect that you're following in your brothers' footsteps and working hard."

"I respect that, too," the woman standing behind him says. Nikki's mom, obviously. "It's admirable. Boys who have drive and ambition will definitely go far in life."

I think I hear Nikki snort when I get her parental approval.

Dr. Cruz pats Nikki on the top of the head. "I see you've met my daughter, Nikki."

"Definitely. I asked her to dance, but—"

Dr. Cruz practically drags his daughter off the chair. "Dance with Luis."

"I don't feel good," she mumbles.

"Come on, sweetheart. At least pretend to have fun."

"I don't want to have fun or pretend to have fun, Dad."

"Don't be rude," her mother scolds, then urges her toward me. "Dance with the boy."

I hold out my elbow for Nikki to take, but she struts her hot little Latina body to the dance floor without waiting for me.

"Good luck," Dr. Cruz calls out to me.

A fast song is playing, and Nikki starts dancing with a bunch of people randomly. I watch her as she pretends to loosen up. I know she's faking it because she's not really smiling . . . she's not frowning, either. She's just . . . here.

I try and dance close to her, watching as her body moves to the music. She's not a good dancer . . . she's downright awful. She doesn't seem to notice she looks ridiculous as she jerks her body like a robot around the dance floor. She won't even look at me. In fact, she's busy moving from group to group so nobody can claim her as their partner.

Until a slow song comes on.

Nikki stops abruptly. I reach out for her waist and gently urge her toward me. We're face-to-face now. She looks up at me with long eyelashes that almost touch her eyebrows and eyes that I could melt into if she'd let me. There's no mistaking the electricity pulsing through the air between us. If we got together, it would be explosive . . . in a really good way. She's intimidating, which is sexy as all hell. I don't get intimidated easily.

"*Hola, corazón*," I say, and wiggle my eyebrows at her.

I expect her to smile.

Or laugh.

I don't expect her to knee me in the nuts and say "Fuck you."

Which is exactly what Nikki Cruz does.

8

Nikki

I didn't mean to knee Luis in the nuts.

Okay, so that's not entirely true. I meant to knee him where it counts. I just didn't mean to do it hard—in front of everyone, including the bride and groom. And my parents. And his mother. And everyone else who happened to be on the dance floor at the time.

While Luis grabs his crotch and winces in pain, I walk away and head for the women's restroom. Sprint is more like it. Maybe if I distance myself quickly, nobody will know that Dr. Cruz's daughter is a complete mess. Fat chance, I know.

I lock myself in a stall, content to stay here forever if it means I don't have to face the rest of the world for a while. After about five minutes of pretending that I don't exist and wishing I were a fictional character in one of Ben's stupid video games, I think the coast is clear . . . until I hear the click of a woman's shoes and a knock on my stall door.

Knock, knock, knock. "Nikki, it's your mother," she says, her knuckles rapping on the door. "Open up."

"What if I don't want to?"

Her response is more knocking.

I open the door slowly. "Hi," I say, forcing a smile.

"Don't *Hi* me, young lady. You completely embarrassed me and your father out there."

"Sorry," I say dumbly.

"I'm not the one who needs an apology. What in God's name came over you, Nikki?"

"Nothing." If I told her, then she'd know about my secret. I can't tell her; not now when I'm trying to figure out what to do. "I just . . . it was an accident."

"An accident?" Mom asks, not convinced in the least. She takes a deep breath. "I don't know what's going on with you, but hurting people and embarrassing yourself and your family isn't the answer."

I know that. But I couldn't stand there while Luis's strong hands wrapped around my waist. I wanted to lay my head on his chest and pretend he was my knight in shining armor willing to avenge my honor. But that was a fantasy. When he spoke to me in Spanish, it reminded me too much of Marco and the biggest mistake of my life. I have no knight, no honor.

"I suppose you want me to apologize."

She nods. "Yes, I do. Sooner rather than later."

I watch as Mom walks out of the room, leaving me alone. It's her way of making the apology my own decision, as if she's not forcing me to do it. I close the door again and lean my head back against the stall door.

I know I'm being irrational. All Mexican boys aren't like Marco, just like all Mexican American girls aren't like me. Actually, most Mexican girls I know speak Spanish and have at least a few other Mexican neighbors. I don't. Maybe I judged Luis harshly, but then again, I probably pegged him perfectly.

I hear the door open and the *tap-tap-tap* of more heeled shoes on the bathroom floor.

"Omigod, I can't believe that girl who danced like a freak *kicked* Luis and left him on the dance floor!" I hear one of the girls say.

I didn't kick him. I used my knee, but I'm not about to clear up her little mistake. Not now, at least.

"Did you get a glimpse of his lips?" the other girl says. "Yum."

I roll my eyes.

"I know, right? I told him I'd help heal his wounds. I'm meeting him over by the pier in five minutes. I'll bring back a report on how kissable his lips *really* are."

There's a pause, so I peek through the little space between the door and stall. The Omigod girl is pushing up her boobs to make her cleavage pop out of her dress like butt cheeks. She turns to her friend. "How do I look?"

I take that as my cue to come out of the stall and show myself. As soon as they realize they aren't alone, they look at me, then at each other. I pretend to fix my hair and makeup in the big mirror right next to them.

I decide to give them my two cents. Not because they asked for it, but because they need it.

"Beware of guys who look like Luis," I say. "Guys like that will use you, then leave you when someone else comes along."

Omigod girl puts her hand on her hip and looks me up and down. "What makes you think I actually care?"

"I'm just trying to help. You know, girl bonding and all that."

"Girl bonding?" the girl says in a mocking tone. "I don't bond with girls who dance like they're having a seizure. And I don't hate guys, like you obviously do."

Her friend is laughing now. Omigod girl joins her. They're laughing at me, just like the girls were at Malnatti's the night I saw Marco kissing Mariana Castillo. I shouldn't care, but I do.

I walk out of the bathroom, leaving Omigod girl and her friend to gossip on their own.

I don't hate guys. I'm just . . . cautious.

My mom stops me as I pass her. "Did you apologize to Luis yet?" she asks.

I shake my head. "I was just about to," I say quickly, then attempt a fake search for Luis.

I wander up and down the beach, taking my time heading back to the party. The lick of the waves against the shore and the fresh smell of the air brings me back to the day I told Marco I loved him . . .

The night I found out I was pregnant.

I'd do anything not to see the disappointment and horror on my parents' faces when they learn that their fifteen-year-old daughter got knocked up by the ex-boyfriend they'd never liked. At some point I need to tell them the truth: that I took a pregnancy test and it came out positive, but just thinking about it makes me want to cry.

While the party is still going strong into the night, I sit on a rock far down the beach and look out at the seemingly endless expanse of water. I sit for a long time, listening to the faint music coming from the wedding. Every now and then I get a stomach cramp that hurts like crazy, but it slowly eases as I breathe in and out with smooth, controlled breaths.

Enough sulking, Nikki. Get up and move on . . . literally and figuratively, a voice inside my head instructs.

I stand up and head back to the party. As I'm walking and thinking about how I'm going to gather up the nerve to apologize to Luis, then go home and have the dreaded talk with my parents, I trip on something soft. I look down and realize I just tripped on clothes. Guy clothes . . . namely a tuxedo.

I look around and see two silhouettes kissing in the water.

Luis and Omigod girl. Her annoying squeal echoes through the air. I can tell she's with Luis because . . . well, every time I glanced at him tonight, his image was etched in my brain. Even in shadow, I instinctively know it's him.

I can't believe he can fool around with Omigod girl knowing that she's just a one-night stand. I realize I'm angry with Marco and transferring my emotions onto Luis, but they're too similar.

Evil thoughts are running through my mind, like snatching his tuxedo so he's left without clothes. I shouldn't do it.

But then again . . .

Without really thinking it through for fear I'll lose my nerve, I snatch up Luis's tuxedo jacket, shirt, pants, boxers, and shoes. I take Luis's wallet from his pocket and leave it in the sand. No use in having him think I stole his wallet, after all.

I toss the clothes behind a rock and head back to the reception area. I wish I could see his face when he has to search, all naked, for his clothes. I left them where he can easily find them . . . in the light of day. He's gonna have to work for it in the moonlight.

Yes! For the first time in weeks, I feel empowered.

"Yo, Nik," Ben says. "Mom and Dad have been looking for you. We're about to leave."

Mom and Dad say their good-byes to practically everyone at the wedding. I stand behind them and add my polite thanks to theirs, without a hint that I've just stashed Luis's tux where he might not find it.

"What were you doing on the beach?" Ben asks me as I get into Dad's car.

"Apologizing to Luis," I lie. Obviously I didn't do that much damage to his lower region if he was fooling around an hour later.

Dad pulls out of the parking lot, down the winding driveway, past the house where the wedding was held, and then onto the small road leading away from a neighboring hotel the guests are probably staying at tonight. Ben, sitting beside me, is busy playing with some app on his phone.

Looking out the window, I see a naked Luis holding his wallet over his crotch while trying to sneak into the hotel. He freezes when we pass, probably hoping to avoid being noticed.

But I notice him.

And he notices me.

With a genuine smile that hasn't crossed my face in forever, I roll down my window and give him a small private wave.

Instead of being embarrassed, he drops the wallet and salutes me with one hand and waves back to me with the other.

Which means he's fully exposed.

Don't look at anything but his face, Nikki. Whatever you do, don't give him the satisfaction of scanning down.

In the end, Luis Fuentes gets the best of me. I couldn't help but look. His body is leaner and more ripped than Marco's, and seeing him in all his glory definitely showcases their differences.

"I'm glad you apologized to Luis," Mom chimes in quietly when we're almost home.

"Yep," I tell her.

Any tiny ounce of glee I might have fades as my stomach clenches again. And again. I feel like I'm going to throw up. A dizziness washes over me, and I close my eyes until Dad pulls into our driveway.

Mom turns around and frowns when we're home. "Don't embarrass us like that again. You're not trash, so don't act like it."

I grab the handle and ease myself out of the car. A sharp pain in my side makes me wince. "I know," I manage to say through clenched teeth.

"You know how to act like a lady," Mom says.

I just need to throw up, then I'll be fine. Ben has already booked it into the house. I can't talk because I'm afraid I'll lose the entire contents of my stomach right here.

Mom sighs in frustration. "Look at me when I'm talking to you, young lady."

"Sorry, Mom," I force myself to say. "I'm just . . . not feeling good."

I walk upstairs, but I stop when my stomach clenches and I keel over in pain. I suck in a breath, not being able to stand it. It feels like something is cutting me open from the inside.

"You okay?" Mom asks as she comes up behind me. "What's wrong, Nikki?"

"I don't know." I look at her and know I can't lie any longer. Especially when I feel a trickle of wetness running down my inner thigh. My heart is racing and I'm feeling faint. Another shot of pain runs right through me.

My knees buckle, and I curl up in the fetal position at the top of the stars because it hurts so bad.

"Raul!" my mom screams.

My dad is kneeling at my side in an instant. "Nikki, where's the pain?" he asks just like a doctor would, but with a hint of panic behind his words. He's a surgeon, but I bet he's not prepared for this.

I can't delay the truth any longer.

I don't look into either of their faces as I cry in a soft whisper, "I'm pregnant . . . and I think something's really wrong."

Now I can see blood trickling down my leg.

Mom gasps, then holds on to the railing for support.

My dad stares at me with eyebrows furrowed in confusion. He's completely stunned for a second, as if time has stopped, but quickly snaps out of it as reality sets in. "All right. Let's get you to the hospital," he says, not in a panic but like a doctor with a purpose. He picks me up and carries me down the stairs while Mom calls our neighbor and asks her to come over to stay with Ben.

My parents help me get in the front seat while the pain increases with every second that passes. In the car on the way to the hospital, I glance at my dad. I've never seen him look this worried or sad. When I started hanging out with Marco almost daily, he warned me to stay away from him. *That boy is nothing but trouble*, he'd said one day when he came home to find us making out in the pool in our backyard. *I don't want you hanging around with him. He'll get you into trouble*. Mom agreed with him.

I thought they were judging Marco just because he lived on the south side. I was wrong.

I look over at my dad. He's got a death grip on the steering wheel, and he's focused on the road.

"I'm so sorry, I'm so sorry, I'm so sorry," I say over and over as the pain gets sharper and sharper.

He sighs heavily. "I know."

"Do you hate me?" I hold my breath, waiting for the answer.

"I'm disappointed in you, Nicolasa," he says, calling me by my formal name he never uses unless he's really upset. He doesn't say anything more than that.

"No matter what, we love you," Mom says encouragingly from the backseat. "How did this happen? When? Where? We don't condone—"

"Maria, not now," Dad tells her.

Mom stops her questions, but they linger in the air between us.

At the hospital, Dad makes sure I get admitted immediately. They do all these blood tests, and the specialist, Dr. Helene Wong, orders an ultrasound. I'm trying to hold in my tears, but it's no use. After the ultrasound, Mom holds my hand. She doesn't say much. I think she's too scared and shocked to say anything, so she lets Dad and the other doctors do all the talking.

After Dr. Wong orders a second ultrasound and I'm put on an IV, Mom sits on one side of my hospital bed and Dad sits on the other. The doctor is standing next to them with my test results in her hand.

"You have an ectopic pregnancy," she says, then explains why I need to have emergency surgery because they suspect my fallopian tube has started to rupture. Mom has her hand over her mouth as tears fall down her cheeks. Dad nods stiffly as he listens to Dr. Wong.

"What's going to happen to my baby?" I ask in a panic.

Dr. Wong touches my shoulder. "There's no way to save the baby," she explains.

I start crying again. The second I realized that I was really and truly pregnant, I'd hoped that the pregnancy wasn't real. Did my negative thoughts make my body reject the baby? Deep sorrow and a mountain of guilt that I know I'll carry around forever settle in my gut.

Another wave of pain hits, and I grab my stomach.

As my parents sign the waivers, the reality of what's happening is making me shake.

"Will I still be able to have kids in the future?" I ask Dr. Wong before she leaves the room to prep for the surgery.

She nods. "One tube will be damaged, but your other one is healthy. You should be able to conceive without too much trouble."

After the IV is in, and they're ready to wheel me into surgery, I look over at my parents. I want to say something to them, but I know if I do I'll burst into sobs.

Mom gives me a small, tight smile. She's disappointed in me. I don't blame her.

Dad holds my hand until I'm wheeled into surgery. "We'll be right here waiting until you come out."

The operating room is cold and smells like canned air. I'm being hooked up to monitors and Dr. Wong tells me I'm going to be feeling sleepy as they put something in my IV. As I fall into a deep slumber, I vow to forget about Marco and forget about our baby who never had a chance.

Luis Fuentes reminded me that I'm still vulnerable. If I'm emotionally unavailable, then I don't have to worry about ever getting hurt. When this nightmare is over, I'm going to be a different person . . . Nikki Cruz will no longer be vulnerable.

9

Luis

Fairfield, Illinois.

If you would've told me two weeks ago I'd be moving back to Illinois after fleeing this place when I was eleven, I'd have laughed. In all that time I came back to Illinois once, for my brother's wedding more than two years ago.

Now I'm seventeen and back for good.

I'm about to start my senior year. I know every teacher, every student, and every inch of Flatiron High in Colorado, where I went for the past three years of high school. If I had a choice, I wouldn't have come back to Fairfield. But I'm Mexican, and my culture is all about loyalty to family.

Duty to family brought us back. Alex and Brittany are living here with my little nephew, Paco. We saw them last night, as soon as we arrived. Brittany's pregnant again, and *mi'amá* says she's not going to miss out on watching her grandchildren grow up.

We're standing in front of the old house we used to rent. It's a two-bedroom house, bigger than a shack but smaller than most homes on my block. It's clear that the Latino Blood don't have as big a presence in

Fairfield anymore. The spray-painted tagging of buildings and street signs is gone, and nobody is looking at cars driving down the street as if they might be rival gang members about to do a drive-by. The presence of a police car parked in the street makes me question my initial observations, though.

I know why *mi'amá* wanted to come back and live in this town, in our old house. It's not just because Fairfield is close to Evanston, where Alex and Brittany live. It's because of the past . . . the memories of *mi papá* she's desperate to hold on to.

I watch as *mi'amá* puts the key in the lock, takes a big breath, then opens the door. She sent in a deposit and a check for the first month's rent while we were still in Colorado, for fear that someone else would snatch it up. I didn't tell her she had nothing to worry about, that nobody would be standing in line to rent the dump we used to call home.

I was wrong.

We stand in the small living room, and I do a double take. The old, ripped carpeting has been replaced by new hardwood floors. The walls have been freshly painted a bright white. I hardly recognize the place.

"Luis, look!" *mi'amá* says as she steps into the kitchen and runs her hand over the new granite counters and stainless steel appliances. She smiles wide, then hugs me tight in excitement. "It's a new beginning for us."

A loud knock on the front door echoes through the house. "It might be Elena. She said she was going to stop by after work," *mi'amá* says, hurrying to open the door.

I'm about to check out the old bedroom I used to share with Alex and Carlos when I hear *mi'amá* exclaim, "Can I help you, officer?"

Officer?

The cops are here?

The only experience I've had with Fairfield cops was when my brothers got into trouble or when they'd question us about gang activity when I was younger. When most of your family have been gang members, the last thing you want is a police officer knocking on your door. Even though Alex is in grad school and Carlos is in the military, old habits are hard to break.

I walk into the living room and watch as a cop in uniform smiles wide at *mi'amá*. He's got dark brown hair in a short military cut and is standing in one of those cop stances that means business. "I saw you pull up and wanted to introduce myself," the guy says, then holds out his hand. "I'm Cesar Reyes, your landlord and next-door neighbor."

Mi'amá reaches out to shake his hand, then pulls it back quickly as she eyes the gun strapped to his holster. "Thanks for introducing yourself, Officer Reyes," she says.

"Call me Cesar." The cop looks down, noticing what she's focused on. "I didn't mean to intimidate you, Mrs. Fuentes. I was about to go to work, and I didn't know the next time I'd catch you home." His eyes dart to me. "Is that your son?"

She opens the door wider and steps back, so now I'm in full view. "Officer Reyes, this is Luis—my youngest."

Reyes nods in my direction. "Welcome to the neighborhood."

"Thanks," I mumble, not thrilled to suddenly be living next to a cop who happens to be our landlord.

"I'm having a barbeque at my place Sunday night. You both should hop on over if you get a chance."

Neither of us answers.

He shrugs. "All right. I guess I'll see you around then." He pulls a business card from his front pocket and hands it to *mi'amá*. "If you need anything, don't hesitate to call."

He walks to his car, then drives away.

"Glad that's over," I say.

Mi'amá closes the door slowly, then sighs as she leans against it.

"You all right?" I ask her.

"I'm fine. Just . . . let's get started unpacking."

On Sunday, Alex calls to say he got me an interview at the Brickstone Country Club in Evanston, which is a twenty-minute walk from our house. I need a job to help out and told Alex to be on the lookout if he hears of any openings. My cousin Enrique has a body shop, but Alex works there already a few days a week, and since the economy turned to shit Enrique doesn't have enough work for two extra employees.

At four I head over to Brickstone. It's a huge place with a private eighteen-hole golf course, Olympic-sized indoor and outdoor pools, and an exclusive dining room solely for club members.

The interview process doesn't take long. This lady, Fran Remington, calls me into her office after I fill out an application.

She puts her hand on her desk and gives me a once-over. "I see here that you're a straight-A student and were on the soccer and swim teams at your old high school. Tell me, Luis, why do you want a job here?"

"I just moved here from Colorado and need to help my mom with bills. I've got college applications due in a few months, and those cost a lot of money."

She lays the paperwork on her desk. "Where do you want to go to college?"

"Purdue University. They've got an aeronautics program," I tell her. "After my bachelor's I plan on applyin' to NASA's astronaut trainin' program."

"You're ambitious."

"Yes, ma'am."

She looks over my application again. "You don't have any serving experience. I really need a server for the dining room."

"I can do it," I tell her. "It's not a problem."

"Our members expect top-notch food and the best service Illinois has to offer. I don't tolerate any bad attitudes, tardiness, or slovenly employees. When members walk into the club, they're treated like royalty by each and every person on my staff. Our members pay a tremendous amount of money to be part of this club. They're demanding, and so am I."

"I can handle it."

The woman hesitates just a few more seconds before smiling at me. "I like a young man with ambition like yours. Even though you don't have experience, I'll give you a shot. You'll start as a busboy for a month, then move up to server if you have what it takes. You can start on Saturday."

"Thank you for the opportunity, ma'am," I tell her. "I won't let you down."

"Good. It's settled then."

Back at home, I find Officer Reyes standing on our front stoop, wearing jeans and a T-shirt. He's got a Budweiser in his hand, and he's talking with *mi'amá*. I wouldn't think anything of it, but the guy has a big grin on his face, and he just touched her elbow as she laughed at something he said.

Oh, man.

I know how a guy acts when he's flirting with a girl, because I do it all the time. There's no doubt in my mind that our neighbor/landlord/cop has the hots for *mi'amá*.

How the hell am I gonna explain that one to my brothers?

10

Nikki

Ugh, I couldn't sleep last night. It's the first day of my senior year, and I'm so ready for it. I'm ready to graduate, get out of Fairfield, and start my life.

I take a shower, get dressed, then head downstairs for breakfast.

"You look nice," Mom says, eyeing my jeans and turquoise silk tank she bought me when she went shopping in downtown Evanston last week. "Here, I made some eggs for you and Ben."

My brother walks into the kitchen, his hair practically falling into his eyes as he reads some gaming magazine. It's his first day of freshman year and he's wearing ripped jeans and a T-shirt that has seen better days. You'd think he'd at least dress up for the occasion, but no.

"Ben, you need a haircut," I tell him.

"No, thanks," Ben responds absently as he reads an article about some new combat game coming out with digital graphics. I only know this because I glimpse the title of the article, which says "Combat Forces II—Stunning Digital Graphics!"

"Ben, you do realize that you're in high school now, don't you?"

"So?"

"So you should take care of your appearance."

He sets his gaming magazine on the kitchen table. "I put on a shirt that didn't have holes in it. That should count for something."

"It says MAY THE FORCE BE WITH YOU!"

He looks down at his shirt. "I know . . . cool, huh?"

I look at Mom for support in this.

"Everybody has their own definition of cool, Nikki," Mom says.

Ben gives Mom an exaggerated wink. "Don't you think it's time to tell Nikki the truth—that I'll be a self-made millionaire by the time I'm twenty and Nikki will probably be asking me for loans?"

Mom sets a plate in front of him and starts heaping eggs and toast onto it. She even pours orange juice into his glass. "The *truth* is that you better sit on your butt and eat your breakfast before it gets cold."

"Social skills count for a lot, you know," I tell him.

"Social skills are overrated," my brother says right before he takes a huge bite of bread.

Mom pats Ben on the shoulder. "Stop antagonizing your sister."

"She makes it so easy," Ben says, then leans back in his chair. "So who wants to name my next Queen of the Dragon Empire in the game I'm in the middle of coding?"

"How about you name her Nicolasa after your sister?" Mom suggests.

"I need a tougher name than that," Ben tells her. "This is a queen who can yield a sword and wear chain mail."

"Why not Bertha?" I jokingly suggest. I hate when Ben starts talking about cartoon characters as if they're real . . . I hate it more when he sucks me in and I actually validate his obsession.

"Queen Bertha? Nope, doesn't work for me."

"Well, I'm sure you'll think of something." Mom gets her keys out. "Oh, I almost forgot. Nikki, you can't take your car today. Your father took it in for repairs this morning when he realized that it was leaking oil. Why don't you two walk to school? Start off the year being active instead of lazy and spoiled."

"I'm proud of my laziness," Ben says, amusing himself. "And what's wrong with being spoiled?"

"Everything." She turns around just as I'm about to finish the last bite of my food and says, "I'll tell you what . . . I'll drive you both to school because I have to go to work anyway, but you can either walk or take the bus home." She smiles serenely.

Having your mommy drive you to school as a senior? "If Dad took my car, let me take his."

"Not going to happen," she says. "Unless you get all As, you're never getting hold of the keys to his Lexus. It's a goal to work toward."

Ben rolls his eyes. "Mom, Nikki has never gotten all As."

"Yes, she has," Mom says.

Ben laughs. "I'm not talking about kindergarten."

I kick my brother under the table. Just because he doesn't try, hardly studies, and gets all As doesn't mean he has to be arrogant about it.

"I'm having dinner with some clients tonight, so I won't be home. I'm decorating their house using all antiques," Mom says excitedly.

"Have fun," I tell her, knowing she will. My mom is an interior designer who loves turning boring spaces into themed rooms she calls "eclectic showstoppers." Each room in our house has a theme and has been turned into one "eclectic showstopper" after another. My life is inundated with themed rooms.

At school, Kendall is waiting for me by our lockers. At the end of junior year we got to pick any locker in the senior hallway for the next year, so

Kendall and I made sure our lockers were right next to each other. That was before she started dating Derek. The two of them have been inseparable since the last day of school, when he showed up at her house with a dozen roses and a song he'd written about her.

I don't trust Derek. I know he likes Kendall, but I also know a lot of girls flirt with him and he flirts back. In a moment of male weakness, he can crush Kendall's trusting heart.

"Just an FYI," Kendall says, wincing as if she's about to share some bad news. "Marco's locker is right across from ours."

A wave of anxiety rushes through me. "Please tell me you're lying."

"I wish I was."

After we broke up, Marco got in really deep with the Latino Blood. I know he's been selling drugs and getting in fights a lot. Something happened last year to the guy who ran the gang, and the LB presence in the south side of Fairfield got broken up. I heard Marco started hanging out with other gangs besides the LB. He's gotten meaner and tougher. I used to think he had a hard exterior but was sweet once you really got to know him. Marco is anything but sweet now.

Derek is walking down the hall, heading straight for us. Of course he's stopped by practically everyone who calls out his name. Girls are enamored with him because he's ridiculously gorgeous with blond hair, a model's face, and a very chiseled body. Guys like him because he's a major athlete. As a sophomore, he made it to the state championships in tennis. When he hurt his shoulder before junior year, he decided he didn't want to play tennis and instead went out for the soccer team. He was voted MVP last year at the end of the season, which surprised nobody.

Derek stands beside Kendall, but she turns her back and pretends to be interested in something in her locker.

"I can't believe you're still mad," Derek says.

Kendall shoves books in her locker. "I'm not mad. You can go to college wherever you want, Derek. You don't have to get permission from me to apply out east."

He puts his hand on the small of her back and leans toward her. "Why won't you even look at Ivy League schools?"

"Because they're not in the Midwest," she tells him. "You want to go far from home, fine. I can't."

Kendall isn't saying it, but she's committed to staying near Fairfield for college because her mother got diagnosed with cancer last year. She's gone through chemo and the doctors say she's in remission, but Kendall doesn't want to be far away.

"What are you saying, that if I go to school out east it's over between us?" Derek asks.

"I don't know."

I decide to put my two cents in the discussion for a reality check. "The percentage of couples who stay together after high school is, like, less than five percent, you guys."

"Thanks for the vote of confidence, Nikki," Derek says sarcastically.

"Just being real," I tell him. "No need to have you guys living in Fantasy Land."

"I hope you never go to Disney World," Derek says to me. "You'll probably tell all the little kids there that Mickey Mouse is just a guy in a costume."

"Probably," I tell him.

Kendall sighs. "Derek, leave Nikki alone. She's just protecting me."

Derek shakes his head, frustrated. "Dammit, Kendall. When are you gonna realize you don't need protection from me."

"Nikki's my best friend."

"And I'm supposed to be your boyfriend." Derek walks away with a bitter look on his face.

Kendall leans her head against her locker. I know she's scared. She was scared of losing her mom, and now she's scared of losing Derek. I know about being scared, which is why I tell it like it is. Yes, Derek might leave her for another girl. Or go to a college far away and forget about how much he loves her. Or maybe he's been lying to her about how much he cares about her. That's reality. Derek might even think he's being sincere . . . but how long will that last?

"He hates me," I tell her.

"No, he doesn't." She turns to me. "He just thinks you're overly cynical."

As soon as she says the word *cynical*, I hear an old familiar voice speaking in Spanish echoing from across the hall. Marco. Just hearing the deep rumble of his voice used to make me grin from ear to ear. Now his voice is like nails on a chalkboard.

I look over at Kendall. She touches my forearm sympathetically.

"Ignore him," she advises.

Of course I'll ignore him, just like I've done the past two years. He's changed way too much, and so have I. I pretend to scratch my chin with my shoulder as I peek across the hall at his locker. Marco is talking to some guy who looks familiar . . .

Wait.

One.

Second . . .

No, it can't be.

It's Luis Fuentes, the guy whose clothes I hid when his brother got married years ago. The last time I saw him, he was naked. That was so long ago, I bet he doesn't remember me. I remember him, though. He's the boy who reminded me that I was vulnerable. The night I met him I became cynical. I glance again.

Oh, no.

He's staring right at me.

Luis

Exotic eyes. Wavy brown hair. An attitude a mile long. Older, but she's still got that unique "angel with an edge" aura about her.

I'd know that girl anywhere. I could pick her out of a crowd of a thousand girls. She denied her Mexican blood, danced like a robot, and dissed me all in the same night.

"That's Nikki Cruz, ¿verdad?" I ask Marco, a friend of mine from grade school. It's kind of weird how it's like I never left. I never realized how deep my roots are in this town, even though I've been gone from Fairfield for almost six years. I came to school early this morning and got my schedule from the front office. As soon as I walked to my locker, I was recognized by a bunch of old friends I used to hang out with.

Marco glances at the girl, then nods. "How do you know Nik?"

"Had a run-in with her a couple years ago at my brother's weddin'." No need to go into detail about how she hid my clothes and left me to fend off the overly aggressive girl I'd been skinny-dipping with that night. "¿Cuál es su historia?" I ask him.

"Her story is that she's filthy rich and has a body made for fuckin' around," Marco says. "She's a *puta*. Keep your ass far away from that *pocha* if you want to stay sane."

I look her way and our eyes meet. Does she remember me?

While Marco talks to a couple guys, I keep my eyes on Nikki. She quickly turns her gaze away, says something privately to the tall blond girl standing next to her, then tosses her hair back and they both strut down the hall without a backward glance.

I fly through my first two classes; it's cool to see old friends that I thought I'd never see again. It doesn't take a rocket scientist to figure out that Marco is hanging with the big boys outside of school. Nobody has to talk about his gang affiliation—it's obvious. Most of the families who lived in my 'hood were connected. Some still are.

The south side of Fairfield might not be overflowing with active gang members anymore, but we're still the poor kids at school. The elementary and middle schools weren't integrated, but the high school merged all the schools from both sides of Fairfield into one multicultural melting pot.

The first time I realize how different things are here than in Boulder is when we have to change for gym class.

"You're sitting in my spot, Mex," some beefy white guy says to me as I sit on a bench in the locker room after being handed my gym uniform. "Move."

I can't help the laugh that escapes my mouth. "Mex? *Did you just call me Mex?*"

"You heard me. Now go sit your dirty immigrant ass somewhere else."

Unlike my brothers, I don't like to fight and I'm not looking to start one now.

I casually take off my shoes and remind myself that this guy isn't worth getting kicked out of school. I'm not gonna let him bully me, though.

"Sorry to break the news to you, *gringo*," I tell him. "But I ain't movin'. It's the first day of school. You don't have a 'spot' yet."

Other guys start piling in the locker room. *Gringo* slams his fist hard on the locker right above my head, causing everyone to look our way.

"I'm warning you," he growls through clenched teeth, then kicks my shoes across the room.

I roll my eyes. He wants me to throw the first punch so I'm the one who gets in trouble. He has no clue that I have the patience of a saint. At least that's what Carlos says, although that isn't saying much, considering his fuse is about as short as an eyelash.

Pedro, a guy who lived across the street from me since before we moved, motions to the back of the locker room. *"Ah, dejalo y mueveté,"* he says to me.

In other words, *avoid the conflict.*

"Listen to your friend," *Gringo* says, then grabs my T-shirt and attempts to push me away from his precious spot.

Not happening.

I push back. He doesn't expect it, because his body slams against the lockers hard. He loses his balance and lands on his ass with a *thud*.

"I'm gonna fuckin' kick your ass!" he screams.

He's about to charge his full weight against me when one of his friends stands between us. "Dougan, chill out. Seriously, man, it's not worth getting kicked off the team."

Dougan stares me down before turning his back and walking to another row of lockers with his friends following behind him. I sit and take a deep breath. I'm not in Boulder anymore, that's for damn sure.

Everyone who has fourth-period lunch ditches the cafeteria and instead chooses to eat outside. The courtyard is filled with students. The south siders sit under the trees, while the north siders have flocked to the picnic tables as if they were personally made for them. I notice Nikki sitting with a bunch of jocks, all vying for her attention. She smiles at them and laughs at their jokes, but I can tell she's being fake. None of them are holding her attention for long.

I sit next to my old friends under a big maple tree.

"So what you been up to, Fuentes?" Pedro asks as he reaches into a brown paper bag and pulls out his lunch. "Besides pissin' off Dougan in the locker room."

I shrug. "Lived in Mexico for a while. Then moved to Colorado."

"What made you come back to this shithole?" Marco Delgado asks. He sits across from me and I catch a glimpse of a pocketknife peeking out of his sock.

"*Familia* brought me back," I tell them.

"Speaking of *familia*," Marco says. "Your brother Alex used to be a Blood, didn't he?"

I nod.

I'd be an idiot not to think that subject would come up sooner or later. My brother was an active member of the Latino Blood, until Hector Martinez betrayed him.

"Chuy got busted a while back. Most of the OGs got sent to the DOC," Delgado explains.

The DOC—otherwise known as the Department of Corrections.

"I heard."

Chuy used to be second in command. Once Chuy went down, the rest of the OGs went down with him. My cousin Enrique almost served time, but Alex helped him get a good lawyer who got the case against him dismissed.

"You think Alex had somethin' to do with the bust?"

Alex, responsible for bringing down the Latino Blood? I don't think so. "My brother isn't a narc," I say. Fuentes pride runs deep, and I'll do anything to protect my brothers and my family name. "*¿Comprende?*"

Marco nods. "I've got no problem with him. It's all good, man."

Mariana Castillo, the girl every guy had a crush on in second grade, sits with us. A bunch of girls follow her lead. Mariana was always the leader of the girls . . . whatever she did, the other girls followed. She's got a flawless complexion, long legs, thick lips, and a gleam in her eyes that reveals a raw and ruthless spirit.

"Well, well. I guess the rumors are true," she tells me. "Luis Fuentes has *definitely* grown up."

Marco laughs. "I think you've got yourself a fan club, Luis."

"You should come out with all of us on Saturday night," Mariana says.

"I've got to work," I tell her.

"That sucks. What if we—"

A blaring voice over the loudspeakers scattered throughout the courtyard cuts her off. *"Luis Fuentes, please report to Principal Aguirre's office immediately. Luis Fuentes, report to Principal Aguirre's office immediately,"* the voice bellows again just in case for some miraculous reason I hadn't heard the first time.

Marco lets out a low whistle. "In trouble with Aguirre on the first day of school, Fuentes?" he asks, amused. "He's probably been alerted that we were friends back in grade school. Got in our share of trouble, didn't we?"

"Sure did." Marco and I had been in the same homeroom and sat next to each other for practically every class. I always earned good grades, but Marco could always convince me to be his partner in crime.

"Did you get called in, too?" I ask him.

"First thing this mornin'. Aguirre's a hard-ass and will try to scare you into playin' by his rules. He'll try to get you to talk, but keep your mouth shut. It'll totally piss him off. It's hilarious watchin' his face get all red."

"I bet it has to do with that fight with Dougan in the locker room," Pedro chimes in.

"Good luck," Mariana says.

"Thanks," I say, hoping that I don't need it.

I find the front office a few minutes later. An old woman behind the front desk looks frazzled as students stand around impatiently requesting class schedule changes or signing up for appointments with the guidance counselor.

I figure I'll wait in line instead of announcing my arrival. I'm not looking forward to facing Aguirre. Marco isn't the only one who declared him a hard-ass. My brothers warned me that their old principal didn't take any prisoners.

The door opens to Aguirre's office and a tall guy wearing a suit and tie appears. "Fuentes!" he yells above the noise. He scans the room until his eyes lock on mine. He doesn't look thrilled to see me. "In my office," he orders.

I weave my way through the crowd.

Aguirre is holding a manila folder with my name typed on it as he sits on the edge of his desk. "Come in, Luis. Sit down."

I sit in one of his guest chairs and look around the room. Fairfield High School memorabilia is scattered on the walls, as well as pictures of Aguirre with old alumni. A tennis player, an NFL quarterback, and a news anchor are a few of the alumni pictures posted. Impressive.

I wonder if in ten years I'll be in a picture with Aguirre that's permanently displayed in his office.

Not right now, though. Right now Aguirre is looking at me with a mixture of annoyance and anger.

"The last time I had a Fuentes called into my office, it was your brother Alex. He was a magnet for trouble." He slaps my file on the table. "I assumed you'd be different, Luis. You were a straight-A student at Flatiron High. That school is ranked as the second-best high school in Colorado for academics. You were in the honor society, active in student council, played soccer, and were cocaptain of the swim team."

I nod. "Yes, sir."

He leans forward. "So why the hell are you getting in fights in the locker room?"

I shrug. "I don't know."

Aguirre lets out a deep breath. "If I had a dollar every time I heard a student say *I don't know*, I'd be a millionaire. No, a billionaire. I have a zero tolerance policy. Whatever altercation happened between you and Justin Dougan in the locker room has become my problem. You want to know what I do with my problems?"

I don't answer.

He leans forward again and speaks in a quiet, slow voice meant to capture my undivided attention. "My problems get a detention. After that comes suspension. Three strikes, and you're expelled."

When he takes a blue slip off his desk and hands it to me, I swallow hard. My first detention. I am not, no matter what, going to get two strikes. Even if it means being called Mex for the next nine months.

"Does this go in my permanent file?" I ask, looking down at the offending blue slip.

"I'm afraid so."

Shit. I briefly have a vision of breaking into the school office in the middle of the night and making the detention disappear. In movies people break into offices and steal files all the time. It would definitely be an adrenaline rush, especially if I was able to pull it off.

"Now get out of here," Aguirre says. "I don't want to see your face back in my office unless it's to tell me you're on the honor roll. Keep your head in your books, and we'll get along just fine."

"Is that it?" I ask him.

"No." He smiles and opens his arms out wide. "Welcome to Fairfield High."

12

Luis had been talking to Marco and Mariana when he got called to
Dr. Aguirre's office. He walked with confidence and purpose out of the
courtyard, and I found myself having a hard time tearing my gaze away
until he was out of sight.

I hope he doesn't remember me, although I have a strange feeling in
the pit of my stomach that he didn't forget our encounter at his brother's
wedding. How could he? The last image I have is him waving to me . . .
naked. He looked ridiculously hot back then, and he's still got the swagger. Just from the way he walks I can tell he knows he's one of those guys
with the "it" factor.

In the halls, girls were staring at him. He nodded and smiled at
every girl who looked his way. Marco was flirting with the girls right
along with him, like they were a tag team.

The next time I see Luis, it's the last period of the day. Chemistry
with Mrs. Peterson. Luis seems amused when he walks in the classroom
and finds me sitting in the back row with Kendall and Derek. When the
pregnant teacher announces that she assigns partners and we'll be sitting in alphabetical order, my heart starts racing. My last name starts

with a *C* and Luis's starts with an *F*. I panic that we could be assigned as partners, until Mrs. Peterson calls out, "Mariana Castillo, you're partnered with Nikki Cruz."

Oh, no. Mariana and I have only one thing in common: our parents were born in Mexico. That's it.

Mariana Castillo hated me when Marco and I dated, as if I took away her property. The few times Marco and I hung out with his friends, she'd always glare at me and make sure none of the other south side girls liked me. I was an outcast in their group, but as long as I had Marco by my side I didn't care. Even though Marco and I aren't together anymore, Mariana still hates me.

"Eww. How come I get stuck with the fake Latina?" Mariana mumbles.

"There isn't anything fake about me, Mariana. You got a problem with me, go tell Mrs. Peterson."

Mariana waves her hand in the air. "Mrs. Peterson, Nikki and I *can't* be partners."

Peterson stops and looks down at Mariana. "Yes, you can and yes, you will. Believe me, Miss Castillo, I get complaints every year, and not once have I changed partners."

"But—"

"Zip it, or you'll get a detention."

Mariana shuts her mouth, but sneers at me as Mrs. Peterson goes down the rest of her list.

Luis is assigned to the table across from ours. Derek is assigned as his partner. I try not to have eye contact with Luis, but I find myself glancing up. Our eyes meet for a brief second before Mrs. Peterson knocks on Luis's lab table.

"So I see I'm blessed with another Fuentes in my class," our teacher says. "Your brother Alex was one of my more . . . challenging students. I guess I should give you the same lecture I gave your brother, Mr. Fuentes. No talking unless it's lab time, and even that isn't supposed to be used for chatter and gossip. It's for work. Get it?"

"Got it," Luis says, giving her a cocky thumbs-up.

"Let's hope you're better than your brother at following directions. Oh, and that reminds me . . ." She regards the rest of the class. "I have a zero tolerance policy. No cell phones allowed, even if it's an emergency from your parents, your friends, your boyfriends or girlfriends, your dog, or even God. They can call the front office if it's important enough. In addition, no gang-related clothing," she says, looking right at Luis and then eyeing the rest of the class, "and no threats against any student or you'll be out of my class permanently. I have detentions ready to hand out for anyone not following my rules. Now, take five minutes and intro- duce yourselves to your partner. Tell them interesting things about yourself, including your hobbies or what you did over the summer. Then you'll introduce your partner to the class."

"I can't believe I have to partner with you," Mariana mumbles.

"The feeling is mutual," I mumble back.

Mariana picks up her notebook and turns to the first page. "So talk, so I can write something down and not get kicked out of class. I know you're a rich bitch who used to date Marco Delgado until he broke up with you. Anything else I should share with the class?"

"Just tell the class that I help disabled dogs get adopted."

"Seriously, that's wack," Mariana says with a grimace. "You tell the class that I got a hundred thousand views on the YouTube video I made."

"Doing what?" I ask, wondering if she did a striptease act. Or maybe it was an instructional video on how to properly take a bong hit. I'm sure Mariana's name wasn't on the drug-free petition some freshman passed around last year for their community service project.

"I sing and dance . . . better than you, I'm sure."

I write that piece of information down to share with the class when it's my turn. Little does she know that dancing better than me is no difficult feat.

Luis introduces Derek, then Derek talks about how Luis moved here from Colorado but used to live in Fairfield when he was younger.

After the introductions there's time left, so Mrs. Peterson takes us on a tour of the lab. She tells us it was updated over the summer, and explains why there's a shower stall in the back of the room.

"Last year we had an . . . incident with some of my students who didn't listen to my instructions. Let's just say that the school board decided that installing a hazardous chemicals washing area might be necessary. None of you should ever need this shower, but if for any reason any one of you gets a chemical on your skin and you're having a reaction, wash it off immediately. You don't need to raise your hand and ask permission."

While we're standing in front of the shower, my phone starts to vibrate. Crap. It's in my back pocket. I totally forgot to turn it off. As if that's not bad enough, it rings so loud that now everyone is staring at me. I ignore it, hoping Mrs. Peterson doesn't realize it's mine and praying that the call transfers to voice mail before the next ring.

"You better turn that off," Kendall murmurs in my ear. "Rumor has it Peterson's got a cell phone collection worth thousands."

Too late.

"Ms. Cruz?"

I squeeze my eyes shut for a moment, wishing I could magically transplant myself to another classroom. "Yes?" I answer meekly.

Mrs. Peterson is standing in front of me now. "Go ahead, answer it."

I hesitate.

"Take your phone out of your pocket and answer it," she orders again. "Before I go into labor, please."

I slide it out of my pocket and press the answer button, when, to my complete horror, Mrs. Peterson motions to hand the phone to her.

She puts it to her ear. "Hello, this is Nikki's phone," she says into the receiver as if she's my personal secretary.

She covers the mouthpiece and whispers loudly so everyone can hear, "It's Dara from Razzle Salon, confirming your bikini and eyebrow wax appointment." Pause. "This is Mrs. Peterson, Nikki's chemistry teacher." Pause. "Dara says she's running late, so she's calling to see if you can come at six instead of four today."

I feel my face getting red hot as comments and snickers echo through the room. "That's fine," I say weakly.

Mrs. Peterson puts the phone back to her ear and says, "Dara, six o'clock will be just perfect. Okay. Yes, I will definitely let her know. You have a fabulous day, too. B'bye."

She turns off the phone, then walks over to her desk and places it inside one of the drawers. Peterson lets out an exaggerated, hefty sigh. "I guess since it's the first day of school I'll be nice and give you an option. Either I get to keep your phone, or you can serve detention after school today."

That's her being *nice*? What's it like when she's being *mean*? I've spent three years at this school without managing to get even one blue detention slip. "I *seriously* thought it was turned off," I say, hoping she'll show some compassion.

She points to her deadpan expression. "Does it look like I care? Zero tolerance. You should have turned it off before you came to class. Or, better yet, left it in your locker. Or at home. It's school policy to keep your phones completely turned off during class, Ms. Cruz. Not on vibrate and not switched to silent. You're a senior. You've had three years to memorize the Fairfield High School manual."

Memorize the manual? From her serious tone, I do think she expects us to memorize the school manual. "I'll take a detention," I say as the bell rings.

While everyone else files out of class, I wait for Mrs. Peterson to fill out the detention slip. She hands it to me, along with my phone.

"Don't let it happen again," she says. "Or you and I are not going to get along."

I don't mention that I'm not feeling particularly optimistic about us ever getting along.

"It's tough love," she calls after me as I walk out of her classroom.

I'd call it something else, but I don't make it a habit to piss off teachers, so I keep my mouth shut and head for my locker. Kendall is standing in front of it, waiting for me. She grabs my detention out of my hand and stares at the offending words written in Mrs. Peterson's handwriting. "I seriously can't believe that woman gave you a detention on the first day of school. Peterson is brutal. Want me to wait for you?"

"Nah, but thanks." My brother is walking toward us, reminding me that we're supposed to walk home together. "I got a detention, so I can't walk with you," I tell him.

"You got a detention on the first day of school?" he asks, completely shocked. "I didn't think that was possible."

"It is when you've got Mrs. Peterson for a teacher," I say.

"I'll give you a ride home," Kendall tells Ben. "But you can't talk about dragon slaying as if it's a real sport."

Ben agrees, although I'm sure he's bummed that he can't talk dragon slaying with her. I feel sorry for my brother, who doesn't have many friends who share his love of gaming. He's very popular online, but the people he plays with are anonymous . . . they're not real friends.

After they leave, I resign myself to the fact that I can't stall the inevitable. I head to the cafeteria, which doubles as the detention room after school. I'm pretty certain I'll be the only one in there.

But as I enter the cafeteria and am handed a sign-in sheet by Mr. Harris, a gym teacher, I see I'm not alone.

Justin Dougan, wearing his letterman's jacket even though it's too hot outside for anything heavier than a T-shirt, is sitting in back with his head resting on top of the table. Either he's sleeping or pretending not to care that he's stuck in this room expected to do nothing but be silent and do homework for an hour.

There's one other person in detention with me—Luis Fuentes.

I sit on the empty lunch table behind him, wondering the entire time how he managed to get himself in trouble. I glance back at Justin, and it doesn't seem so impossible anymore. Justin isn't exactly known for being the nicest kid in school. He must have provoked Luis. And Luis must have fought back.

Fights aren't allowed at Fairfield High without consequences. Neither are cell phone calls during class.

I sit for a half hour, attempting to study because some teachers don't think the first day of school is meant to be a blow-off day. I force myself to look down at my math book, but I can't focus and I'm totally lost. It's because Luis is here. I'm so aware of his presence in the room that it's distracting.

"Hey, Nikki," Luis whispers.

I look up and realize that Mr. Harris has walked out of the room. "What?"

Luis slides off the cafeteria bench and straddles the one right across from me. "We didn't really have a chance to talk in Peterson's class. Remember me from a couple of years ago?" he asks.

I shake my head. "Nope," I lie.

He puts his hand on his chest. "Luis Fuentes. I met you at my brother's weddin'."

As if I'd ever forget. I wish I didn't remember Luis Fuentes and his arrogant, annoying smile. Or the fact that he went skinny-dipping with a girl he met after flirting with me.

He's looking at me with his head tilted to the side, assessing my response.

I look away. Then look back at him. He's got one brow arched questioningly. It's no use, because he'll know the truth sooner or later. I can't keep up the charade any longer.

I shrug. "Okay, I remember you. Happy now?"

He casually props a foot up on the bench, and I can imagine him being a model at a photo shoot doing that pose. "Are you still bitter 'cause we never got it on that night? You didn't have to steal my clothes to get a peek at the goods, you know."

"I did *not* steal your clothes. I just hid them. And I don't remember seeing your . . ." I gesture to the general area of his crotch. "It wasn't memorable, obviously."

But it was. I've replayed that image of him, in all his glory, not looking one bit insecure or ashamed of his nakedness, many times. I hate myself for remembering him and everything he'd said to me that night in detail.

The beginning of a smirk tugs at his lips, because *he knows*. He knows I remember that moment just as clearly as he does.

Luis leaps back to his original seat as Mr. Harris walks back in the room.

"By the way," Luis whispers to me, "you got numbers three and seven wrong."

I look down at my math homework. "How would you know?"

He taps his head with his forefinger. "I'm kind of a math whiz. In both questions you forgot that the left-hand side requires the chain rule since y represents a function of x."

I look down at my paper. After a minute of retracing my steps, I find out that he's right. I look up at him in shock, but his back is turned to me again and Mr. Harris is scanning the room to make sure we're quiet.

After an hour, Mr. Harris announces that we've completed our detention requirements and are free to leave. Justin is the first to go. He glares at Luis as he passes him. Luis must either pretend not to notice or he doesn't care.

I walk out of the room. Luis walks next to me. "Looks like you need a math tutor."

"I don't hang out with south siders," I tell him, not stopping as I push open the front door to the school and walk out into the scorching summer heat. "Or date them."

"You don't date south siders?" he asks, chuckling.

"Not anymore I don't."

"I don't want to hang out with you or date you, Nikki." He flashes me a killer smile he's probably practiced in front of a mirror until it was perfect. "I suppose I wouldn't mind messin' around with you, though. Whenever you're up for it, let me know."

13
Luis

The best thing about surviving the first week of school is that you appreciate weekends and being able to sleep in. That is, except when your little nephew trots in the room while you're sleeping and mistakes your head for a drum.

"Hey, *muchacho!*" I say, picking him up and having him sit on my chest. "If your diaper leaks, you're outta here."

He flashes me a four-toothed smile.

Now that Paco is almost two years old, it's time he learns how to pronounce my name. "Say *Luis*," I tell him.

"Weese," he says.

"Not quite, but we'll work on it."

"Weese," he says again, getting excited now. He's bouncing up and down on me, like I'm his horse. "Weese, Weese, Weese!"

Brittany peeks her head in the open doorway. "Paco, are you bothering *Tío* Luis?" she asks.

"Nah," I tell her. "He's cool."

After entertaining him for a bit, I take my nephew into the living room, where Alex and Brittany are talking to *mi'amá*.

"Hey, bro," Alex says, then gestures to my boxers, which have the word *Colorado* written all over them in random colors. My friends gave them to me before I moved. "Nice pj's."

"Thanks." I put my nephew up on my shoulders, which makes him really happy. "I got Peterson for chemistry. Feel sorry for me?"

Brittany and my brother smile at each other.

"Definitely. She's brutal," Alex says. "Brit, didn't she give us detentions like every other day?"

"I've tried to block those days out." Brittany cringes. "I really hated you back then, Alex."

He slides the back of his hand slowly across her arm. "Come on, *chica*. You wanted me, but you were afraid to admit it."

Brittany bites her bottom lip as she looks into my brother's eyes. He cups her cheek in his hand and pulls her close, then kisses her.

I slide my nephew off my shoulders and shield his eyes. "Seriously, guys, aren't you past the honeymoon stage by now? You're on your second kid already."

"I don't want to get past this stage," my brother says.

"Me neither," Brittany coos.

Mi'amá wags her finger in my direction. "Don't you get any ideas, Luis. Keep your head on straight and don't lose sight of your goal." She holds out her arms for me to hand Paco over to her, then she takes him in the kitchen.

"I almost didn't recognize the place," Alex says, eyeing the furniture and hardwood floors.

"This place looks amazing," Brittany agrees. "The neighborhood has completely changed, too."

"Tell me about it," I say. "We've even got a cop livin' next door."

Alex shakes his head in confusion. "A cop?"

"Yeah. He also happens to be our landlord." I leave out the part that I think the guy was making a move on *Mamá*.

Alex sits up, really interested now. "Your landlord is *a cop*?"

"I don't think he's realized that this side of town is dirt poor. I've got the feelin' he wants the south side of Fairfield to be the next Wrigleyville." Wrigleyville is the upscale yuppie neighborhood where Wrigley Field, home of the Chicago Cubs baseball team, is located. Wrigleyville is nothing like Fairfield, even if Officer Reyes wants to think it is.

"*La policía* livin' in south Fairfield," Alex murmurs, almost to himself. "Glad he wasn't here when I was in high school. I definitely didn't play by the rules like you do, Luis."

What he doesn't know won't hurt him. I wonder what rules I'll be tempted to break tonight with Marco, Mariana, and their friends after I get off work.

"Want to go to Brookfield Zoo with us after breakfast?" Brittany asks. "Paco goes crazy walking through the bat house."

I laugh. "While I'd love to stroll around the zoo with you guys, I've got homework. Then I work from three to ten tonight."

My brother raises an eyebrow. "You got the job at Brickstone?"

"You're lookin' at the club's newest busboy, Alex."

"A busboy?" My sister-in-law shakes her head. "I don't think you should do it. You're ridiculously smart and athletic, Luis. They should have put you as a lifeguard, or at the front desk or something. Don't settle."

"It's money," I tell her, shrugging.

"It's degrading," she shoots back.

I shrug again. Brittany was brought up rich and white and has no clue what it's like to be poor. Or Mexican. I know we need the money, and the place pays decent. So what if I'll be pouring water and handling people's dirty dishes. It's not a big deal. Mexicans are notorious for doing jobs white people don't want to do. I'm cool with it. And I know I'll do a good enough job to get that promotion to server in a month.

Alex and Brittany leave with Paco after breakfast. I get a few texts from Marco asking me to hang out with him and a bunch of other guys before I go to work, but it'll have to wait till later. I've got to keep my grades up. If I don't, I can kiss the aeronautics program good-bye.

After studying for next week's math assessment and US history quiz, I walk to work. It's still nice out, but I know it won't last long. Spring in Illinois is just a tease before the scorching summer. Then fall hits with a vengeance. But what really brings you to your knees is the frigid winter cold with winds that'll slap you in the face and make you wish you lived where they don't even know what snow is. Chicago snow is totally different from Boulder snow.

Fran Remington meets me by the front desk and has me work with a guy named Richard, a middle-aged dude with feathered hair that doesn't move across his scalp. It's either hairsprayed to death or a hairpiece.

In the employee locker room, I'm handed my uniform—white pants and a crisp white shirt with the word *Brickstone* embroidered in a small crest on the chest. Richard gets to wear black pants and a white shirt complete with a black jacket and tie. He looks like he's going to a wedding. I, on the other hand, resemble a guy who sells ice cream from a vending cart.

I spend the night shadowing Richard. Guests pile into the dining room as the night goes on. I help Richard serve the food, I clear dishes, refill glasses, and pretty much float through the night without a problem.

Until Nikki Cruz walks in with a group of friends. They're all white except for her, which shouldn't annoy the shit out of me, but it does. It's no wonder she disses her Mexican side . . . she doesn't associate with anyone who's Mexican. I don't recognize any of them, but one of the guys in the group is wearing a black golf shirt with the words *Chicago Academy Golf Team* embroidered in gold letters.

Everyone knows that Chicago Academy is the exclusive private high school that kids with a lot of money go to. They're known for being complete snobs who drive high-priced, gas-guzzling cars. I bet none of these *pendejos* could tell the difference between a carburetor and an alternator.

Nikki's got on a low-cut pink sundress that shows off her curves. Damn, she looks hot. I'm not the only one who notices, because the Chicago Academy dudes walking in behind her are not subtle about checking out her ass.

Richard taps me on the shoulder. "You almost spilled water on Mrs. Steinberg," he says in a not-too-thrilled tone.

"Sorry," I murmur. Shit. Seeing Nikki here is distracting me.

I watch as the hostess leads Nikki and her friends to a table in a secluded corner by the window. Just my luck it's in Richard's station.

"Pour them water," Richard says, gesturing to Nikki's table. I hear her quiet laughter from across the room over something one of the girls says to her.

I go over to the table with a pitcher of ice water. I'm in charge of water—all types of water. The assistant waiter is in charge of all other drinks.

"Would you like tap, sparkling, or bottled water?" I ask them.

Nikki looks up at me, wide-eyed. "Luis, what are you doing here?"

"I work here."

"You *know* him?" one of the Chicago Academy guys asks Nikki. The guy eyes me, obviously sizing me up, then says to her, "Is he your cousin?"

Because we're both Mexican he thinks we must be related? Idiot.

"No. We, umm . . ." Nikki stumbles on the words.

"We go to school together," I say, finishing her sentence.

"That's cute," the guy says. "My dad went to Fairfield before they merged Fairfield South and North together. He said it's trash now."

"You're such an elitist," Nikki says, more amused at his comment than annoyed. "Fairfield is diverse, unlike that white-bread school you go to."

"You're as much of an elitist as I am, sweetheart," the guy says.

Derek and his girlfriend, Kendall, walk in and join the group. Derek reaches out his hand, and we shake. "What's up, man? You didn't tell me you worked here."

"My brother knew some—"

The elitist guy taps me on the elbow. "Get us some sparkling water," he orders, interrupting me.

Derek scowls. "Yo, Hunter. Don't they teach you at that fancy school of yours not to cut someone off when they're talking?"

The snob rolls his eyes. "I just played eighteen holes, Derek. I'm thirsty. Sue me for asking the kid for something to drink."

"It's cool," I tell the snob, but I'm thinking, *Kid*? A dude my age, named *Hunter* no less, just called me *kid*. Unbelievable.

When I come back from the kitchen with the sparkling water and a small bowl of limes in hand, I pour the guy water.

I pour Nikki water, too. I wish I didn't get a whiff of her sweet perfume as I leaned down next to her.

After finishing all of their drink orders, I busy myself with the rest of the customers. I don't linger around Nikki's table, and only go back to clear dishes or give refills. There's something about Nikki that makes me want to know what it would be like if we got together. It's her feisty spirit, and the fact that nothing I've done has made her loosen up. She's a challenge that I definitely want to take on.

I hate the fact that there's a part of me that's embarrassed being a busboy in front of Derek, Nikki, and Kendall.

When Nikki's table gets up to leave, Hunter holds out a fifty-dollar bill. "Here you go," he says, making a show of handing it to me like I'm a charity case. "Don't spend it all in one place."

"Thanks, man," I say, even though I'd like to shove the money back in his face. Or up his ass—where it looks like he stashes the rest of his cash.

"Hey, Nik," I call out as she's about to walk out of the room.

She stops and looks back at me.

I know the rest of the guys are watching, so I step close to her and whisper in her ear, "Ditch these guys when I get off work and hang with me, *mi chava*."

She pulls me close and whispers in my ear, "Dream on," then struts out of the room while the guys look dumbly at her, then back at me.

"You shouldn't flirt with her," Derek says to me before following the rest of their friends out of the dining room.

"Why not?"

"Because Nikki has claws. Big ones, and they'll come out when you least expect it."

"She doesn't scare me," I tell him.

He pats me on the shoulder. "She should."

Twenty minutes later, I recognize Nikki's parents as they walk into the dining room and are also seated in Richard's section.

"Luis, you look familiar," Dr. Cruz says as he looks at my name tag.

"My brother is Alex Fuentes. I met you and your family at his weddin'."

"Ah, yes. That's why you look familiar. It's been a long time."

Mrs. Cruz smiles in a reserved, almost rehearsed way. "Alex told us you were moving back to Chicago. If you need anything, be sure to call us."

I nod, not sure if she really means it or if she's just saying it to be polite. "Thanks."

Being in the presence of Dr. and Mrs. Cruz makes me forget that I'm supposed to be serving other tables. Until I get a nudge from Richard, reminding me that I have a job and I better do it well or risk being fired.

I stand up straight and get back to business. "Would you like sparkling, bottled, or tap water?"

14

The guys from Chicago Academy are all the same. They've got big egos and think they're studs. After dinner, my friends and I hang out by the Brickstone volleyball courts. My brother disappeared before dinner to go to the game room because he found out someone beat his high score on a simulated motorcycle game. My parents are at some lecture in the Brickstone auditorium.

Hunter McBride is sitting next to me, along with a bunch of guys and girls from Chicago Academy. They live in my neighborhood so I've known them forever, but ever since junior high they've gone to private schools while the rest of us went to public schools. My mom wanted me to go to CA, but since all my friends were going to public schools I chose to stay with them.

I look over at Kendall and Derek sitting on the other side of the court deep in discussion. I don't know which one of them looks more miserable. Ever since they had the whole "where are we going to college" discussion, they haven't been getting along. I think they finally realize that their relationship won't last forever.

Hunter nudges me and says, "Nikki, truth or dare?"

I throw my head back. "Not this stupid game again. The last time we played truth or dare, I ended up having to eat three burgers and threw up afterward."

"I'll let you start, then."

All eyes are on me. I sigh, wondering how I get myself into these situations. I need Kendall to get me out of this, but she's caught up in her own problems with Derek right now.

"Come on, Nikki," a guy named Mason says. "It's your turn to get Hunter back for the burger-eating incident."

I'll play, but only because I get the upper hand to start with. "Okay . . . Hunter, truth or dare?"

He doesn't hesitate. "Dare."

Now I've got to think of something that I know he won't do. That'll teach him to start playing this stupid game with me. "I dare you to jump in the pool with your clothes on."

"Fine."

"Really?" I didn't think he'd agree to it, mainly because I think he probably only owns clothes that need to be specially dry-cleaned and hand pressed.

"Yeah," he says, "but you have to come with me as a witness."

Fair enough. The rest of the group waits for us at the volleyball courts as Hunter and I walk across the grass to the outdoor pool.

"Are you really gonna jump in?" I ask.

"Absolutely." He wiggles his eyebrows. "I'd do anything you tell me to do."

I roll my eyes. Hunter can't stand the fact that I won't just go out with him because of who he is. He's told me it's his life goal to make me say yes to a date, so he's made asking me out a game. Most girls are dying to know what it's like to be with Hunter McBride, son of the biggest real estate mogul in Chicago. He goes out with girls once or twice, then gets sick of them. He knows we'll never get together for real, but that doesn't stop him from trying.

I shouldn't play along, but I do. Hunter is a harmless rich guy who needs friends like me in his life to bring him down to earth. It's not easy . . . years of being spoiled and getting everything he wants is rotting his brain. Kendall thinks he's hopeless, but I think of him like one of the dogs at the shelter I volunteer at—he just needs some training.

We open the gate to the outdoor pool at Brickstone, which is officially closed to guests because it's past ten o'clock.

"So what's the deal with you and that busboy guy?"

"Nothing."

"Yeah, right. He was looking at you the entire time. I saw you checking him out more than a few times."

"I was not. You're changing the subject," I say because I can feel my face getting hot just talking about Luis. "You better hurry and jump in before security comes."

Hunter sits on a lounge chair and pulls off his shoes.

"I said with your clothes on, Hunter."

He laughs. "These are my custom Edward Green shoes, sweetheart. I'm not about to get them wet."

I take one of his precious shoes, stand at the edge of the pool, and pretend to toss it in the water.

His eyes go wide. "You better not."

"What if I did?" I ask, tossing the shoe back to him. He needs to know material things shouldn't mean so much.

He puts both shoes neatly under the chair. It makes me wonder if the clothes in his closet are neatly folded and color-coded.

"If you tossed my shoe in, I'd do this!" he says, then surprises me by picking me up and jumping into the pool with me securely captured in his arms.

I come up sputtering. "I'm gonna kill you!" I swim toward the edge of the pool, completely drenched and contemplating how I'm going to explain this one to my parents. I hoist myself out of the water and wring out my hair. "I hate you."

"No, you don't. In fact, I think you like me a little."

"That's where you're wrong. You owe me a new pair of shoes," I tell him."

"No problem. When can I take you shopping?" Hunter gets out of the pool. His shirt is sticking to his chest, his pants are sticking to his legs . . . and he's looking right at my chest. I look down and realize that my dress is clinging to my skin.

"Never. I'll e-mail you my size and a picture of them."

Hunter stares down at my heels. "What designer are they?"

"I don't know. I got them at Target."

He laughs. "Do you know how cute you are?"

"Not when I'm wet and makeup is running down my face. I'm sure I look horrible, thanks to you."

"You look hot, Nik. Superhot." He steps closer. "We're both wet. You know what this means, don't you?"

"That I'm done playing truth or dare?"

"No. It means that we've got something in common. I might not have the Mexican thing goin' on, but we're both soaking wet."

"You're grasping at straws, Hunter. Being wet does not mean we have something in common."

"Just shut up and roll with it. You know, I'm always game if you want to fool around. You don't have a boyfriend, I don't have a girlfriend . . ." He leans in to kiss me, but I put my hand on his chest and stop him.

"Seriously, don't make me laugh."

"Come on, Nik." He looks down at my breasts. "Your body is telling you something."

If he's referring to me being nippy, it's because a gust of wind just blew over me and I got a chill for a second. We're in the suburbs of Chicago—no girl is immune to the Chicago wind.

"The pool is closed for guests," a guy says from the gate. A bunch of employees are standing behind him, ready to jump in the pool for employee "after-hours" swim time. Luis is there, too, talking to the hostess from the dining room.

"The pool is closed?" Hunter asks as if he wasn't aware of it. Hunter winks at me to play along. He's good at playing dumb, I'll give him that.

"You'll have to come back tomorrow," a security guy says. "It's only open to staff after ten."

"Sorry." Hunter grabs his shoes, then takes my hand in his and leads me out of the pool area.

"Hey," Luis says as Hunter and I pass him.

"Hey," I say back dumbly.

I take my hand from Hunter's grasp. "Remind me never to play truth or dare with you again."

Hunter laughs. "Are you kidding? That was fun. I bet I could have paid that security guard off and we could have stayed. You'll have to come over to my house next time and go in our hot tub with me."

"Keep dreaming."

Over by the volleyball courts, I see my parents talking to my friends.

"What happened to you two?" Dad asks us when he catches a glimpse of our drenched clothes. "You're both soaking wet."

I'm not about to admit I was playing truth or dare. It's better to play the stupid teenager role. "Hunter thought it would be funny if we went swimming with our clothes on," I tell him.

Hunter opens his mouth wide in mock shock and points to me accusingly. "She made me do it."

Mom shakes her head. "I think the party's over, Nikki. Time to go home."

"I'm coming with you," Kendall says, joining us. She leaves Derek sulking by himself.

As we walk to the car, I look over at the pool area where the employees are still hanging out. Though it's not fully lit, I can see Luis on one of the lounge chairs still talking to the hostess.

"We ran into Luis Fuentes," Dad says when we start driving home. "You remember him, don't you, Nikki? He's Alex's brother. Very smart boy."

"I know," I say. "He's in my chemistry class."

"I suspect Luis has a wild streak now that he's moved back to the south side," Mom says in a warning tone. "Don't get involved with him."

"I've hardly said two words to him," I say to my overprotective mother, but really feel like moaning in defeat.

It's been easy to reject advances from guys like Hunter because I don't feel a connection with them. When Luis and I are in the same room, I'm so aware of him that I wonder how long I can keep the wall of protection up before he chisels through it. His swagger, his confidence, his advances . . . they make me weak and I have to continually remind myself that a boy like Luis can make me lose control.

Staying strong has never been so hard.

15

Luis

On Monday morning, Nikki is waiting for me at my locker the second I get to school.

"What are the chances that I can convince you to get another job?" she asks me.

She says it as if I can find another job with a snap of my fingers. "What's the problem, *chica*?"

"The problem is that I don't want my friends questioning how we know each other or guessing that we have some unfinished business between us . . . because we don't."

"Why do you care about what other people think?"

"I just do," she says. "Everyone knows I don't have a boyfriend or want a boyfriend."

I laugh. "So who was that guy you were with in the country club pool Saturday night?"

"Hunter is just a friend." She crosses her arms on her chest, doing a pretty good imitation of our chemistry teacher. All she needs to complete the image is a glare that can melt steel.

"So you go around bonkin' guys who aren't your boyfriend? Nice," I say.

"I don't bonk."

Marco sticks his head between us. "Yes, Nikki, you do. I've got first-hand knowledge." He pats me on the chest with the back of his hand. "But she likes to call it makin' love. Ain't that the truth, *puta*?"

"Lay off, man," I tell Marco in a stern voice, but as I look at his eyes and see they're completely bloodshot I know he's wasted.

"Why should I lay off?" Marco drapes his arm around Nikki and kisses her cheek mockingly. She doesn't move a muscle. "Nikki here likes gettin' down and dirty, don't you, baby?"

She winces. I push him away from her and say to him, "Come on, man. Don't be a *pendejo*."

In a flash she runs down the hall and disappears.

"Since we broke up all she does is hang out with rich white dudes. Every once in a while she needs to be reminded what it was like to be with a Latino stud," Marco says.

I take my books out of my locker and head to class. "You should probably go home and sleep off whatever you're on, *ese*."

"Need to stay in school," he answers. "If I'm absent, they won't let me try out for the soccer team."

Soccer tryouts are today and tomorrow after school. Soccer wasn't a popular sport at Flatiron High, but at Fairfield it's obviously big because everyone is talking about it. Even some of the girls talked about watching the tryouts.

I don't see Nikki until the end of the day, in chemistry. She's standing at the lab table across from me. "What's up?" I say.

She doesn't respond.

"Marco didn't mean what he said this mornin'."

"Yes, he did. You guys are all alike. Leave me alone."

"Why does Nikki hate me so much?" I ask Derek.

He laughs. "Nikki hates every guy who reminds her of Marco. You're Mexican, he's Mexican . . . and worse, you're friends. 'Nuff said."

"So she goes for guys like Hunter instead?"

He shakes his head. "Don't ask me. I'm having enough troubles with my own relationship; the last thing I want to do is try to analyze someone else's." Derek and I start getting our lab station ready while we wait for Peterson's instructions. "You ever have a girlfriend?" he asks me.

"Not a serious one—nothin' that lasted more than a couple of months." I dated a girl when I lived in Mexico, but her parents didn't like me. They said they didn't want their daughter running with some poor dude. I bet if her parents knew I was living back in the U.S. they'd be pissed we broke up. Getting a one-way ticket to the States without sneaking across the border like a fugitive is like winning the lottery.

"A bunch of us are gonna watch you at soccer tryouts," Mariana says to me as she leans across the lab table. "I hear you've got moves."

Nikki snorts.

"Table one, I hear talking!" Peterson yells from across the room. "Do you four want a detention, because I have some detention slips in my desk collecting dust. You know how much I hate dust."

After the final bell rings, Derek and I head for the locker room. During tryouts, the social divide is blurred. The coach puts Marco and me on the same team and we dominate. The other side can't even score.

Justin Dougan, who happens to be our goalie, pushes me from behind when I get close to our net to block a ball.

"What the fuck, Dougan. If you haven't noticed, we're on the same team."

"Oops," he says sarcastically, then holds out his hand so anyone watching would think he's about to help me up.

I whack his hand away. "Were you born a prick?"

"Shut up, Fuentes. We might be on the same team, but we'll never be in the same league."

Derek stands beside me. "Dougan, get over yourself."

"It's cool," I tell Derek, and ignore Dougan the rest of the time.

At the end of practice, all the guys walk to the hot dog place a block away from school. Derek has been preoccupied the entire walk over. He pulls out his cell phone and starts texting the minute we get our food and sit down.

"You been datin' Kendall a long time?" I ask him.

"Since this summer," he says. "She doesn't trust me. She thinks I'm gonna cheat on her or find someone else if we go to different colleges." He grabs a fry. "I love her, you know. I can't even see myself with anyone else."

"Does she know you're in it for the long haul?"

"Shit, Luis, I tell her all the time. Nikki's been putting negativity and doubts in her head ever since we started going out. Don't get me wrong . . . I think Nikki's cool, but she thinks we're all out to screw as many girls as possible. I wish she had a boyfriend so she'd loosen up." He nods in my direction. "Would you date her?"

I think of Nikki's feisty attitude mixed with her delicate vulnerability that intrigues me to no end. She's also crazy beautiful with a body that has inspired more than a few fantasies. I'm afraid if I dated her, I wouldn't want to let her go. I'd have to, though. I have a long-term plan, and it doesn't include being tied down to a girl.

"So, would you date her, or what?" Derek asks again.

"I'd go out with her," I admit.

"I'm supposed to have Kendall come on my boat next weekend. You should come with us . . . I'll have her bring Nikki."

"Nikki won't go if she knows I'm gonna be there," I tell him.

"Leave that up to me."

A kid I don't know walks past us. "Hey, Ben!" Derek says.

The kid gives a half wave as he heads to the game room off to the side.

"That's Ben Cruz, Nikki's brother," Derek explains. "He's a freshman and is completely antisocial if you're not into gaming."

"Gamin', huh?" I say.

"Yep."

I wander into the game room after I finish eating and most of the guys have left.

Ben is playing some alien shooting game when I walk up to him. He's in the zone and doesn't look up until the game is over.

"You're Nikki's brother, right?" I ask before he slips another token in the slot.

He looks at me, then goes back to playing the game.

"I'm Luis Fuentes," I tell him.

He starts shooting aliens. "I know who you are. You're Alex's brother."

"How'd you know?"

He shrugs. "Photographic memory, I guess."

Gamers love when you speak their language. "You ever play World of Warcraft?"

"Of course."

"They've got some sick graphics." I had played WoW, but the free trial period ended and there was no way I could afford the monthly fee. "Awesome game," I tell him.

When he finds out I've played WoW, his entire face lights up. "I've been playing for two years," he says. "I'm designing my own adventure game with awesome graphics and levels just like Warcraft. Nobody really cares except gamers."

"I'll bet it's cool." I definitely appreciate strategic computer games.

"I'd show it to you . . ." He hesitates. "But you probably don't want to come to my house."

"Why not?"

"Because I'm a geeky freshman and you're a senior who hangs with the tough kids and jocks. On top of that, I heard my sister telling her friends that you're a jerk."

Marco yells out, "Yo, Luis. We're goin' over to Juan's house to hang out. Come on, I'll give you a ride."

Ben stiffens as soon as Marco's voice bellows through the air. The poor kid is scared shitless of Marco. Is it because of Nikki? Or did Ben and Marco have a problem in the past?

"I'm gonna stay here," I tell Marco.

He laughs. "All right. But when you get bored playin' with the geeks, call me."

Ben pretends not to hear the insult. We talk about online games versus traditional arcade games. It doesn't take long before Ben insists I come to his house so he can show me the new game he's developing that would mix the two. The kid is more excited than I would be if I got a Camaro.

When I follow Ben up the driveway of his house, it's hard not to be impressed. Inside, each room is decorated in weird patterns and colors. They have a computer room decorated in a jungle theme complete with a stuffed tiger in the corner.

Ben has a superhigh-tech computer with a huge monitor that looks like a television screen. I bet the whole thing cost close to four Gs.

Ben explains how to play the game he's designing. I choose to be a dragon slayer and my mission is to battle the badass dragon who's guarding my princess. In the middle of my battle, the dragon freezes. Ben takes the controller from me.

"I need to fix that bug," he says. I try and help him, although computer coding is not my strong suit.

"What are you doing here?" Nikki asks me when she walks into the computer room.

"Playin' video games with your brother."

"He's a *freshman*," she says.

"So? Luis's a gamer," Ben tells her proudly. "Just like me. Us gamers have to stick together."

Nikki sneers at me. "Luis is *not* a gamer, Ben." She huffs in frustration and storms out of the room.

"Be right back," I tell Ben, then I follow Nikki. She's heading for the stairs, but I grab her elbow and force her to look at me. "What's your problem?"

"I don't like you."

"You haven't even given me a chance."

She laughs. "I don't need to. You're too cocky for your own good."

"It's a cover-up for my extreme insecurity when it comes to you. Maybe if we kissed it would prove whether we have chemistry or not."

"Just one kiss?"

I nod. "You don't know what you're missin'."

She closes the space between us and, before my brain has time to contemplate what's about to happen, Nikki grabs the back of my hair and pulls my head to hers so our lips are just barely touching.

Talk about an adrenaline rush.

"Do you kiss with just lips?" she whispers, then brushes her lips against mine. "Or do you spice it up a bit?" Her tongue darts between my lips in a slow, sensuous rhythm that sends images of us together in a more intimate setting rushing through my head.

I keep my hands at my sides, letting her control this. That means I'm in control of myself, even if she's controlling the kiss. I know she's fucking with me, making me all hot and bothered just to dis me after.

I've got this. In fact, I think she's the one losing control.

"I definitely like to spice it up." I glide my tongue against hers. It's hot and wet and feels fucking incredible. A small moan escapes from her mouth that I swear sounds like, "Oh, Luis," and that's where I lose it.

Nikki is an adrenaline rush just being herself. I pull back and cup her flushed cheek gently in my palm.

We just stare at each other. "What are you doing?" she asks.

"Lookin' at you. We got major chemistry, don't we?"

"Nope." She doesn't break eye contact, probably wanting me to look away first. When I don't, she steps away and a huge, cocky grin crosses her face. She *tsk*s and shakes her head. "Sorry, Luis, but you need a little practice. Your tongue action was a bit awkward. I mean, it wasn't *all* bad. You have potential, but obviously we're not compatible."

As I'm standing there stunned, I'm thinking that this girl is a witch and not an angel. She's definitely put a spell on me, and I'm practically panting, ready to beg her for the chance to do it again—now. That wasn't just *fun*, and my tongue action is anything but awkward. I've had *fun* with other girls. Lots of 'em. Nobody has complained before.

When I looked into her eyes, and her eyes were locked on mine, there was something there. It was undeniable.

Nikki wipes her lips with the back of her hand. "Don't you *dare* tell anyone we kissed."

Why, because I'm a poor Mexican and after Marco the only guys who are worthy of her have fifty-dollar bills they wave around like pieces of scrap paper?

Ben walks in the room and asks, "What were you guys doing?"

Nikki says "Nothing" at the same time I say, "Your sister and I were just makin' out."

16

Nikki

Sometimes things are better off forgotten. The fact that I kissed Luis is one of them. So it wasn't as bad as I made it out to be . . . and in reality I can't stop thinking about doing it again. But he doesn't need to know that. All week during school I've managed to avoid talking to him, which is great. Except it takes a lot of energy to avoid someone you can't help but notice.

Sunday mornings I volunteer at the animal shelter near my house. When I get there, the manager, Sue, tells me that a new dog named Granny came in this morning.

"She's blind," Sue tells me, and my heart breaks a little. "Bulldog. Probably around nine or ten years old. Her elderly owner died, and nobody in the family could take the dog."

I've seen old dogs die in their cages at the shelter, because few people want to adopt a dog only to pay the higher medical costs older dogs usually have. On top of that, people don't want to adopt a dog that won't be around much longer.

"Where is she?" I ask.

"Cage thirty-three. You can walk her, then start cleaning out the west side cages."

I immediately go to cage thirty-three. Granny is lying down in the corner with her head on the ground.

"Hey, girl," I say as I unlock the cage.

She picks her head up when I pet her, and leans into my lap. I learn pretty quickly that Granny likes her tummy rubbed. I take her for a walk, leading her to the open grassy area in the back so she can sniff around.

I walk the other dogs, but the entire time I'm thinking about Granny. I go back to her cage to give her tummy rubs five more times.

"I'll come back tomorrow to check on Granny," I tell Sue during my break.

"You're not on the schedule."

"I know. But I noticed her bowl was full. I hand-fed her. If she doesn't eat tomorrow, I'll help her."

Sue rolls her eyes. "She'll eat, Nikki. Healthy dogs don't starve themselves."

"Depressed ones do," I say back. "And she's depressed."

"Too bad we don't have the budget for a dog therapist, huh?"

"You've got me, though," I tell her.

I spend the rest of the time handling the other dogs until I leave the shelter and head home for a shower.

When I pull into my driveway, Kendall is already waiting for me. She stares at the mud stains on my jeans. "Are you full of doggie germs?"

"Yep."

She holds her hands up. "Ugh. Don't touch me. I'll wait outside while you take a shower. Hurry!"

We've had plans for a while to go on Derek's boat in Fox Lake. It's not actually his boat, it's his parents'.

Twenty minutes later I run out of the house all showered and ready to spend the rest of the day relaxing and tanning on the boat.

"So . . . ," Kendall says. "Want to elaborate on what's going on between you and Luis since 'the kiss'?"

I'd called Kendall after our kiss and told her everything. "Nothing. You know I just made out with Luis to prove a point to myself . . . and to him."

"And that point is . . ."

"That I can kiss a guy without getting emotionally involved."

"And how did that work out for ya?"

I look out the window. "I'm not as emotionally immune as I want to be. I'm just glad we're going out on the boat so I can clear my head. I don't want to get involved with anyone, Kendall. Especially someone like . . ."

"Like Marco?" Kendall says, finishing my sentence.

"Yeah. I can't do that."

Kendall shrugs. "What if Luis is different, Nik? What if he likes you, and you like him, and it's all good?"

"It doesn't work that way. You love Derek, and Derek loves you, but you guys still have problems."

"I'm going on the boat today, aren't I? I'm trying to live in the moment instead of obsessing about our inevitable future."

"And that's what you think I should do?"

After the forty-minute drive, she pulls into the gravel driveway. "I think you should be happy. You've been punishing yourself for two years, Nikki."

"I don't want to get hurt again." I smile and give her a hug. "I love you for wanting me to be happy, though."

Kendall was there after I lost the baby. She listened to me cry hour after hour, day after day, night after night, until I had no more tears left. When I needed her to talk, to just say anything to get my mind off of what had happened, she came through for me. She talked about everything and nothing until her throat was sore. And when I didn't want to talk, we sat silent for hours. She bought me ice cream and Hallmark sympathy cards with encouraging words on them, and told me one day my heart would heal even if my body was scarred forever.

"Just try to have fun, okay?" We walk around Derek's lake house and head for his private pier.

"Hey, girls!" Derek yells from the boat. "You're late."

"Nikki had to wash dog germs off her," Kendall tells him. For the first time in a week, Kendall wraps her arms around Derek and gives him a kiss. I'm glad things are better between them, even though I admit I have my doubts.

I'm shocked to see Luis sitting on the bow wearing nothing but a pair of long swim shorts, revealing naturally tanned washboard abs and a thin line of hair, which extends from his navel and disappears beneath his swim shorts, which ride low on his hips.

Whoa. I hate that I'm tempted to stare.

"Who invited you?" I ask.

"Obviously not you," he says.

"Give the guy a break," Derek chimes in as he sits in the captain's chair.

"Don't think this is a date," I tell Luis quietly as he offers a hand to help me in the boat.

Luis furrows his brows. "Who said anythin' about a date? I didn't say anythin' about a date. Yo, Derek, did you say anythin' about a date?"

"Actually, *you* did. You said you wanted to ask Nikki out, but were too chickenshit to do it."

"Well, this is turning out to be an interesting afternoon. Luis, nothing is going to happen between us. We kissed. It was awkward. It's over."

Luis smacks his lips together and winks. "Whatever you say, *mi chava*."

"Stop calling me that."

"Uh-huh," he says dismissively.

Derek starts the boat and soon we're flying over the water. Derek and Kendall are by the wheel, and Luis and I are up front. I sit across from Luis instead of next to him, mainly because I'm afraid I'll grab on to him for dear life when we jump the waves. I love boating, but I like going slow. Unfortunately Derek doesn't have that same philosophy. I hold on to the side rail and pray we don't capsize.

I glance at Luis. He's looking down, fascinated, as he watches the water crash against the side of the boat. He's definitely enjoying the ride.

When we ride over the bumpy wake of another boat, I close my eyes and grip the rail tighter.

"Are you afraid?" Luis says over the roar of the engine. He's suddenly at my side. I can feel the heat of his body next to mine, and I'm tempted to reach for him to hold me. I open my eyes and look around as the scenery whizzes by.

I don't need a guy to make me feel secure. I can do it on my own. I grab the rail tighter. "I'm fine."

"You're lyin'. If you hold on to the rail any tighter you'll cut off the circulation in your fingers." He slides his body closer. "I want to hold you, Nikki. Will you let me?"

17

Luis

I don't know what it is with this girl. She's vulnerable and strong-willed at the same time. She makes me want to protect her, and at the same time peel back the layers of that wall she puts up.

"Let me hold you," I say again.

She shakes her head. "No."

I lean away from her. She's shutting me out.

"Is it because of Hunter, or some other dude?"

"No. It's because I don't want to get serious with any guy."

I shrug. "So let's not be serious. Let's just have fun with each other and see where it goes. I won't pressure you or give you attitude. Just the real me."

I know she's thinking about it. At least she didn't shut me down right away.

"That was a rush, wasn't it?" Derek yells after he anchors the boat. He tosses a raft in the water, then does a backflip off the side.

Kendall jumps in next. "Come on, you guys!" she yells from the water.

Nikki strips off her shorts and tank top, revealing a red bikini with black trim. I watch as she stands on the edge of the boat with the tips of her toes hanging over the side. I'm mesmerized, but trying not to show it.

"So . . . Luis?" She looks back at me without her usual animosity. I notice the playful challenge laced in her voice. "You said we should have fun. Are you brave enough to take the plunge?"

18

Nikki

I only asked if he'd take the plunge in a moment of pure weakness.

I don't have long to analyze his physique when he stands over the side, extends his muscular arms over his head, and dives in the water like an Olympic swimmer. I peer over the side of the boat, waiting for him to emerge from the water. When he doesn't, I start freaking out.

"Where is he?" I ask in a panic.

"You lookin' for me?" he asks. His voice echoes from the opposite side of the boat.

Instinctively, my hand flies to my chest. "Don't do that again, Luis. You scared me half to death. I thought you'd drowned."

"Considering he's an all-state champion swimmer," Derek says as he swims by Kendall, "I don't think you have to worry about that."

I arch an eyebrow. Luis, an all-state champion swimmer? I jump into the water, feet first. It's not graceful, but I'm not an all-state champion swimmer—far from it.

"Let's see how fast you are, Fuentes. How about a race?" Derek points to his left. "To the buoy over there and back. Girls get a head start."

Kendall and I immediately start racing toward the buoy. The boys wait, but not for long. It's not a fair race, because Luis and Derek pass us in less than five seconds. Derek is on the swim team at Fairfield and can definitely hold his own. Luis passes him easily, though, way before they reach the buoy.

Derek and Luis both stop at the buoy and wait for me and Kendall to catch up.

"What's the holdup?" Derek calls out.

Kendall attempts to splash Derek, but he's too far away. "You guys are such show-offs."

"It's the testosterone," Luis says, treading water with seemingly no effort.

I swim harder, but too quickly I'm out of breath and need a second to rest.

"You girls have no stamina," Derek says.

"I'll show you stamina," Kendall calls out, doing a pretty good breast stroke back to the boat. Derek follows close behind her, while Luis swims over to me. "You okay?"

Water drips off his lips, chin, and hair. He looks younger right now, kinda like he did when I first met him.

"I'm done racing, if that's what you mean," I tell him. I float on my back to give my body a rest.

Luis floats next to me, but grabs Derek's abandoned raft that has floated near us and we both hang on to it. We stay silent for a while, riding the wakes of other boats skimming across the water while we stare up at the sky.

He points to one of the clouds. "Looks like a dog, doesn't it? See the ears and long tail?"

"Looks like a snake to me. It can't be a dog because it doesn't have legs."

He laughs. "Nobody's perfect."

"No, they're not. I learned that the hard way," I blurt out, then point to another cloud so he doesn't analyze my comment. "That one's shaped like a rainbow."

"No, that's a turtle," he says. "See its head pokin' out?"

"You're wrong. That's not a head. It's the pot of gold at the end of the rainbow," I counter in an Irish accent, reaching up to the sky and tracing the rainbow and the pot of gold with the tip of my finger.

"You sure?" he asks.

"Absolutely. I'm an expert on cloud formations."

"Did you ever think what the earth would look like from space?"

I've never wondered about it. "I've seen pictures and video. Looks like a big marble."

"I mean experience it, like be up there lookin' down on earth. Would you go if you had the chance?" He lets go of the raft and puts his arms behind his head, floating on his back and looking up at the sky. "Man, I'd do anythin' to go up there."

"You could die on the way up . . . or down."

"I don't care. It's worth the risk for the ultimate adventure. Bein' so close to the moon and stars . . . knowin' the universe is endless."

"You're daydreaming, Luis. Come back to earth." I splash him.

He cocks his head to the side and says boldly, "Just so you know, I retaliate."

I splash him again.

"I'm warnin' you . . ."

When I splash him the third time and say "Bring it," he ducks under the water. I kick my feet, wondering what he'll do. "Luis, if you scare me or pull me under I'll kill you. I swear it. I was kidding when I said 'bring it.'"

I keep kicking. There's no sign of Luis, not even a ripple in the water indicating he's near me. The suspense is driving me nuts. I wait, still kicking. I know he's around here somewhere, unless he really is a fish and is breathing underwater in some magical underworld. He'll come up . . . but when?

He bursts out of the water right beside me, making a big splash with his entire body. I let out a very geeky yelp, which makes him laugh.

He swipes the water off his face with his hand. "You're not as brave as you think you are, *mi chava*."

"I'm brave when guys aren't creeping up on me."

"I don't creep."

"Stalk?"

"I don't do that, either. When I like a girl, I'm not subtle. In third grade I put a love letter in Selena Ibarra's desk."

"What happened? Did she read it?"

"Yeah. She laughed. And then she showed it to everyone on the playground. I got made fun of until my brother Carlos threatened to kick anyone's ass who gave me shit. Nobody really bothered me after that. Carlos is intimidating when he wants to be."

"Do you think he'll kick my ass if I give you shit?"

"He's in the military, stationed overseas. I think you're safe."

"Good," I say. "Then he won't mind if I do this." When I reach out to dunk him, he goes down easily. When he comes back up, we're face-to-face.

My breathing gets harder and faster. I don't know if it's because I've been in the lake for too long, or because he reminds me so much of Marco. Suddenly I can't see clearly and my head spins.

"Whoa," I say.

"What's wrong?"

"I'm suddenly light-headed." I reach out and frantically grab his arm for support.

"You okay?" he asks, concern in his voice. His free arm reaches around my waist and holds me in a firm, protective grip . . . like a hero. Our legs touch under the water and it feels intimate even though it's not.

I quickly take my hand off his arm. "Sorry. I just . . . got dizzy for a second. I'm fine."

I thought Marco was my hero, but he wasn't. Heroes are just made-up characters in fairy tales. They don't exist. At least in my universe, they don't. Luis is close to being one today, though.

He leads me back to the boat, staying by my side the entire time and asking periodically if I'm okay. Before we climb back up, he taps my arm. "Nik?"

"Yeah."

"Just so you know, I'm havin' a good time."

I nod and give him a small smile. "Me, too. It's a good thing we established this wasn't a date."

"I should warn you that I plan on spendin' the rest of the day changin' your mind," he says with a big grin on his face.

19

Luis

After soccer practice on Monday, Marco and I hang out at his house. He rolls his eyes when I insist on doing my homework before we go off and party with some of the other guys.

After I'm done with my homework, Marco and I get in his black SUV with tinted windows and ride around town.

"I've been hangin' out with Nikki," I tell him when we turn down Green Bay Road.

"I know."

"You got a problem with that?"

"What I got a problem with is you hangin' with Derek and Ben—guys from the north. You belong with us, Luis. You're one of us."

"I'm not dissin' you."

"Just know where your loyalties lie. ¿*Comprendes, compa*?"

"*Sí*."

"*Bien*. Now let's go party at the beach, where the real Latinas are."

I don't tell him that Nikki is a real Latina, and I can't get her out of my head. After our non-date on Derek's boat, she said she needed space. I'm giving it to her, but I can't deny I want to be with her.

Marco drives toward Lake Michigan. He doesn't park near the public beach. Instead, he takes a right and heads for the secluded part of the beach where the Blood used to hang out.

"Why here?" I ask. The Blood aren't active in Fairfield anymore, so I figure this part of the beach is deserted.

But it's not.

"You didn't hear the news?" Marco asks.

"What news?"

"Chuy Soto got out of the DOC on Friday."

I freeze. Chuy is one dangerous motherfucker. I don't suppose being locked up has reformed him. If he's back, does that mean the LB is about to get stronger?

I've seen gang deaths, beatings, and bullshit. But I've also seen the honor and loyalty the guys in gangs have to their friends.

The beach is filled with guys from my 'hood; *my* people. Guys I haven't seen since I moved back have come out of the woodwork for this welcome home party for Chuy.

We play football on the beach for a while. Afterward, Marco grabs a can of beer from a cooler. He gulps the alcohol until the liquid is running down the sides of his mouth. When he's finished, he swipes his mouth with the back of his hand, tosses the empty can on the ground, and slaps his knees together as if he just made a touchdown.

Marco tosses me a can. "Your turn."

I open the can and chug it in hopes the alcohol will erase the image of a soaking wet Nikki in a bikini from my mind. Unfortunately, it doesn't. I reach in the cooler and take another can. I take big gulps, waiting for the buzz. I've haven't gotten shit-faced drunk often, but then again, it isn't often a girl invades my mind.

"Luis, come here!" Marco yells, waving me over.

I head over to where Marco and his boys are talking. "'Sup?" I ask.

"That's Chuy Soto." He nods in the direction of the newest person to walk down the beach.

The guy is as big as a bear, has tattoos completely covering his arms and neck, and walks with an intimidating don't-fuck-with-me-or-you're-dead swagger. To top off the look, a cigar hangs out of the side of his mouth.

Everyone is silent. Chuy stops when he reaches me. If I hadn't grown up with gang members my entire life, I'd probably be shittin' in my pants right about now.

"I heard a Fuentes had graced Fairfield with his presence," Chuy says as he holds out his hand for me to shake.

"I brought him," Marco says, proudly taking credit.

I shake Chuy's hand with a strong, sure grip. Guys like Chuy respect anyone who doesn't shiver in their boots when approached.

"*Caballeros*, let me talk to Fuentes alone," Chuy says.

It doesn't take more than that for Marco and the other guys to disperse. Marco joins the rest of the *ganga* who are surrounding a big pile of wood and sticks they're about to light up.

"I asked Marco to bring you here tonight," he says.

That doesn't make sense. From what I heard, Chuy thought of my brother as a traitor ever since he got jumped out of the Blood. Why the sudden change of heart for a Fuentes brother? If Chuy considers Alex an enemy, why am I safe from his wrath?

Unless he expects me to replace Alex in the gang.

"I thought you were in jail," I say.

He smiles, with the cigar still hanging out of the side of his mouth. "Let's just say I got out on a technicality." He leans forward and talks in a low voice. "Listen, I need to rebuild the Latino Blood, and you're gonna help me do it."

"Why me? I'm not connected."

"That's where you're wrong, Luis. You were born a Blood." He pats me on the back. "And you'll be an LB until the day you die."

"If I were an animal, I'd most likely be . . ." by Luis Fuentes

Normally I like writing essays. Last year I wrote a paper in English about why certain aspects of Mexican culture had been integrated so completely into American society. I got an A, of course. Mr. Heilmann somehow got it printed in the local newspaper, which was pretty cool.

But now I'm stumped, which rarely happens. I bet most guys in my class'll choose a lion, the king of the jungle. I'm not the king, and never have been.

Thinking of a king reminds me of Chuy Soto.

My pen is poised over my paper. I wonder if I was drunk last night or if Chuy really did say he expects me to help him rebuild the Latino Blood. I gaze at a picture of Alex, Brittany, and Paco on the wall.

Mi'amá has the day off. I realize she's not cooking like I thought. She's got a cigarette perched between her fingers as she stands over the sink.

"I hate when you smoke," I tell her.

"It relaxes me." She takes a drag of the cigarette and taps the ash in the sink. "I got offered a job yesterday, as a receptionist. It's at the hospital where Elena works."

"That's cool."

"It's decent money, and includes health benefits," she says, then lifts the cigarette to her lips again.

"You okay, Ma? You look like you're freakin' out."

"*Estoy bien.*" She blows out smoke. "Well, everything's not fine. I got a call today that Carlos was injured."

I start to panic as horrific images of soldiers who've come back in wheelchairs and lost limbs swirl in my head. "What happened? Give it to me straight."

"Nothing serious, but bad enough that he's coming home to recuperate."

"What do you mean it's nothin' serious?" I ask. "If he's comin' home, it's got to be bad."

"It's his leg. He had to have surgery and couldn't join the rest of his unit, so they're forcing him to take a medical leave. He also has to decide if he wants to reenlist. I want him home, but . . ."

"You heard that Chuy Soto got out of jail."

"Elena just found out from Jorge." She points the cigarette at the doorway. "You just make sure you stay away from him. I don't want you or Carlos getting messed up with him, or the LB."

Too late for that. I rub the knot forming in the back of my neck. How do I say this? I hesitate and my palms get sweaty. "Ma, did I get 'blessed in' the LB?"

"Where did you hear that?"

"Chuy Soto said somethin' to me about bein' born a Blood and, well, I didn't know what he meant."

She points to me, her finger shaking. "You don't listen to Chuy, Luis. You hear me? Just stay away from him."

"He's runnin' things again. He wants to rebuild the LB."

I know I have a crazy, dangerous streak—an urge to charge into danger. For the most part I've controlled it, but when I met Chuy last night . . . I kinda got an adrenaline rush at the prospect of facing him head on—to make him pay for his part in Alex's jumping out, which almost cost him his life.

Mi'amá takes another drag of her cigarette. "Just keep your distance and don't ask questions."

"Don't I have the right to know why the new head of the Blood thinks I'm one of them?" I ask her.

She cups my cheek in her hand. "No, Luis. No questions. We're always better off not asking questions. You're safe. We're all safe as long as you stay away from Chuy."

I don't tell her that I don't want to stay away, because I want to find out what Chuy has planned. The more power he has, the less power the rest of us in Fairfield have. If Chuy has control, he can order revenge on Alex. If my family is in danger, I need to know.

Getting close to Chuy is my only option.

20

Nikki

Derek always has a party on his birthday because his parents are always out of town at a yearly sales conference at the same time. It's something everyone at Fairfield looks forward to. I was really excited to come to Derek's party tonight. I haven't opened up physically or emotionally with Luis since we went on Derek's boat two weeks ago, but I've thought about it every day.

Kendall and I arrived at the party early to decorate the house. Derek took his older brother's ID and bought a few kegs. Normally I don't drink, but Luis texted me and said he was definitely coming here tonight.

"What are you doing?" Derek asks as I fill a plastic cup to the rim with beer and start to gulp it down.

"Losing my inhibitions," I tell him. "What does it look like I'm doing?"

"You don't drink, Nikki."

I raise my cup in the air. "I do now."

"Kendall!" Derek yells, obviously not knowing how to deal with me. "Come here!"

Kendall peeks into the kitchen. "What's up?"

Derek gestures to me. "Your best friend is having a solo pre-party."

Kendall laughs as I take another gulp. "Umm . . . not a good idea, Nik."

"Yes, it is. Luis is coming here tonight." I'm starting to feel less stressed about being with him the more I drink.

Kendall and Derek give each other knowing looks.

"It's not what you think," I tell them. "I just want to know what it would be like to pretend we're a couple."

"Pretend? Just admit that you like him," Kendall says. "And deal with those feelings. Getting drunk is like a bandage that won't stick."

"I told you, I don't have feelings for him." I laugh at the thought.

Kendall pats Derek on the chest. "Derek, do something . . . say something."

Derek holds up his hands. "I'm not touching this conversation with a ten-foot pole." He quickly leaves as the doorbell rings.

I've almost downed the entire cup, and pour myself more. "Do you know Luis was the first guy I kissed since Marco?"

"I know," Kendall says.

"I think about it a lot. More than a lot, actually. Luis is the perfect one to practice on, right?"

Kendall takes the cup out of my hand. "I don't think you should use a guy for practice. You'll hurt him."

"No, I won't," I assure her. "He's admitted he's a player, just like Marco. He's the one who said we should just have fun. I'll make sure he knows whatever happens between us is just casual."

"Girls like Mariana do casual hookups, not you," Kendall says. When I grab another cup and fill it to the rim, she drops the subject. "Don't say I didn't warn you."

"I'll be fine. You tell me I need to loosen up. Luis tells me the same thing . . . I'm gonna give it a try."

An hour later music is blaring and the place is crowded. I'm definitely buzzed, and want to find Luis. I down the rest of whatever's in my cup, toss it in the garbage, and push through the crowd to find him. He's nowhere in sight. I ask around, but nobody's seen him.

"Hey, Nikki," Justin Dougan says, smiling wide with teeth that are so white I bet a blind person could see them. "You look hot."

"Umm . . . I kinda had plans with . . ." I'm about to say *Luis*, but *we* don't really have plans. *I* have plans. I just assume Luis will go along with them. And hanging out with Justin Dougan is definitely not in my plans.

"Go upstairs with me," he says, taking my elbow and urging me away from the throng of partiers.

"I'm not going upstairs with you, Justin." He's not the one in my fantasies.

"Trust me," Justin says. "I won't try anything."

"I don't trust any guy who says 'trust me.' I . . . need some air."

"Fine. Then walk outside with me."

Before I can protest, Justin leads me outside to the pool deck. The entire time I'm craning my neck to see if I can catch a glimpse of Luis, with no luck. He said he'd be here, but maybe he changed his mind.

Justin is drunk, too. I can tell by the way he stumbles across the deck before sitting on one of the lounge chairs. "Sit next to me," he says, then grabs my wrist and urges me down. "You look like a hot tamale."

"That's not really a compliment," I tell him.

He leans toward me. I don't know if he's falling on me or trying to feel me up. Either way, he smells like beer and sweat. It's not a good mix. I push him off me.

"Hey," I hear Luis say as he steps into view.

He looks good in jeans that hang off his hips just the slightest bit and a T-shirt that looks so worn it's probably as soft as silk.

Justin glances up at him. "Go away, Mex."

"Nikki is also Mexican, you dumbass," Luis says.

Justin stiffens. "Who you calling a dumbass?"

"Nobody! He didn't mean it," I say. "Right, Luis?"

"Not really," Luis says. "I meant it."

Justin is about to get up and challenge Luis when Derek grabs Justin's arm and steers him away from Luis. "Dougan, I need your help."

"With what?" Justin asks.

"Just . . . something." Derek leads him into the house, leaving me alone with Luis.

Luis is looking at me as if I've betrayed him. "What were you doin' sittin' with that *pendejo*?"

"I didn't actually sit with him . . . Okay, I did but . . ." I sigh. Tonight is not going as I planned. I'm buzzed, and I don't know how to explain that I've been waiting for him this entire time. I can show him, though. "Follow me."

He hesitates.

"Come on," I say, taking his hand and leading him toward the pool house. I know the key is hidden in the planter. I take it out and open the door with one thing on my mind: to let go of my inhibitions and kiss Luis like I did in my house. This time, we won't be interrupted. Luis attempts to turn on the light switch, but I put my hand over his.

"Lock the door," I tell him.

He does.

I walk farther into the room. "I didn't want to be with Justin tonight. You're right, he is a *pendejo*."

"I didn't like seeing you with him," he says. "I don't think I'd like seein' you with any other guy . . . besides me."

Right now I have a desperate need to be held by him. This isn't going to define me. This is about having fun and living out the fantasy.

"Hold me," I say. "*Please*."

"You're drunk," he says.

"Just a little buzzed, that's all."

"Nikki," he whispers as he gets closer. As soon as I feel his body heat I reach out and slowly run my hand down his arm.

"Don't talk," I whisper. If he talks, he might say something to ruin the moment. To be honest, I'm afraid of what he'll say.

Being here, in the dark, makes this surreal. It's like a mixture of fantasy and reality all meshed in one. I'm totally okay with living in Fantasy Land right now, because that's what I need. If this felt too real, I wouldn't be able to go through with it.

I brush my lips across his face to his ear. "Hold me, like you wanted to on the boat."

The second he wraps his arms around me, a sweet calmness washes over my entire body. It reminds me of when he held me protectively when we were in Fox Lake. I'm not deluding myself into thinking this incredible feeling will last forever, but I revel in his embrace. I'm living in the moment, and it feels so amazingly good I never want it to end.

His arms are caressing my back slowly, the warmth of his strong fingers searing my skin through my silky top.

I've pushed him away for so long, but tonight the pressure is off. With renewed determination, I reach up and touch my fingertips to his face.

He pulls back. "You sure about this?"

"Definitely," I say. "You're my fantasy tonight. Is that okay?"

"Fantasy, huh?"

"Yeah. As in the opposite of reality." I laugh, giddy just being here with him. I'm excited to put my plan into motion. "Just for tonight, let's see what happens."

"And tomorrow?"

Tomorrow? "I haven't thought that far ahead. I just want to make out with you right now. You game?"

"That depends."

"On what?" I ask.

He leans forward and kisses the sensitive spot right under my ear, then whispers, "If you want to stop at kissing, or go further."

When he brushes his lips slowly down my neck, I throw my head back and hope he continues to go slow. I'm not used to slow.

"That feels so good." I moan as he lets his lips rest on the spot where he can feel my pulse. He kisses the spot lightly. "Keep doing that."

He kisses it again. And again. And again. "Your pulse is racin'," he whispers against my skin.

"No shit," I say, which makes him laugh.

I put my hand on his chest. Through his shirt, I can feel his heart beating hard and fast against my palm. "Yours is, too."

"Mmm," he says before I feel the softness of his warm, wet tongue replace his lips on my pulse.

Whoa. I suddenly get dizzy and grab his shoulders for support. His strong arms lock around me immediately and hold me steady, as if he's more than willing to be my hero tonight.

I need a hero.

It's romantic. The shades are closed and we have total privacy from the chaos outside. A few slashes of dim light between the slats break through the darkness of the room. I don't know if it's the alcohol I drank that's making me want him so much, but I've never felt this way—not even with Marco.

I wish this could last forever.

When his lips sear a path down my neck and he gently pushes the straps of my shirt away to kiss the top of my shoulder, I can't take it anymore.

"If you don't kiss me I'm going to die." I pant. "Forget going slow."

"I thought you said my tongue action needed work."

"I lied. Want to try again?"

"Oh, yeah," he says. "Real bad."

He hesitates for a split second, but then I feel his palm cup my cheek while his thumb moves back and forth like a soft caress across my lips. I close my eyes and kiss his thumb.

"Does this feel good?" he asks, replacing his thumb with a touch of his lips.

"Yes," I whisper back. My hands weave into his hair.

I must be more than buzzed, because all I can think about when his lips brush against mine is that I wish we could stay like this forever.

A flick of his tongue against my lips makes my breath hitch.

"Let me taste you, *mi muñeca*." He moans.

I clear my head from all thoughts and inhibitions as my tongue reaches out for his. He's a breath away, waiting for me. When our tongues collide, it's hot and wet and slippery and slow . . . it feels dirty and sexy and beautiful all at once.

I melt into him as he holds me close. Our mouths are open and tasting each other. I feel like my insides are molten lava as he cups his hands over my butt and urges me closer. I feel him against me, and his obvious bodily reaction to our kiss makes my body ache for his touch.

We're both breathing heavily now. The place has no air-conditioning, and I'm starting to sweat. In one motion, I break our kiss and pull my shirt over my head. I'm standing here in my shorts and my bra.

I take his hand and place it over my bra. His breath catches, and the hot air around us seems electrified.

His fingers skim the silky satin of my bra and the sensitive skin between my breasts. His hands are skilled and slow. He's teasing me, and I'm breathing harder in anticipation of him pulling the material aside.

Waiting is complete torture.

I can't wait anymore. I reach around and unhook my bra, then let it fall to the floor. I wish I could see his face right now.

"Your turn," I say playfully, then tug on the bottom of his shirt. "I want to feel your skin against mine."

He hesitates again.

"It's okay," I tell him. "Don't overthink this. We're having fun. Isn't that what you want?"

Without further hesitation he rips off his shirt and immediately pulls me against him. My breasts crush against his hard, lean body.

While he caresses my bare back and his hands move down to cup my butt again, I wrap my arms around his neck and my legs around his body. His hands hold me suspended in midair until he carries me to the nearest wall. He presses against my body, holding me against the wall while we grind against each other. His hardness presses against my softness, and I wish we were naked but at the same time I'm glad we're not, because right now I'm not in control. I've lost it, and I have the feeling he has, too.

"Tell me to stop." He groans against my lips.

I don't. I can't. Instead, I wrap my legs around him tighter, urging him to keep moving. He does.

I bite down hard on his bottom lip when things get too intense, too emotional. My hands are on his hot chest and I can't hold back anymore.

I wrap my arms around him tighter and whimper against his neck. My entire world explodes around me, and the feeling won't stop. Then I feel him grab me tighter while he comes apart in my arms. It's just . . . wow.

"That was amazing," I say weakly after I come down from the high and catch my breath. "To be honest, I was nervous all week. But . . . this was a great fantasy, wasn't it?"

He tenderly touches my hair, then gently runs his fingers through it. "It was more than that, *mi chava*."

"Yo, Luis!" Marco's voice calls from the outside of the pool house. *Knock, knock, knock.* "Luis, you in there?"

21
Luis

Nikki quickly covers her nakedness with her hands and whispers in a frantic voice, "It's Marco. What's he doing here?"

"I don't know." My body is still coming off the high and I can't think straight. I've hardly had time to recover, and I know there's a good chance the evidence of what we just did is probably gonna be visible. Not good.

Knock. Knock. Knock.

"I'll get rid of him." I pick up her clothes and hand them to her.

I watch as Nikki clutches the bra and shirt to her chest. "Thanks," she whispers.

She rushes past me, but I take her hand and gently urge her to face me. "Are we cool?" I know it's a stupid thing to say, but no other words come. I want to tell her more, a lot more, but I can't.

"Yeah, we're cool. Just . . . go."

She locks herself in the small bathroom while I make sure my shirt covers any evidence of our encounter.

"What the fuck took you so long?" Marco asks.

Shit. Think of something fast. "Takin' a piss. What're you doin' here? I thought you didn't party with north siders."

"I might not party with 'em, but I've got business with 'em."

By *business* he means drugs. "You're *loco.*"

"And proud of it."

He peers over my shoulder and scans the pool house, but the lights are off so he can't see anything. I close the door and head out, hoping to guide Marco far away from Nikki. It's obvious she doesn't want him knowing what happened between us. Hell, she might want to deny we fooled around. Or maybe she was so buzzed she won't even remember it in the morning.

Marco and I walk into the main house. "This place is lame. Let's bounce," he says, pushing through the crowd of people who are eyeing us suspiciously.

"Who invited the wetbacks?" Justin Dougan calls out as we leave. He's on the front lawn with a bunch of the guys on the football team, and they're not sober. They're all laughing and giving Dougan high fives for insulting us.

Marco and I both halt, give each other knowing looks, and in unison turn to face Dougan and his crew.

"What the hell did you just call us?" Marco asks, ready for a fight.

"You heard me," Dougan says. "We only allow immigrants to clean our houses or mow our lawns."

"Really?" Marco says. "'Cause when I screwed your sister in her bedroom two weeks ago she didn't say anythin' about that. In fact, I know firsthand that she loves eatin' big, fat burritos."

Oh, man. Dougan's nostrils flare, and his group advances toward us. "You're dead, Delgado."

"Did you really screw his sister?" I mumble out of the side of my mouth so only Marco can hear.

He grins mischievously and nods.

"Go back to Mexico where you animals belong," Dougan says, then spits at us like we're the animals he accuses us of being.

Without hesitation, Marco charges him. I've got his back, though, when two of Dougan's friends pull him off and start pummeling Marco with their fists. It doesn't take long for my own fists to start flying.

And it doesn't take long for a crowd to gather.

I don't get into fights often, but when I do the beast in me unleashes with a vengeance. Maybe Dougan is right and I am an animal. The instinct to fight is in my Fuentes blood. Two guys are holding me down while a third is kicking my stomach. It doesn't even hurt . . . with each blow the rage rising to the surface makes me stronger. I break out of their grasp and bring two of them down before I scramble to get up and pull a guy off of Marco.

I fight one guy to the ground, punching until he stops fighting back. Then Dougan and I get into it. He throws a punch that hits me square in the jaw. I retaliate with a punch of my own that brings him down.

I don't even notice the flashing blue lights of a cop car until two cops pin me to the ground. One puts his knee on my back and starts to handcuff me. I look over and see another two cops handcuff Marco.

"Get up, Luis," one of the officers orders.

Huh? I know that voice. I turn to look at the officer. Holy crap. It's none other than Officer Reyes, my next-door neighbor and the guy who's been flirting with *mi'amá*.

"Shit," I groan. "Not you."

"You know this kid?" another cop asks Reyes.

"Yeah. And I know his ma ain't gonna be happy he got in a fight." Reyes looks on the ground right next to me. Two packets wrapped in blue cellophane are lying in the grass. "What are those?" he asks me. "Those come out of your pockets when you were fighting?"

"No."

He picks up the packets.

"Looks like blow to me," one of the cops holding Marco says. "You two been dealing tonight?" he asks us.

Marco shakes his head. "No, sir."

"Cesar, I swear they're not mine," I tell him.

I glance up at the crowd and see Nikki, standing with her hand over her mouth in shock. When our eyes meet, she turns away in disgust. She doesn't believe me.

From the look on Reyes's face, he doesn't believe me, either.

He lets out a slow breath and shakes his head in frustration. "All right. You two, over by the squad cars. Now!"

I'm told to spread my legs so Reyes can pat me down.

"Got any weapons, drugs, or needles on you, Luis?"

"No," I say.

"You high or drunk?" he asks, his hands patting up and down my legs.

"No."

"Then why were you fighting?"

I shrug. "Just felt like it, I guess." I'm sure he doesn't give a shit if the *pendejo* called us wetbacks and thinks Mexicans should be second-class citizens.

"Think hard, because I'm the one who's gonna have to call your mother to explain why I have you in custody and suspect you were dealing some pretty serious shit. I'd rather give her a reason why you thought it was a good idea to come all the way to the north side of town to cause trouble."

What, does Reyes think that poor Mexicans are only allowed on the north side to mow lawns and clean houses, too? "I didn't come here to cause trouble," I tell him.

"Really? Why are you here?"

"He was invited," Derek's voice calls out. "By me."

"And who the hell are *you?*" Reyes asks.

"I live here."

"Let me see some ID." Derek pulls out his ID and Reyes examines it.

Reyes gives a short laugh. "Happy birthday."

"Thanks."

"Listen, I'm sure you're aware that the legal drinking age in Illinois is twenty-one. You're eighteen." Reyes *tsk*s and shakes his head. "Where are your parents?"

"Vegas."

"So you thought you'd host yourself a birthday bash while they were gone?"

Derek nods. "Seemed like a good idea at the time."

"Uh-huh. Get everyone out of your house, lock it up, and come to the station with us so we can call your parents," Reyes says.

Derek is one cool *gringo* to come out here and vouch for me. "Don't take him in, Reyes," I say. "Give the guy a break. It's his birthday."

Reyes shakes his head. "Birthdays aren't a license to break the law, Luis."

I'm led to the back of one of the squad cars, while Marco and Derek are led to the other. Two officers drive them away while Reyes walks over to Dougan and his buddies. He talks to them for a while, taking notes the entire time. After a while Reyes and his partner walk back to the squad car I'm in.

Reyes gets in the driver's seat and turns to me. "You really screwed up tonight."

"Tell me 'bout it."

"Listen, Luis. I care about your mother. You being involved in fighting and drug dealing is gonna hurt her real bad."

"I already told you the *coca* wasn't mine."

"Was it your buddy's stash?"

I shrug. "I don't know."

"Here's the deal. I'm gonna let you and your friends off tonight after calling their parents, because I didn't find the drugs on your person and a few witnesses said that you and Marco were harassed before the fight. But I'll be watching you like a fucking hawk from now on. If I find out you're dealing or getting into more fights, I'll be on your ass so fast your head will spin."

Shit, this guy is worming his way into *mi'amá*'s life, and now he's going all parental on me. I've lived without a father my entire life, and have done just fine.

"You're not my father," I remind him.

"You're right. If I were, I'd lock you in juvie for the night to teach you a lesson."

22

Nikki

I let my guard down, which was not in the plan. Tonight, when Luis and I were in the pool house, I allowed myself to believe Luis and Marco are completely different.

That was before I saw him fight.

Luis and Marco were on the same side, fighting Justin and some guys from the football team. Luis's fists were flying, and the worst part about it was that I think he liked it—as if the fight fed some need in him.

I don't know who started the fight. It doesn't matter, really. Luis didn't walk away. Instead, he was the last man standing, ready to take anyone on that would dare challenge him. He didn't stop until the cops physically restrained him.

And then I saw the drugs on the ground right by his feet.

I can't be with someone who fights and deals drugs. Marco used to fight so much he'd get suspended. Principal Aguirre says he has a zero tolerance policy, but quickly realized when our class entered Fairfield freshman year that if he gave everyone three strikes and then expelled them, there'd hardly be any students from the south side left. Aguirre still threatens to expel students, but rarely follows through.

I need to force myself to stop thinking about Luis. As I fall into bed after I get home, I can't help but hate myself for feeling so vulnerable tonight. I let go of my inhibitions and knew what I was doing. But Luis didn't tell me he was dealing drugs—that's a game changer.

Sunday morning comes and I wake up hoping Granny has started eating on her own.

"How is Granny doing?" I ask Sue.

"She won't eat much. She's definitely depressed."

I go to her cage and sit with her.

Granny sniffs the air as soon as I open her cage. "Hey, girl," I say as I reach out and lead her to my lap. "Did you miss me?"

Her answer is a wag of her tail. She looks thin. Too thin.

I pet her behind the ears and she rolls onto her back. When she seems content, I pick up the food in her bowl and hand-feed her. She eats from my hand when I put the food to her nose.

"Want me to take you home?"

She answers by nuzzling her nose into my leg.

"I just have to convince my parents to let me take you," I tell her.

When I'm home and I tell my parents about Granny, they both say I can't have her.

"You have too much going on," Mom says.

"And when you're off to college, then what?" Dad says.

"But she's old, and blind, and living in a cage! If you were old and blind, would you want to spend your last days in a cage?" I argue.

Mom pats my hand. "Nikki, we think it's admirable for you to want to help the dog, but—"

I sigh. "Just . . . can you meet her? Meet her first, then make a decision, okay? I'm sure she'll be a great pet, and I know when you take one look at her you'll have the same opinion that I do about her."

They both look at me as if I'm pathetic. I know what they're thinking, that I'm trying to take care of a needy animal because I need to be wanted. We've covered this ground before. Maybe they're right. I can't help but have a special bond with the less fortunate dogs who come into the shelter—the ones who seem helpless. I root for the underdog, every time.

"I'll tell you what," Dad says. "Next weekend, if Granny is still there, your mother and I will go meet her."

A big grin crosses my face. "That's awesome! Thanks so much!" I hug both of them.

"We're making no promises, Nikki."

"I know, I know." Well, I do know. Once they see Granny they'll fall in love with her.

On Monday, the buzz about the fight at Derek's house, the arrests, and the drugs found by Luis's feet is running rampant. I can't walk down any hall without hearing something about Luis, Derek, or Marco.

I get some sideways glances, too. Everyone at school knows Marco and I dated, and some still associate us together.

I avoid eye contact with Luis even when he calls out my name, and during lunch I sit in the library and study for my calculus exam so there's no chance of meeting with him or Marco. I know I'll be seeing Luis in chemistry, though.

I time my arrival so I get to chemistry just as the bell rings.

"You can't ignore me forever," Luis whispers behind me when Mrs. Peterson instructs us to go to the sink in the back of the room to clean out our test tubes.

"Yes, I can," I tell him.

"What about Saturday night, in the pool house?"

I freeze, remembering the moment I let go of all my inhibitions. That was a mistake, and the wall is up again. "I'm trying to forget it."

"You can try, but it's not gonna work." He leans closer. "I can't forget it either, you know."

His words stir something deep inside me, and I need to lash out at him to push him away. "You know what sucks, though? You starting a fight just minutes later with Justin Dougan and finding out that you were dealing drugs."

He steps back and weaves a hand through his hair. "Yeah, that was a bummer. You know what sucks even more, though?"

"What?"

"That you're so desperate to believe everythin' bad you hear about me. You're obviously not a supporter of the 'innocent until proven guilty' concept."

"Mr. Fuentes," Mrs. Peterson calls out. "Stop the chatter. Are you aware there are people in back of you who need to use the sink?"

Luis looks right at our teacher and says, "To be honest, Mrs. P., I don't really give a shit."

23
Luis

I'm done worrying about getting detentions—staying after school for an hour is obviously going to be a common occurence so I might as well embrace it. In fact, the last time I had a detention I actually got some homework done. The problem is getting a detention from a teacher who insists that you serve the detention in her classroom instead of in the cafeteria with all the other delinquents.

I'm sitting on my usual lab stool and I pull out homework. I'm about to work on math problems when Peterson stands over me.

I look up at her. She's giving me the evil eye, which would make me laugh if I didn't think she'd give me another detention if I did.

"Hi," I say.

"Don't *Hi* me. What's going on with you?" She crosses her arms on her chest, and I can just sense the wrath of Nadine Peterson is about to hit like a tornado. "You know better than to cuss in my class. You also know having private spats in the middle of a class experiment is unacceptable."

"I'm havin' a bad day."

"From the look of the bruises on your face, I'd also say you had a bad weekend. Want to talk about it?" she asks as she sits on Derek's chair and leans on the lab table. I get the sense that she's parked in that spot and isn't about to move until I spill.

"Not really."

"Okay, don't talk. I'll do the talking, and you can listen."

I put a hand up, stopping her. "You can save your breath."

"My motto is you can't have too many lectures. Ask your brother to confirm my philosophy.

"Sometimes you're on a great path, and you reach a fork in the road. Sometimes you decide to go straight, and all is fine and dandy. But then sometimes the other paths look a little interesting, so you choose to switch things up a bit."

"And your point is?"

"Don't switch things up, Luis. I've known your family since you were eleven years old. You're smart like Alex, you have the drive like Carlos, and you've got a boyish charm all your own that's endearing. You can lose it all like this," she says, snapping her fingers.

"Sometimes you have no choice about what path you follow. Sometimes you're forced into it," I respond.

She sighs. "I know it's not easy. Alex started out on a destructive path, but found a way to make it right. I know you will, too." She waves a finger in my face, acting like the stern teacher she's always been. "And if you cuss in my class again, I'm going to personally drag you down to Dr. Aguirre's office."

"You're not as mean as you think you are, you know," I tell her. "Your zero tolerance policy has too many gray areas."

She gives a harrumph and slides off the stool. "It's the pregnancy. I assure you after I push this kid out I'll come back to school meaner than ever."

"Somethin' to look forward to," I say sarcastically.

After detention, I head over to Brickstone.

"You're late," Fran says as I pass her in the lobby.

"I know. My chemistry teacher made me stay after school. It won't happen again."

"Make sure it doesn't. I don't tolerate tardy employees." She narrows her eyes and steps closer. "What happened to your face?"

Oh, hell. I could lie and tell her I fell down the stairs, but I doubt she'll believe me. I might as well just fess up. "I got in a fight."

She motions for me to follow her into her office. "Sit down," she says, pointing to the guest chair. She folds her hands on top of her desk and leans forward. "I've hired and fired more employees in my career then I'd like to admit. I know you're a new employee, but today you're late and have bruises on your face. My guests don't want to be served by delinquents. I've seen kids like you who are on a downward spiral that only gets worse. I've given them chance after chance, but to be honest, it never works out in the end. I wish I had better news for you, but my instincts tell me I'm going to have to let you go."

"I've had a bad week. Just give me another chance," I say, but she's already walking toward the door.

"I'm sorry. Your last paycheck will be sent to your home." Fran glances at her watch, a sign that my time is up. "I wish you all the best in your future endeavors. Bill!" she yells out. "Mr. Fuentes here is no longer an employee. Please escort him off the property."

First she fires me, then she gets a bouncer to kick me out. Talk about adding insult to injury.

I follow Bill to the front entrance. "It's not you," he says as I hand over my name tag and am told to get in his security vehicle, also known as a golf cart. "We've had some incidents in the past with former employees who stayed on the premises to cause havoc."

"No prob, man. You're just doin' your job."

After being escorted off of Brickstone premises, I take my time walking home. How the hell am I gonna explain getting fired to *mi'amá*? It's bad enough she hasn't talked to me since she picked me up from the police station on Saturday night. On top of that I've got Chuy telling me I'm already a Latino Blood; Nikki, who thinks I'm a piece of shit drug dealer; Peterson breathing down my neck; a cop making moves on *mi'amá*; and now I get fired.

Talk about a week from hell.

A big black SUV pulls up beside me. It's Chuy. "Hey, Fuentes. Get in the car."

When I was a kid I knew to stay away from Chuy. I once over-heard Alex tell Paco that Chuy was a crazy motherfucker who'd pro-fess to be your best friend one minute and point a gun at your head the next. Chuy's older now, with weathered skin and empty eyes. *Mi'amá* warned me to stay away. I'm not afraid of him, and I want to know what he's up to. I don't know if that makes me tough or just plain stupid.

I get in the car and admire the clean leather seats and sweet sound system. "Where are we goin'?"

"The warehouse." He blows out smoke from his cigarette. It lingers in the car before slowly disappearing. "You ever been there?"

"No."

"It's time, *amigo*." He drives through town. I notice him looking through the rearview mirror and glancing around, probably making sure we're not being followed. He makes a quick turn onto a small street between the railroad tracks and an industrial park. It doesn't take long before we drive through a wooded area and come upon a building that has a big sign on it saying QUINTERO SHIPPING AND RECEIVING. It's always been a front for the Latino Blood hangout. And now that Chuy is back, the place is buzzing again.

I take it all in, wondering how come this guy trusts me.

"Come on," Chuy says. "You and I need to have a little chat."

A few guys are hanging out front. He flags the Latino Blood gang sign, and they flag back, before parting and letting us pass.

He leads me to a room off to the side, with a huge leather couch facing a big flat-screen TV.

"Sit down," Chuy orders as he pulls out another cigarette and lights it.

I want to know what the hell he wants from me, without the bullshit. "I'm fine."

He shrugs, then sits on the couch and puts his feet up on the coffee table in front of him. "I want to be friends. I've kept an eye on you since you left Fairfield. You're a smart kid, Luis. Smarter than most *pendejos* out there."

"You kicked the shit out of my brother and left him for dead. You don't want to be friends, Chuy. You want to use me as a pawn."

"We're all pawns, Luis. The bottom line is that the Blood needs you, and it's your time to step up. Everyone has to step up sometime."

"To fill my brother's spot?"

"Sure, if you want to rationalize it that way. The Blood is comin' back to Fairfield. You're either with us or against us. Alex knew the score and was smart enough to come on board. He knew the consequences of not joinin' when approached to be a part of our brotherhood. He's out. The burden is on you now."

"What are you sayin'?"

He pulls out a Glock from the waistband of his jeans, places it on the coffee table with a loud *thud*, then looks up at me with a stern, serious expression. "You want to keep your family safe, don't you?"

24

Nikki

I am a big believer in the justice system. The fact that Luis insinuated I judged him unfairly is just . . .

Okay, maybe I did judge him. But the evidence was right there, at his feet.

During dinner, I can't eat. The hurt look on Luis's bruised face after I told him he was dealing drugs makes me feel horrible. After dinner, I go to Kendall's house.

I plop myself on Kendall's purple beanbag chair in her room and spill everything. "I called Luis out, and he got pissed that I judged him before hearing his side. I feel like crap now. Luis and I fooled around in Derek's pool house right before the fight. It was intense." I get butterflies in my stomach remembering how far we went. "I don't remember it ever being that intense with Marco, and it scared me. I can't get sucked into a relationship with a guy who's gangbanging and dealing."

"I agree with you there," Kendall says.

Oh, how I wish I could turn back time and make Luis ignore Marco's knock on the pool house door. "I told Luis it was fun fooling around with him, but to be honest it was more than that. It *felt* real, and I got carried away because of it."

"You told him it was just some casual *fun*?"

"What else was I supposed to do, Kendall? I don't want him thinking that I want to trap him in some exclusive relationship and I'm falling for him. He'd probably laugh in my face anyway."

From the first second I met Luis two years ago, I knew he was a player. He didn't even try to hide the fact that he wanted to get with me the night we met. When I rejected him, he moved on to someone who was more than willing.

Kendall gets a phone call, but she ignores it. "Did you ever think that Luis wouldn't consider it being trapped to be in a relationship with you?"

"No."

"You, my friend, have issues that you still need to work on."

Tell me about it. "Just the thought of bringing up the word *relationship* scares me. It's a moot subject, though, because we've pegged Luis as a gangbanger."

Kendall sighs. "I don't know. If he's dealing drugs, get out now before you get sucked in. But Derek thinks he's not doing that stuff. They've become friends."

Ugh, I'm so confused. I was so sure after Luis got in the fight and I saw the drugs on the ground right there that he was guilty. Now I'm second-guessing myself. "You think I should go talk to him?"

"Talk to who?" Derek says, walking into the room and giving Kendall a kiss like they're a married couple in love.

"Luis," I say.

"I saw him get escorted out of Brickstone by security about two hours ago. I tried calling his cell, but he's not answering. He looked pretty bummed," Derek says.

"What happened?" I ask in a panic. "Why did they fire him?"

He shrugs. "Don't know. I asked some of the staff, but didn't get any answers."

With renewed determination, I get off the beanbag and grab my keys. "I'm going over to Luis's house to talk to him." I feel sick, as if somehow his detention and getting fired from Brickstone is connected to our argument in chemistry class. I never gave him a chance to explain everything because, in the back of my mind, I was looking for an excuse to push him away.

I took the coward's way out.

"Nikki, wait!" Kendall grabs her purse. "We're going with you for moral support."

"Thanks, but I need to do this on my own."

Kendall gives me an understanding, sympathetic look. "Just remember that if it was meant to be, it's all *good!*"

It makes me wonder if it wasn't meant to be, how *bad* can it get?

25

Luis

I walk home, glad *mi'amá* is working so I can be alone and lock myself in my room. The second I walk in the house, I realize that's not an option. Both of my brothers are sitting on the couch in the living room. I haven't seen Carlos in over a year, and wasn't expecting him to be released from the hospital in Germany until next week. He looks fine, but when he gets up I can tell it's not without pain.

"Hey, bro!" I say. "They let you out early?"

I couldn't stand bein' in the hospital, so I made them release me early. I almost don't recognize you," Carlos says, giving me the once-over. "You're sportin' some badass bruises. How does the other guy look?"

"You mean the other five guys?"

Carlos whistles in appreciation as he turns to Alex. "Our little brother has turned into quite the fighter while I was away."

"Tell me about it," Alex mumbles. "Ask him who he's been hangin' with."

Carlos raises an eyebrow. "Who you hangin' with, Luis?"

"None of your business. Alex, where's Brit and Paco?"

"At her parents' house for dinner. I got out of goin' when I heard Carlos was flyin' in today. So, Luis . . . I got a text from Julio a few minutes ago sayin' you got the boot. What happened to your job at the country club?"

"That's also none of your business."

"You're our little brother," Carlos says, advancing on me like a soldier on a mission. "Everythin' you do is our business."

The last thing I need is my brothers giving me shit, especially now. I would push Carlos away, but supposedly he's got a nasty gash complete with a shitload of stitches on his leg from shrapnel that wedged itself into his muscle.

"Lay off," I tell him, but my words fall on deaf ears.

Carlos attempts to pin me to the wall like he did when we were kids. I'm too fast and slip out of his reach, but not before he grabs my T-shirt and pulls it hard to get me to face him.

"You're packin' heat, aren't you?" he says as he lets go of my shirt.

Shit. Busted. Alex is up in a flash. He stands next to Carlos and both of my brothers form a human wall, preventing me from escaping.

"Give it to me," Alex growls.

Carlos shakes his head. "What the fuck, Luis? You gangbangin'?"

I hear the front door open and *mi'amá*'s voice call out, "What's going on?"

Reyes is standing behind her in uniform.

Carlos immediately blocks me protectively. "You got a warrant?" he asks.

"Carlos," *mi'amá* snaps in a scolding tone. "Don't be rude. I invited Cesar over for dinner."

"Who the hell is Cesar?" Carlos asks.

"Our next-door neighbor," I explain. "And landlord."

Carlos looks from me, to Alex, then to *mi'amá*. "Is this some sort of joke?"

"I'm afraid not," Alex says.

Mi'amá sets down her groceries in the kitchen, then comes back in the room. "What are you doing home so early, Luis?"

"I got fired."

She blinks a few times in shock. "*Fired?*"

"They didn't want an employee with bruises from a fight servin' customers."

Mi'amá shakes her head in disappointment and sighs. Damn, I think she's about to cry. I wonder if it's because Officer Friendly is here. She excuses herself and sullenly escapes back to the kitchen.

Reyes steps forward and holds out his hand to Carlos. "You must be Carlos. Your mother is really proud of your service. It's nice to finally meet you."

While Carlos and Reyes shake hands, Alex slaps me on the shoulder. "Luis and I will be right back," he tells them.

In my room, which used to be *our* room, Alex goes all father-figure on me. "You better not be dealin' drugs," he says in a harsh whisper so Reyes can't hear us.

"I'm not."

"Why did you get fired? Don't bullshit me."

"It wasn't for gangbangin', Alex. I already said I got fired for havin' bruises on my face . . . and for bein' late for work," I add.

"Why were you late?" Alex asks, not letting up on his interrogation. I think he chose the wrong profession.

"Peterson gave me a detention. Now lay off, bro. I'm not strapped, and I'm not dealin' drugs. Seriously, Alex, stop puttin' your shit on me."

I pull up my shirt and show him that I'm hiding a black rolled-up notebook in my waistband. I pull it out. "I don't have a gun in my waistband. I have this."

Carlos, who just popped in the room, pulls the notebook from my hand. "What's this?"

"The gun you thought he was hidin' in his pants," Alex says. "It's a notebook, Sherlock."

Carlos opens the notebook and starts reading the first page out loud.

"Nobody really knows her
Except the chosen few
Her secrets are kept hidden
Behind that sun-kissed hue."

"Give me that!" I yell as I try to grab the notebook back. Carlos yanks it out of my reach and continues reading.

"If I reach out to touch her
She'll just run away
My Forever and Always
Will have to wait another day."

"Holy shit, bro. That's deep. Alex, I would've bet that you were the sappiest one in this family, but I was wrong. Luis beats you, hands down." Carlos rolls the notebook back up and hands it to me. "Who's the lucky girl?"

"Doesn't matter. She thinks I'm scum."

Carlos laughs. "That means she likes you, bro. Shit, the first time I met Kiara, she thought I was an asshole."

"You *were* an asshole," Alex chimes in.

"Damn straight," Carlos says, completely proud of it. "Girls like assholes; at least they did when I was in high school. We're a challenge for 'em. Kiara was different." He laughs just thinking about his girlfriend. "Kiara, on the other hand, was *my* challenge. She didn't make it easy for me."

Nikki's not making it easy for me, either. Man, life used to be so simple until we moved back to Fairfield. I had a solid, foolproof ten-year plan. Now that I'm back, all my plans have turned to shit. Today I was forced to make a choice between my family's safety and my own future.

I had to take the detour. *Mi familia* comes first. They'll always come first.

I had to take the gun Chuy put on the table. I pledged my loyalty to the Blood after that, which screws everything up. How long can I keep the truth from my brothers when they're already suspicious?

"Alex! Luis! Carlos! Come help set the table!" *mi'amá* calls out to us.

My brothers practically jump to attention when they hear her voice.

"We'll talk about this later," Alex promises.

I play it cool until everyone is occupied in the kitchen. It's my opening to find a place to hide the gun.

When Reyes came in, I maneuvered the Glock so it was hidden in my shorts. Nobody saw me slip a notebook from my backpack and roll it up. I didn't think I could pull it off, but I did. I swear a few times I thought the gun was about to slip down, but by some miracle it held until Alex walked out of the room.

Now I've got to stash it so my brothers won't find it, and Paco won't accidentally get hold of it when he comes over and mistakes it for a toy. Without having time to think, I rush to my closet and shove the Glock in the pocket of the one and only suit I own. I've worn it to weddings, funerals, and a few *quinces*. The suit is in the back of the closet, so I'm confident it's safely hidden. I walk back to the kitchen and hope I don't have guilt written all over my face.

"Hey, Ma. Did you know Luis has a crush on a girl?" Carlos says when we're all eating at the small kitchen table. Even Reyes is still here, but since he's gotten the hint that we're not thrilled he's in the picture, he's been quiet.

"That's news to me," *mi'amá* says. She doesn't even look in my direction, clearly still pissed at me for getting in a fight and losin' my job.

I'm glad when the doorbell rings and interrupts the silence.

"Expectin' anyone?" Alex asks as he moves toward the front door.

"No," *mi'amá* says.

My cousin Elena stomps in the house like a tornado. Everything about Elena is big. She's got big hair, a big personality, and . . . well, let's just say she doesn't need silicone implants. Elena is hilarious, but she is one scary Latina when she's pissed. "Is the bastard here?" she asks.

Alex shrugs. "And the bastard would be . . ."

"Jorge. You know, my cheating husband."

Mi'amá rushes to Elena's side. "What happened?"

"I found him at Homestyle Buffet with that tramp Nina Herrera."

"Who's Nina Herrera?" I ask.

"His high school girlfriend. I caught them in the act."

"You caught them having sex at Homestyle Buffet?" Carlos chimes in, confused and maybe a little amused.

"No. They had dinner! When was the last time my sonofabitch husband took *me* to dinner, huh? Huh? *Huh?* Anyone want to answer *that* question?" She gestures to each of us, then sneers when she focuses on Reyes. "Lorena, are you aware that you've got a *cop* sitting at your dinner table?"

"I'm Cesar," he says, standing as he introduces himself.

She stares at the handcuffs secured to his uniform, just waiting to be slapped on an unsuspecting criminal. Considering Elena herself had run-ins with *la ley* when she was younger, she doesn't trust cops any more than the rest of us do. She takes a step away from Cesar as if he has some infectious disease.

"Yeah, umm . . ." She turns to *mi'amá* and murmurs fast and furious, "What the*fuck*areyoudoingwithacopinyourhouse?"

She says it as if it's all one word.

Mi'amá's response is, "He's a friend."

Elena nods as slow as her brain is processing the information. "He's a friend? Since when did you become friends with cops? Wait, maybe this is a sign!" She plasters a big smile on her face and turns to Reyes. "I need you to arrest my cheating husband."

"While I'd really like to help you," Reyes says, "I can't legally do that."

"Who said anything about doing it *legally*?"

"She's kidding, right?" Cesar asks *mi'amá*, who shrugs with embarrassment.

"Not really." Dismissing Reyes because he can't help her cause, Elena stands next to Carlos's plate and reaches out to take a bite of his *taquito*. "I forgot to welcome you home, Carlos. How's your leg?"

"I got to be honest, Elena," Carlos says as she kisses him on the cheek and leaves a big red lipstick mark. "Since you came in, I haven't felt any pain. You're more entertainin' than television, and more effective than Vicodin."

She takes her attention off of Carlos and focuses on me. I moan as she takes my cheek and squeezes it between her fingers. "I love you Fuentes boys like you were my own. *Mwah!*"

She comes in close. I can clearly see a stray chin hair she needs to pluck, and her strong perfume burns my nostrils.

Her lips start to pucker and I cringe. "Please don't get lipstick on me."

"Oh, you know you love it," she responds. I try to shield my face, but she plants a wet one on my cheek with her big lips.

"Did she get me bad?" I ask Alex.

Alex cocks his head to the side, analyzing the mark. "Yeah. She got you good, bro."

Alex doesn't wait for Elena to make her mark on him. Instead, I watch as he opens his arms out wide for a hug. When she goes to kiss him, he ducks and plants one on her cheek.

"You're sneaky," she says, wagging her finger. "If you ever cheat on Brittany, I'll seriously cut your dick off."

"You'd have to get in line behind Brittany if that ever happened. Listen, Elena, I'll call Jorge and see what's up. He's not havin' an affair."

"Anyone home?" Jorge's voice echoes through the house.

My chair scrapes the floor as I make a quick move to help Alex restrain Elena so she doesn't go all ape shit on Jorge. When Reyes wants to get involved, I hold a hand up to stop him.

"This is normal," I tell him.

"For who?" he responds.

"I wasn't cheatin' on you," Jorge says, looking like a mess. "Nina wanted someone to talk to after she broke up with her boyfriend, that's all. Stop actin' like a jealous wife."

"I'm not jealous," Elena cries out, clawing through us to get to him.

"*Culero*, get a clue. When an ex-girlfriend wants to talk to you, that's code for 'I want you back.'"

The doorbell rings again.

"I'll get it," Alex says. I'm not paying attention until his loud, commanding voice carries across the house, saying, "Luis, you have a visitor."

26

Nikki

I stood outside Luis's house for a few minutes before I got up the nerve to ring the bell. They're obviously having a party. I can see a house full of people through the front window.

Alex answered the door. He knows who I am. Every few months my parents invite him and his wife and son to our house for dinner or Sunday brunch. He calls Luis to the door and my heart pounds in anticipation.

Luis comes to the door with a big red lipstick mark on his cheek. "What are you doing here?" he asks, his voice tense. He's obviously not happy to see me.

"Come on in," Alex says, putting his arm around me and urging me inside.

"You still got that lipstick crap on your face, bro," Alex mumbles to Luis as we pass him.

Luis curses, then starts wiping his cheek vigorously. "My cousin likes to mark us," he explains. "It's kind of an unnecessary and annoyin' tradition."

I pass a police officer standing next to Luis's mom. Carlos is here, too, along with another couple. The couple must be having a heated argument, because they don't look happy with each other.

Carlos points to me. "Is this *the* girl?" he asks Luis. "The one from the poem."

"What poem?" I ask, suddenly curious.

"There is no poem," Luis insists. "My brother is delusional from the pain meds he's on. Don't listen to him."

"Are you okay?" I ask Carlos.

Carlos lifts up his pant leg, revealing a nasty cut stitched together with a row of staples traveling from his thigh all the way down to his calf. "This is proof that freedom ain't free."

"Ouch. How did it happen?" I ask, cringing. Just looking at it is painful.

"Shrapnel from an IED." He narrows his eyes at me. "You *Mexicana*?"

"Carlos!" his mom calls out in a scolding tone.

"Seriously, bro, shut up," Luis says.

Carlos holds up his hands in surrender. "What, it's a crime to ask a girl if she's Mexican?"

"No. It's just rude," Luis says.

Carlos laughs heartily. "Bro, when have you known me *not* to be rude?"

I answer Carlos, "I'm American more than Mexican. Does it matter?"

"Only if you deny your heritage. Don't want to dilute the culture, you know."

"Carlos is one to talk," Alex chimes in. "His girlfriend is as white as they come."

"Are you kiddin', Alex? Have you looked at your lily-white wife lately?" Carlos argues playfully.

"Hey," Alex says. "Before you rip on white people, you might want to remember that your nephew is half white."

"Not the half that counts," Carlos says proudly. "Listen, I'm an American and fight for this country, but that don't mean I ignore my Mexican heritage like it's somethin' to be ashamed of."

"I'm not ashamed of it," I say. "I don't know Spanish or walk around waving a Mexican flag. I'm not going to fake it, when I don't know much about it."

"It's not too late to learn," Carlos says.

"Luis, are you going to introduce me to your friend?" his mother cuts in.

Luis hesitates, so I step forward. "I'm Nikki," I say with a smile.

"Nikki *Cruz*," Alex says. "Dr. Cruz's daughter."

"Ah, I remember you." She tilts her head, deep in thought. "Weren't you at Alex's wedding?" I silently pray she doesn't mention that I kneed Luis's nuts on the dance floor. That's an incident I'd rather not dredge up right now.

Carlos isn't going to let this one slip by. He perks up. "Oh, yeah! Nikki, weren't you the one who kicked Luis in the—"

"Nikki goes to Fairfield," Luis explains. "We're in chemistry class together."

So now everyone is silent, waiting for me to talk. I turn to Luis and mumble quietly, "Can we talk?"

"Yeah. Follow me." I follow him through the kitchen and out the back door. "All right," he says. "Talk."

I clear my throat and look up at the sky, knowing that Luis wants to go up there one day. Will he pursue his dreams, or has he changed his plans? "I was thinking about what you said in chemistry today. You know, the part about me judging you before I had all the facts. Well, after thinking about it . . . you were right."

He shrugs. "It doesn't really matter."

"It does to me," I say.

"Why? You've made up your mind about me." He gives a short laugh. "Everyone has."

"Tell me right now you're not dealing drugs and I'll believe you. Look in my eyes and tell me the truth."

He looks me straight in my eyes. "I'm not a dealer," he says, his gaze not faltering one bit. "The drugs weren't mine. I'm not Marco, so stop puttin' both of us in the same category."

"You're friends with him."

"I'm also friends with Derek. Listen, I don't know what the hell happened between you and Marco. To be honest I don't really want to know, 'cause if I did I'd probably want to kick the shit outta him."

"I don't need you to protect me."

"What if I want to?" I watch as he looks up at the sky and stares at the stars. "Damn, Nik, you have no clue what crazy thoughts have been runnin' through my head since we were on Derek's boat, and then after hookin' up Saturday night . . . You want to ignore what happened, but I can't."

"The truth is, I can't, either." I swallow the lump forming in my throat. "I have to know if you're in the LB, because if you are I can't do this."

"Look at me," he says. When I do he sighs. "I'm not a gangbanger, Nik."

"You were right to call me out. I wanted to think the worst about you, because if I did I could ignore the connection I feel when we're together. It's like I *get* you, and you *get* me, and then Saturday night when we were alone in the pool house—"

"You said it was *fun*."

"I told you it was fun just to throw you off. Hunter once told me most guys can screw a girl they love just as easily as they can have a one-night stand. Marco was the last guy I dated, and he practically destroyed my heart and soul and everything in between. It was more than fun Saturday night, Luis. I need to know if you think we can make it work."

"Wow. The way my week has been goin', that's the last thing I expected to hear." Luis runs a hand through his hair. I can sense the stress radiating off him. "My life is so fuckin' complicated right now."

"Sorry," I say. "I don't mean to complicate things more." I focus on the ground because I don't want to see his face when he tells me that I'm delusional.

"It's not your fault." He takes a deep breath, then slowly lets it out. "Nik, I gotta be honest. I don't know if it's a good idea to get involved with me right now."

"I get it," I say. "You don't have to explain." He hadn't tried to hide the fact he was a player from the second I met him. I was stupid to think getting closer to him and feeling a connection meant I'd suddenly changed him.

"No, you don't get it." The sides of his lips turn up in a small smile. My breath hitches when he reaches out and slides his hand to the back of my neck and urges me to look at him. "I don't want to be with anyone else, *mi chava*. I want you to be my girlfriend."

"Really?"

"Yeah, really."

His words soothe my increasing doubts. "I don't want to be with anyone else either," I say.

I haven't wanted to let anyone get close to me, but that was before Luis came back into my life. Maybe this push-pull thing is us trying to figure out where we stand. Times have changed, I've changed, and I'm ready to put the past behind me.

A moment passes and I feel a sense of peace cover me like a blanket. I hope he doesn't see tears threatening to fall from my eyes.

"Come here," he says, pulling me close. "You're shaking."

I close my eyes and a tear falls down my cheek. Luis has managed to slice right through my invisible protective armor and I feel so vulnerable. "I'm scared."

"Me too." He holds me tighter, then kisses the top of my head.

It feels so good to be held again by him. I bury my head in his chest, soaking up the warmth of his embrace. "Promise me you'll always be honest with me, Luis."

"I promise."

27

Luis

The second lie I just told my new girlfriend is that I'd be honest with her. The first is that I'm not in the LB. If she knew I have a task to do for the Latino Blood, and I'm ordered to pack heat to prove my allegiance, I'd lose her. I understand that makes me a selfish bastard, but I don't want to give up the chance at having Nikki be a part of my life.

The back door opens. It's Brittany, holding Paco in her arms. The second she sees us, she gasps. "Oops, sorry," she says, backing up. "I didn't mean to interrupt. Paco was looking for you, Luis, and your mom said you were outside. I didn't know you were with someone." She squints in confusion as recognition sets in. "Nikki Cruz, is that you?"

"Yeah," Nikki says, stepping away from me.

"Oh. Wow, okay. I didn't know you and Luis were, um, friends."

"We're kinda more than that," I tell my sister-in-law.

"What's going on? Are you guys, like, *dating*?"

I drape an arm around Nikki, because it feels right and I want her close. She looks up at me, and I swear I can stare into her expressive dark brown eyes forever. "Yeah, we're datin'," I say without looking away from my girl. "Right, *mi chava*?"

Our eyes are still locked on each other as Nikki smiles up at me and nods.

"Does your mom know?" Brittany asks.

"Not yet," I tell her.

Brittany laughs. "I think she's got a pretty good idea. I caught her peeking out the kitchen window at least a dozen times since I came in. I had no clue you were out here with a girl . . . which completely explains why she was snooping. *Mamá* Fuentes protects her boys like a mother hen. I'm sure I won't be any different when my son starts to discover girls. You remember that, Paco."

"Weese!" Paco yells, and squirms to get out of his mom's grasp.

"Paco, *Tío* Luis is busy," she tells him. "He can't play with you right now."

"It's okay," Nikki says, tearing her gaze away. "I have to go home anyway."

As soon as Brittany lets him down, Paco runs over to me.

"How's my little *taquito*?" I ask, picking him up and giving him a high five. "Shouldn't you be asleep by now?"

"Yes, he should," Brittany chimes in, exasperated. "My son likes to be up all night and sleep all day . . . just like his father." She places a hand over her growing stomach. "This one keeps me up all night, too. God help me."

"He's a Fuentes," I tell her proudly. "Right, Paco? You're gonna have a little brother to boss around soon?"

He nods.

Brittany doesn't. "Hopefully this one's a *girl*. The male Fuenteses in this family are exhausting me. I don't know how your mom survived living with three of you boys under one roof."

"Never a dull moment." I faintly hear Carlos laughing. "It's still not dull."

Alex calls Brittany back to the house, leaving me holding Paco.

"Remember me?" Nikki asks, tickling my nephew's stomach. "I'm Nikki."

"*Ki-ki!*" Paco yells. "Ki-ki-ki-ki. Ki-ki-ki-ki." He bobs his head from side to side as if he's singing a song.

"We're workin' on his verbal skills," I tell her.

She gently smoothes a hand over Paco's hair. "He's perfect."

"So are you." I lean in to kiss her, and for an instant an image of us repeating this moment in the future flashes across my mind . . . me, Nikki, and a child of our own.

Nikki says, "I really have to go. We have school tomorrow, you know."

"I don't want you to go."

"I know that you made the soccer team. I could watch your practice after school. We can hang out after."

"I've got to do something after practice." A little task Chuy gave me that Nikki doesn't need to know about. "But I'll meet you later on."

"Okay," she says, nodding. I can't tell if she's skeptical or not.

We walk back in the house. Everyone is, unfortunately, still here. And, unfortunately, all eyes are on us.

"I'm gonna walk Nikki to her car," I announce to my family. I hand Paco to my brother.

"Bye," Nikki says, smiling shyly as she gives a nervous, general wave to everyone in the room. She walks up to *mi'amá*. "It was really nice seeing you again, Mrs. Fuentes."

"Thank you," *mi'amá* responds politely. "Give my regards to your parents."

Regards to her parents? Suddenly *mi'amá* has turned into a mild-mannered socialite. Is she putting on an act for Officer Reyes? Whatever it is, I'm grateful.

Nikki and I walk to her car parked out front. She leans against her car door before opening it. "Hey," she says, then bites down on her bottom lip nervously.

"Hey."

"You know that's our routine, right?" she says. "You always say 'Hey' to me, and I say 'Hey' back. Or I say 'Hey' to you, and you say it back to me."

I smile. She would pay attention to something like that. I look down at those sweet lips I'm dying to taste again. "Hey," I whisper as I bend down to kiss her.

"Hey," she whispers softly against my lips. She puts a hand on my chest. "Um, before we go ahead and make out . . . I think you should know that your family is watching us."

I glance back at the house. The lights are suddenly off, and I can make out the shadows of my family spying through the front window.

"This is embarrassin'," I mumble.

"Call me later," she says as she opens her car door.

"Wait, aren't we gonna kiss?" Seriously, now that I have a girlfriend, I'm gonna reap the benefits. Hell, the way my week has been going I figure being liplocked with her will keep me sane.

She gives me a peck. "There."

"My cousin Elena's stupid kisses are better than that, Nik. Come on, *mi chava*, throw me a bone here."

"I told you, we have an audience," she says.

I shrug. "I don't care. Let's give 'em somethin' worth watchin'. My back is facin' them, so they won't see much."

She wraps her arms around my neck.

I moan, loving the feeling of her body leaning against mine.

It's dark and quiet outside with only the streetlights giving off a yellow glow. Nikki knows how to get me fired up with a mere touch of her lips, and she uses that to her advantage. Her soft lips brush against mine, over and over. We start making out. Good thing my back is hiding our hot embrace.

A car driving by honks repeatedly and stops beside her car, ruining the moment. "Gettin' lucky, Fuentes?" a familiar voice yells out the window.

It's Marco.

Nikki freezes, then buries her face in my chest in an attempt to hide her identity. It's no use, though, because her car is a dead giveaway. My hands are braced against the car, shielding her even though I know it's useless.

"What's up, Delgado?" I ask.

He sticks his head out the window. "Obviously not as much as you and Nikki. Just a tip: she likes it when you lick her behind her ear."

"Thanks for the advice, man, but I think I can figure it out on my own," I tell him. "Now get the fuck out of here."

Marco's laugh lingers as he screeches away and disappears down the block.

"Is he gone?" she asks, her voice muffled because she's still got her head buried in my chest.

"Yeah. Don't worry. I'll tell Marco to lay off." I tip her chin up so I can get lost in her soulful eyes again. "My goal is to make you forget you ever dated him."

I lean down to kiss her again, but she pulls back. "I just, you know, need to say something before I leave. I don't want to be worrying about it all night."

"Hit me with it."

"I won't have sex with you," she blurts out.

Her words slam into my libido like a bucket of water on a flame full of testosterone. I think my dick just twitched in protest. "Like, *ever?*" I ask.

"I just don't want our relationship to be about sex and nothing else," she says. "If we remove the sex expectation right now, it'll be better."

Better for who?

"I don't want us to be all about sex, either, Nik, but I got to be honest . . . I was hopin' it'd be part of it at some point."

She glances to her left and right, as if she wants to make sure nobody else can hear our conversation. "I just can't. Too many complications, you know."

No, I don't know. Do I even want to know? Shit. Is this about Marco? Or is this all about me?

"I'll understand if the no sex thing is a deal-breaker for you," she says shyly.

I'm not gonna lie. Just lookin' at Nikki makes me horny, but it's more than that. I like her. A lot. Enough to want to call her my girl-friend. I like just sitting with her and talking. The rest will come when she's ready.

"All right," I tell her. "I'm cool with the no sex rule. But, uh, can we keep the option open to talk about it in the future? You know, just in case you change your mind."

"Yeah," she says, lightly kissing me on the lips. "But don't hold your breath that I will. We can do other things, though."

I raise my eyebrows, interested. "Like what?"

"I'll show you later." She covers her mouth when a smile crosses her face. "I can't talk about this when your mother is watching. I'll see you tomorrow."

She gets in her car and pulls away just as *mi'amá* opens our front door. "Is there something you need to tell me?" she asks before I step in the house and face the rest of the family.

"Yeah. I have a girlfriend."

"Don't you think a girlfriend will complicate your life?"

"*Sí, Mamá.* It will complicate my life." But not in the same way she thinks. The Latino Blood is a black cloud over my head. I wish finding out what Chuy is up to didn't include me getting caught up in the Blood. But it has. "It'll all work out."

"College is most important," she says. "More important than girls. Don't let anything sidetrack you from your goals, Luis. You'll regret it the rest of your life."

Right now my goal is to get past tomorrow after soccer practice, when I'll be going into Evanston. It's my first errand for Chuy and another way to prove that I'm willing to take risks for the Blood. I'd be lying if I didn't admit a part of me was looking forward to the challenge.

28

Nikki

In the morning, I wake up and immediately turn my phone on, hoping to have a text from Luis. I get butterflies in my stomach just wondering if he might have been thinking about me when he woke up this morning.

A text pops up on the screen. It's from Luis. I can't help but grin when I read his perfectly thought-out message.

Luis: Hey

The message was sent twenty minutes ago. I quickly type the only appropriate response and press SEND.

Me: Hey

I rush to the bathroom, but bring my phone with me just in case he texts me back. While I'm brushing my teeth, I hear the chime on my phone. Another text. I hurry to finish brushing, then pick up my phone.

Luis: u ok?

Me: About what?

Luis: Us. Me.

Me: yeah. Why?

Luis: just checking.

At school, Luis and I sit on the floor in front of my locker before the bell rings.

"I didn't do my math homework last night," I tell him as I pull out the sheet Mr. Gasper gave our class. "After I got home I couldn't concentrate. I hardly understand it anyway. My brain doesn't compute calculus. I don't even know why we have to learn it. It's not like I'm going to use it in real life."

"Depends what you do for a livin'." Luis slides the sheet onto his lap and studies it. "Come on, we have ten minutes before the bell rings. I'll help you finish it."

I try hard to focus on anything else but him. I move my hand over his and draw invisible circles on the back of his hand with my fingers.

"You're distractin' me," he says.

"I know."

He laughs, then pulls his hand away. "Don't you want credit for the homework, *mi chava?*"

I kiss him. "Yeah, but I'd rather just hang out with you."

"I don't want my girlfriend flunkin' math and havin' to take it over in summer school. Focus," he tells me.

"Okay, okay." I put my pencil on the paper, ready to work. "I'm focused."

We work until there's a minute before the bell rings. All I know is that Luis has the patience of a saint. He was able to explain stuff to me at my level, instead of Mr. Gasper's way, which is way too confusing.

"Thanks," I say as I slip the sheet into my folder.

"Sit with me at lunch today," he says.

"With *your* friends?"

"Yeah." He laces his fingers through mine.

"I don't really get along with them. They hate me."

"It'll be fine, I promise."

Kendall and Derek come walking down the hallway. "I guess you two worked it out last night, huh?" Kendall says.

I squeeze Luis's hand. "Yep."

Luis and I part when the bell rings. I know I'm not going to see him until lunch, but I do see Marco. He's in my gym class. I usually ignore him and he ignores me.

Today I'm not so lucky.

"So you've finally found another guy to obsess over?" Marco asks as we run around the track surrounding the football field.

I run faster, but he keeps up with me. Mr. Harris, our gym teacher, is holding a stopwatch. "Keep up the good pace," he calls out as we pass him.

"This thing with you and Luis won't last, you know," Marco says. He stops talking as a couple of runners pass us. "When he dumps you, are you gonna make him feel like dirt and turn everyone on the north side against him, like you did to me?"

I didn't turn anyone against Marco. We broke up at the same time that he joined the Latino Blood. Coming to school with gang tattoos didn't really help his popularity with the people I hang out with. I know almost everyone on the north side ignored Marco after we broke up. I just don't think it had anything to do with the breakup and everything to do with him flaunting his gang affiliation.

I keep running and ignore every word that comes out of Marco's mouth. I wish I had headphones in my ears to block him out completely.

"If you tell Luis what I said, I'll pass around that naked picture I took of you on my cell." He leans in close. "When I told you I deleted it, I lied."

Tears threaten to sting my eyes, but I hold them back. When gym is over, I rush to the locker room and pray that Marco is bluffing.

At lunch, I spot Luis in the hall just as we're both entering the cafeteria.

"Hey," he says.

"Hey. I'm eating lunch in the library," I tell him. "I've got to study, and I can't do it when everyone is around. I'll see you in chemistry, okay?" I need to get away from Marco and his threats.

He starts to follow me. "I'll go with you to the library."

"No. You're the biggest distraction for me right now. I need to focus."

"Seriously?" Luis asks, unconvinced.

"Seriously." I kiss him, loving the feeling of his warm lips on mine that make me forget Marco's threat for the moment. Being with Luis makes me believe everything will be okay in the end.

"Hey, you two. No PDA," a teacher calls out. Oh, no. It's Mrs. Peterson. She taps us on our shoulders. "Break it up."

Mrs. Peterson waits for us to part, then crosses her arms. "Nikki, I'm going to have Dr. Aguirre send you home with another Fairfield High student handbook. You obviously haven't memorized the rules. If you'd like to stay after school and go over them together, I can help you." She raises an eyebrow at Luis. "That goes for you, too, Mr. Fuentes."

"Haven't you ever broken the rules, Mrs. P.?" Luis asks her.

"No," she retorts, but then thinks about it more. "Well, there was this one time in high school . . ." Her voice trails off. "Never mind. I don't want to catch you two kissing in the hallway again. I didn't make up the rule, but I have to enforce it."

Shocker. Mrs. Peterson just admitted to being a rule breaker herself. And maybe she even disagrees with some of the rules. Luis looks pretty pleased with himself that he got her to admit it.

"I'll see you later," I call out as I head to the library. "Go eat with your friends."

I sit in one of the private study carrels and pull out my lunch and a book from the fiction section that I just picked off the shelves. I don't really have to study. I just don't know how to tell Luis that I can't hang out with his friends.

29

Luis

In chemistry, Peterson watches us like a hawk. Damn, that woman might not have made up the rules, but she sure does get off on enforcing 'em. Today Peterson is lecturing the entire class. I glance at Nikki and find her looking right at me. She smiles. I'm the luckiest dude on earth. I'm gonna hate leaving her after practice today.

The bell finally rings. Nikki and I walk to our lockers together.

"I'll meet you on the field," I tell her, then pull her close.

She pushes me away. "You heard what Mrs. Peterson said. No PDA in the halls."

"She's not lookin'. Besides, school's over."

She shakes her finger at me. "You're living on the edge, Mr. Fuentes," she says, imitating Mrs. P. "Promise me you won't get another detention."

"I can't do that, *mi chava.*"

In the locker room, Dougan comes up to me as I put my soccer jersey on.

"Nobody likes the idea of you and Nikki together," he says. "Well, besides Kendall and Derek."

"I don't really give a shit what anyone thinks," I tell him.

I sit down on the bench and get my cleats on, hoping Dougan will just disappear.

He doesn't.

He sits next to me. "You know her parents are gonna have a fit when they find out she's dating a dude in the LB. I know you're one of them . . . no need to deny it. Just so you know, I'll be there to comfort Nikki when she realizes you're just another Mexican scumbag."

I finish fastening one cleat and put on the other. I don't want anyone, especially Dougan, interfering with my relationship with Nikki. I know Alex and Brittany had similar issues. All of their friends tried to warn them their relationship would end up in disaster, but in the end it didn't matter what anyone else thought. That's how I want it to be with me and Nik—the two of us figuring this out without interference from anyone else.

"You don't know shit, Dougan."

"I know more than you think."

I finish tying my cleats and scan the area to make sure we're alone. "Yo, Dougan. If you tell Nikki anythin', I swear the LB will be all over your ass." Without waiting for him to respond I head to the field, where the coach is having the team do laps for warm-up. Nikki is sitting in the stands with Kendall, watching us, with a bunch of other girls.

Marco jogs beside me. "What's up, Fuentes?" He nods toward the bleachers. "I see you got a fan."

"If you have an opinion about my girlfriend, keep it to yourself," I tell him. "Seriously, stop givin' her shit or you'll have to answer to me."

"What are you, her bodyguard or boyfriend?" he jokes.

"Both." I glance at the bleachers. Nikki doesn't look too happy that I'm talking to Marco.

"I think it's entertainin' that you and Nikki have a little thing goin' on," Marco says, then pats my back. "Good luck with that, bro . . . while it lasts."

He sprints to the side of the field to talk to the coach before I can say anything back.

Derek is a midfielder who can kick the ball farther and more accurately than I've ever seen. Marco and I are forwards, and we read the game as if we're of one mind. Instinctively we know what to expect from each other, and what we're both thinking.

The only distraction I have is Nikki. Each time the ball goes out of bounds, I find myself looking for her in the stands.

"Fuentes, what are you doin'?" Coach yells. "Sal just threw the ball inbounds to you and you were staring off into La-La Land."

"Sorry, Coach," I say.

"Get off my field until your head is back in the game," he yells, then motions for another player to replace me.

I jog off the field and stop at the water station. I squirt water in my mouth, then douse my head to cool me off.

"I'm distracting you, aren't I?" Nikki asks.

I turn around and see her leaning on the chain-link fence. The sun is shining on her dark hair, showing off hints of natural red highlights.

Is she distracting me? Hell, yeah. "I missed that ball 'cause I was lookin' for you."

"Don't do that," she says. "Do you want me to leave? It's not a big deal. I don't want to piss off your coach."

I wink at her. "You know I don't want you to leave."

"Nikki Cruz, stop distracting my player, or I'll make this a closed practice and kick you out!" Coach yells.

"Go make a goal to appease the poor man," she tells me.

"Will do."

The rest of the practice I keep myself focused on the drills and not on Nikki. After practice, Marco and I are talking about strategy as we walk out of the locker room. Nikki is waiting for me in the hallway.

"Hey," she says.

"Hey." I pat Marco on the back. "I'll meet you at your car."

He sighs. "All right. But don't take long. We need to bounce, bro."

I put my arms around Nikki and bend my head down to kiss her, but she pulls back. "You have plans with Marco?"

"Yeah." I shrug. "He wants me to help him out with somethin'."

"Why didn't you tell me?"

"Because I didn't want you to know, all right? Listen, you've got issues with the guy and I didn't want to piss you off. I'll come over right after, I swear."

"I'm sorry. I don't mean to question you." She pulls my head down and kisses me. "I have trust issues."

"I know. I'm on a mission to cure you of that."

I put my arm around her and we walk to the parking lot. Marco is waiting out front in his car. He beeps when he sees me. "Come on, *pendejo!*" he yells impatiently out the window.

"I'll see ya later," I say to Nikki, then kiss her again before sliding into Marco's car.

A few minutes after we drive off, Marco motions to his glove compartment. "Open it."

When I do, five little packets of white powder packed in blue cellophane stare back at me.

"Chuy wants us to unload this shit for seventy-five dollars a pop. We get to keep twenty-five."

I slam the compartment shut. "Dude, that's *yeyo*. You know, that stuff I almost got busted for over the weekend."

"Tell me somethin' I don't know. Here," he says, pulling out a sheet of paper with an address scribbled on it: 2416 Newberry Drive. Evanston. "Chuy said we could unload it by sellin' it to this *culero*."

We drive on Sheridan Road through Fairfield, winding down the tree-lined curvy road until we reach Evanston. I'm silent the entire time, looking out the window at pedestrians and wondering what they think of us. Do they see two Mexicans in a car and immediately think we're drug dealers? Today they'd be spot on. It's not a big shipment that could put us in jail for ten years, but it's enough to get us arrested.

Chuy's threat runs through my head. *You're either with us or against us. You want to keep your family safe, don't you?*

Yeah, I want to keep my family safe. I have to do this for my brothers, my nephew, my sister-in-law, and *mi'amá*. Doing drug deals for the LB is an obligation as much as it is a way to find out insider info. I'm pretty sure Alex did it, I know Carlos did it . . . now it's my turn.

It's still light out, so it's not hard to find the address. We arrive at the house. "This place is a dump," I say, staring at the random pieces of scrap metal and wooden skids piled up in the yard.

"I'll wait in the car," Marco says.

I shove the five packets in my pockets. I've never done anything like this before and feel like a complete poser. "Why don't you do it?" I ask Marco. "You're the veteran."

"Chuy told me to make you do it. Somethin' about you provin' yourself." He checks his rearview mirror. "Look, I wouldn't be surprised if this guy is one of Chuy's buddies checkin' up to make sure you're gonna follow through."

Shit. "You got my back?"

"Yeah . . . Yeah, I got your back." Marco is acting all cool, as if he's done this a thousand times and it's not a big deal. "Go on already. Stop stallin'."

I reach into the small duffel I stashed in Marco's car this morning before school and pull out the Glock. I shove it into my waistband, then walk to the front door. On it is a sticker that says NO SOLICITING. I'm about to sell drugs. Is that soliciting? I could probably do a kick-ass essay on the topic, making an argument for and against it.

Okay, I am stalling. *You can do this*, I tell myself as my heart is pumping hard and fast. I ring the doorbell and hear footsteps as someone comes to the door. It opens. A guy with a shaved head that resembles a cage fighter I once saw on TV is standing in front of me. I'm gonna guess he hasn't showered in a week, because he smells like shit.

"Who the hell are you?" the guys asks.

Umm . . . what do I say? It's not easy thinking this stuff up on the fly. "Umm . . . I think I got stuff that you want."

I sound like an idiot.

"What kind of stuff?" the guys asks, unfazed at how stupid this conversation sounds.

I start to pull one of the packets out of my pocket when the guy grabs my shirt and pulls me into his house.

"Don't ever do that again, you hear. Pigs drive around these parts lookin' to bust guys like you. He sees you flashin' coke and you and I will both be arrested. All right . . ." He sniffs a few times and his hands are shaking in anticipation. "Show me what you got."

I pull out the five packets. "Seventy-five dollars each. Three seventy-five for all five." I was always good in math.

"How about three fifty?" he counters.

Seriously, are you even allowed to counteroffer on a drug deal?

He obviously thinks I'm a rookie. I am, but if Chuy is monitoring this, I better not back down. If I don't do this, my loyalty will be questioned.

"What the fuck do you think I am, a wholesaler?" I say in a pissed-off tone, slipping into the tough gang member role easily. "Three seventy-five or I'm out." Listen, as long as I'm here, and risking it all, I might as well get the full amount. "I've got ten more guys who'll give me four bills for shit this pure. Either you take it, or they will."

I took AP economics—the supply and demand model is powerful stuff. If this dude thinks the supply is low and demand is high, chances are he'll play the game my way.

He hesitates for a split second. I take my chances and go for the bluff, heading for the door.

"Okay, fine!" he calls out. "I'll be right back with the money. Just . . . just wait right there."

I hold the packets in one hand and reach around for the Glock with my other. If this guy is about to shoot me, I better be ready to fire back or get the hell out.

Shit, what have I turned into? A gangbanging drug dealer getting off on being a badass. How easy it's been for me to do a complete 180. The only thing keeping me here is the fact that if I don't, I won't know what Chuy has up his sleeve. It's something that involves me. I know that for sure. I can't go to the cops. Chuy's got eyes and ears all over the streets, and even hinted that he's got some of the cops in Fairfield on his payroll. For the first time in my life, I can't do the right thing.

The thought that this *pendejo* about to buy drugs from me can be an undercover cop enters my mind, but the way he looked longingly at the *yeyo* and started sniffing over the prospect of havin' the stuff within reach makes me forget that thought.

The guy comes back in the room with a bunch of bills in his hand. "Here," he says, shoving the money at me.

Do I count it now, before I leave, or is that considered a dis? I don't know the protocol here so I'm making this shit up as I go along. I briefly glance down at the money, then hand over the *yeyo*.

As I walk back to the car my heart is still pounding. This adrenaline rush gives me a natural high that makes me feel invincible, like I felt when I free solo'd it back in Boulder. The chance I'll get bitten by a snake here is rare, but lying to Nikki and my family could have worse consequences.

"Let's get out of here," I tell Marco as I slide into the passenger seat.

I get a text as we speed away from the house.

Nikki: Hey. what u up to?

I don't answer.

30

I tell Luis to meet me at the animal shelter. When he pulls up on a motorcycle, I do a double take. He pulls off the helmet and walks over to me.

"Is that *your* motorcycle?" I ask him.

"It's my cousin Enrique's. He let me borrow it. He said I could work at his auto body shop a few days a week since he knows I lost my job at Brickstone and business has started to pick up." He puts his arms around me and holds me for a long time. "I missed you, even if you do smell like wet dog."

"I gave Granny a bath."

"Granny?"

"She's my favorite dog here. You want to meet her?"

"Definitely."

"Come on." After introducing him to the staff, I take him back to Granny's cage. "Isn't she adorable?" I ask as I bend down and pick her up. "She's blind, but she can hear you perfectly."

Luis takes her from me. "Yo, Granny, what's up?" She nuzzles her nose into his shirt as he pets her. "You want to take her home, don't you?" he asks me.

"How did you know?"

"By the way you look at her."

"My parents don't want me to get a dog, but I'm working on them. I think they'll cave soon. I even had them come meet her." I look off into the distance. "I think they're afraid I'll freak out when she dies."

"Will you?"

I stroke Granny behind her ear. "Yeah, probably."

"How long does Granny have left?"

"How long do any of us have left?" I ask him, getting a thoughtful smile from Luis in return.

I introduce him to more dogs, and point out all of their stories and quirks. Jake the beagle doesn't stop howling, Hannah the shepherd mix likes her crate mate a little too much. The puppies that came in today will probably be adopted by noon. "Everyone loves the puppies."

"Except you. You love the pathetic ones, like Granny."

I push him playfully. "She is not pathetic. She's needy."

"I took psych last year. If I was a psychologist, I'd probably diagnose you as a person who likes to feel needed."

"That's a fair assumption," I admit. It's better than being needy. "What about you, Mr. Fuentes? Are you needy?"

"I can be if you want me to be," he says, which makes me laugh.

I show him the makeshift studio I set up to take pictures of the dogs to post on the adoption website I created. I pick up the camera and show him the pictures I took of all the dogs at the shelter.

"Maggie sleeps a lot, so I put a pillow down and had her lie on it," I explain. "And Buster loves to play catch, so I took this one with three balls in his mouth so people would know he's a playful guy. I try to show the personality of each dog in the pictures."

"I'm impressed," he says, eyeing me with admiration as he scans through the pictures. "These are good. I can see them in a book."

"My goal is to get them adopted," I tell him.

"You're a saint."

I think of the picture that Marco said he didn't delete. "I'm far from it. I've done some really dumb things in the past."

"We all have." He holds out his hand. "Remember these scars? I wasn't lyin' when I said I got bitten by a snake and fell off a cliff right before my brother's weddin'. I didn't wear a harness."

"Why not?"

"Because I like livin' on the edge sometimes. Don't you?"

"No. Not anymore, at least." He keeps flipping through the pictures. The last one in the camera is of Granny. It didn't do her justice. "Wait here." I get Granny and put her in his arms. "Sit over there with her."

He sits by the light and pets Granny while I snap pictures. When he turns her over and scratches her stomach while she lies upside down and practically smiles into the camera, I know I have the perfect picture. Granny might be blind and old, but she's going to be the perfect pet for me. The fact that Luis is smiling warmly as he pets her makes me want to print out a copy to post on my wall at home. I feel like she's already mine.

"Your turn," he says, giving Granny to me. I hold her while he takes a picture of us on his cell phone.

My mom calls, telling me I have to come home and help her hang new drapes in our living room. She's into abstract flower patterns that remind her of some artist named Georgia O'Keeffe or something. "I've got to go," I tell him.

Luis and I head to the now empty parking lot.

"Do you think we're rushing into things?" I ask him.

"Don't stress about it, *mi chava*. It's all good." He slips the helmet over his head and revs the engine to his motorcycle.

"Don't kill yourself riding that thing!" I yell.

He gives me a thumbs-up, then waits until I get in my car before speeding out of the parking lot.

I come to the realization that my boyfriend is an adrenaline junkie. Can I keep up with him?

31

Luis

High school soccer games don't usually have police and security guards at them, except when Fremont plays Fairfield. Our team is pumped on Saturday morning when we play Fremont. We're rival schools and rival towns with rival gangs. I guess after an incident where a Fremont player got stabbed by a Fairfield player last year, they decided to hire police to patrol the stands and the sidelines just in case all hell breaks loose.

In the end, we win five to four. Alex, Brittany, Carlos, and Paco stay after the game to talk to some old friends from Fairfield.

I'm holding Paco when Mariana and a bunch of her friends walk up to me. "Cute kid," she says.

Paco is a complete chick magnet. He gives them all high fives, and even calls Mariana *"chica"* like Alex calls Brittany. It actually sounds like *cha-cha* and the girls find it hilarious. Man, the kid already knows how to flirt with the chicks. My nephew is advanced in that department, but I wouldn't expect anything less from a Fuentes.

Carlos is standing next to me, shaking hands with this dude I've never seen before. "Tell your sister I said hi," he tells the guy.

"Who was that?" I ask after the guy walks away.

"Destiny's brother."

Destiny. His ex. I don't know if he's seen her or talked to her since they broke up years ago. I do know that Carlos was obsessed with the girl and had pictures of her taped above his bed. I know Carlos was bummed when she broke up with him and would have done anything to get her back. That was before Kiara was in the picture, though.

I look around for Nikki. She's standing in the bleachers talking to a couple of her friends.

"Hey, Nik!" I yell up to her.

She glances at me, then looks away.

What the hell?

I'm still holding my nephew as I walk up to her. "What's up?"

Her friends say a quick hello, then scatter.

Nikki crosses her arms on her chest, her Latina attitude clawing its way to the surface. "To be honest, I'm kind of jealous you were all chatty-chatty with Mariana."

"Seriously, you were jealous?" I ask, amused. "That's cool." It means she cares.

"It's not funny. You were flirting with her."

"I was not. Paco was. I don't know if you could blame a kid who's not even two years old, though." I cock my head to the side and change the subject. "Did you see the two goals I made for you?"

"For me?"

"Didn't you see me point to you after I made them?"

"You were pointing to the sky, Luis. Toward God."

"Same thing."

"It was not, and you know it." She takes Paco from me. My nephew plays with her hair, and suddenly I'm the one who's jealous. "Why are you making a joke out of this?" she asks.

"Because it's stupid, Nik. There's not even room in my day to think about someone else." Paco starts kissing her on her cheek with big, sloppy wet ones. "He's suckin' up to you."

"At least someone is."

"You tryin' to fight with me? Before you answer, I should warn you that I find you ridiculously sexy when you've got attitude."

"I just . . . forget it," she says. "If you don't even recognize that you're a flirt, it's useless to talk about it."

My brothers laugh when they see her giving me the cold shoulder. "Oh, man," Carlos says. "I think our little bro is in big trouble."

Carlos drapes his arms around both of us. "Kiss and make up, you two. Kiara is comin' here in less than an hour and I've got a task for you guys. You too, Alex."

"What kind of task?" I ask.

"I need you to dig for *mi'amá*'s jewelry box."

Oh, no. Not this again. When Carlos was younger he thought it would be brilliant to pretend he was a pirate hiding his treasure. *Mi'amá*'s jewelry box doubled as the booty. Ended up it wasn't such a brilliant idea because Carlos forgot where he hid the box. *Mi'amá*'s wedding ring and every piece of jewelry she'd owned was in there. For years we dug in that small wooded area by our house and came up empty-handed.

"I don't think Nikki is gonna want to go treasure huntin'," I say.

"I don't mind," she says. "Where is it?"

"That's a good question. I hid it by the ravine near our house." Carlos rubs the top of his crew cut and winces. "I kinda need it pretty bad.

Kiara's comin' and, well, I just need to find that damn thing. I tried lookin' this mornin', but my damn leg gave out."

When Carlos leaves to go pick up Kiara from the airport, the rest of us head over to the ravine with shovels. Nikki had me pick up this German shepherd named Hank from the shelter so he can help with the search, because she swears she can tell he was specially trained at one point in his undocumented life.

In the woods above the ravine, Alex sections the place out. Alex, Brittany, and I are not optimistic. But Nikki and Hank have enough optimism and energy for all of us. Hank sniffs the air and walks over the sticks and leaves as he and Nikki head to their designated section.

Brittany waves the small garden shovel in the air, like she's raising her hand. "How deep do we have to dig?" she calls out.

"I don't know," Alex tells her. "I figure not too deep 'cause Carlos was a kid who hated breakin' a sweat."

I start digging, spacing my holes about ten inches apart in a grid pattern so I don't miss anything. The jewelry box was white, so it should be easy to find. I look over at Nikki. She's talking to the dog and instructing him to "go find it!" Seriously, is a dog supposed to know what *it* means? I laugh as Hank sniffs away. The second he settles on a spot, Nikki starts digging away. She's so intent on her task, she doesn't look up.

Which means I can watch her.

I know what she's thinking. In her mind, Carlos needs her. He's desperate to find the jewelry box, and I know she's more than motivated to find it for him. I wouldn't be surprised if she dug in every spot Hank sniffs until darkness falls. My girl is on a mission. I don't have the heart to tell her that Hank might be sniffing for a place to shit, not because he's actually following a scent.

I wonder what she'd say if I told her I need her, too.

After twenty minutes and about five false alarms, I hear Nikki screaming, "I think Hank found it!"

My head pops up and I see Nikki on her knees, waving her arms back and forth so we can see her. Sure enough, when I get close I see she's dug out a tiny section of what looks like it could be a jewelry box. Hank is barking now, crazy excited.

"That dog is a fuckin' genius, Nikki," Alex says, taking his shovel and digging the rest of it out. Moments later, I help lift it free.

"I'm textin' Carlos and tellin' him we found it," I say as Alex pries open the rotted top.

Nikki's got a huge grin as she praises Hank and gives him a treat she stashed in her pocket. I'm still in shock and can't believe the dog had anything to do with it. Maybe it was just plain luck, but then again, when I look down at the dog I think he's got a proud grin on his face.

Alex takes out *mi'amá*'s engagement ring and holds it up to the light shining through the trees. The diamond glitters in the light.

Back home, Nikki announces the good news to *mi'amá*. *Mi'amá* opens the box and takes out her wedding band and engagement ring. She slips them on as tears run down her cheeks. "It's been so long," she says, choking back the words. Paco asks her if she's got a boo-boo because she's crying. "Yes," she says to him. "I have a boo-boo."

Ma places the rings back in the dirty box just as Carlos and Kiara walk in the door. Kiara is yelling at Carlos for carrying her luggage in the house when he's not fully healed, but he's just ignoring her protests. Kiara should know by now that he's one stubborn motherfucker. They're checking into a nearby hotel later, but he didn't want to leave her expensive luggage in the car while it was parked in front of the house.

"Are you two seriously fightin'?" Alex asks. "You haven't seen each other in over a year."

"We like to argue," Carlos tells him. "It's one of the two things we do best. Right, *mamacita*?"

Kiara rolls her eyes. "Remind m-m-me why I'm in love with you again?"

Carlos gives her a mischievous grin as he pulls her close. "I'll show you later."

Kiara seems content with that answer as she hugs me, Brittany, and Alex.

"This is my girlfriend, Nikki," I tell her, then point to the dirty dog panting on the floor. "And that's Hank the orphan."

Nikki isn't prepared for Kiara to hug her like a long-lost sister, and then go over to pet Hank, who rolls onto his back for full exposure.

Brittany and Alex leave to pick up Shelley, Brittany's sister. She lives in a care facility for people with disabilities, but spends most weekends at Alex and Brit's place. Paco loves riding in her wheelchair and has no clue she's disabled. Nikki and Shelley obviously know each other from previous interactions and, when Shelly arrives, immediately start chatting about dogs and the shelter. Nikki promises to take Shelley to the shelter one day, which makes Shelley squeal with happiness and Brittany smile with gratitude.

At dinner when our entire family is together, it really hits me that Nikki and I are a couple. My arm rests on the back of Nikki's chair and she leans into me. I hate to admit I'm falling hard and fast. Just the thought of losing her because of my involvement with the LB stresses me out. Especially when I get a text from Marco to meet him later tonight at the warehouse.

I reach for Nikki's hand and squeeze it under the table. She squeezes back, then looks up at me.

"You okay?" she asks quietly while the rest of my family is pigging out. "You've been quiet ever since we got here."

"I was just thinkin'."

"About what?"

I lean in close and whisper in her ear, "Renegotiatin' the terms of our relationship."

Her face turns beet red and she whispers back, "We'll discuss that later."

"Just so you know, I got an A in debate," I tell her.

She looks up at me with a grin on her sexy ruby lips. "So did I."

32

On Monday, Luis surprises me by coming over to my house after soccer practice.

"You could have just texted me," I tell him.

He shrugs. "Yeah, well, I thought you could use a calculus tutor. I'm offerin' my services," he says, then adds with not a small hint of cockiness, "for free."

Oh, man, I am in trouble. The more time I spend with Luis, the more I want to be with him. I force myself to keep distant, and tell myself that I'm not going to let him get too close. I'd like to, though. When he puts his arms around me, I feel protected and safe. My mind tells me it's a false sense of security. I'm constantly trying to determine which of my emotions is centered on reality.

I even get the sense that when he says he's going to work at his cousin's auto body shop, he's actually doing something else. I'm probably being paranoid. I told him to be honest with me, and I want to trust him. But I have my doubts. It's easy to push all doubts to the back of my head when I'm with him, though.

"I do need some help in calc," I admit.

"Hi, Luis," Mom says as I lead him to the kitchen table where my books are spread out.

"Hi, Mrs. Cruz," Luis says politely.

"You two have been spending a lot of time together lately," she says, stating the obvious.

Luis nods. "Yes, ma'am."

"Well, I hope it's not too serious. Nikki has to concentrate on her college applications and keeping her grades up."

I cringe. "Mom, don't embarrass me."

"It's okay, Nik," Luis tells me. "My ma said the same thing."

I'm tempted to prove to them both that we don't have to compromise our future just because we're together.

"Can Luis eat over, Mom?" I blurt out, changing the subject before she asks him for his dating credentials. I know she worries about me, and doesn't want a repeat of what happened between me and Marco. Both my parents have grilled me about any boy I talk to. What they don't know is that all friendships I've had with guys after Marco were just that— friendships. This thing with Luis . . . it's much more. But I told my parents we were just friends so they won't freak out.

"We're ordering Chinese, Luis," Mom says. "Do you like Chinese?"

He shrugs. "I can eat anythin'."

"You're more than welcome to join us for dinner." She says it without a smile on her face, like she's only saying it to be polite. I hope Luis doesn't notice. She looks at our schoolbooks spread on the kitchen table. "You guys better get cracking on that homework."

Luis and I sit at the kitchen table. He helps me with my calculus, then moves across the table to start on his own homework. I'm working on a poem for language arts. Our teacher said we should write about someone who had an impact on our lives, whether it was good or bad. I want to write about Luis, because he makes me want to change . . . he makes me want to love again. I'm still holding back, but to be honest, I don't want to.

I glance at Luis for inspiration.

I catch him checking me out at the same time. Nervous butterflies flutter in my stomach as I fantasize about what it would be like if we were alone together.

I expect him to look away, but he doesn't.

"Why are you staring at me?"

"I'd ask you the same thing," he says.

"Do your work," I tell him, trying not to let on that I'm tempted to go sit on his lap and wrap my arms around his neck. He looks down at his social studies folder. "I can feel your eyes on me," he says after a minute.

"Sorry." I stare at the blank page and start my poem. My first attempt is about a hero, who has come to save me before my heart turns completely to ice and cracks in a million little pieces never to be healed. No, that sounds too paranormal. I hope what I have with Luis is real, but after my bad judgment in the past, I don't **trust** my instincts.

"Want to come over on Sunday?" he asks me. "*Mi'amá* will be at work, and my brothers are gonna barbeque."

"Sounds great."

"I'm gonna warn you, though. They've already talked about playin' Panty Discus." He laughs when he sees my expression. "It's not what you think. It's a game played with a tennis ball and panty hose . . . the kind that women wear. You have to see it to really appreciate it."

"I'm sure," I say, unconvinced. "Are your brothers competitive?"

"Let's just say I suspect Carlos started trainin' for it months ago while he was stationed overseas. Alex has always won, but now that we'll be playin' in pairs I think we've got a good shot at winnin' the whole thing. Brittany is kind of a lightweight when it comes to strength."

"What do you win?"

"Braggin' rights." He shrugs. "They're kind of a big deal in my family."

When my mom goes to pick up the Chinese food, I bite my lip wondering if I should bring up The Talk. I look up at Luis and know I'm going to have a hard time keeping to my original conditions.

"Umm . . . didn't you challenge me to a debate or something like that the other night?"

His head shoots up. "Yeah. I'm ready."

I laugh. "For what?"

"The debate, or, you know . . . whatever you're ready for . . . I'm all in."

"This isn't the World Series of poker."

"I know what it is, *chica*."

I twirl my hair on my finger nervously. "I have to admit I've been thinking about *being* with you a lot."

"Me too. Come here." He pulls his chair out and motions for me to sit on his lap. Hoping my mom won't come in, I sit on his lap and wrap my arms around his neck. I look down at his dark, mesmerizing eyes. "Nik, I won't hurt you. I'm not gonna ditch you afterward."

"I know. It's just hard for me and . . . I'm afraid."

"Of what?" He rubs my back affectionately. "Talk to me."

I don't say what's really on my mind. *Marco. The miscarriage. The betrayal. Luis's secrets.* I'm afraid of making myself vulnerable. I bury my face in his neck and squeeze tight. Despite all of my inhibitions and

all of my suspicions, I'm falling for Luis. Being able to resist him physically is beginning to be impossible.

"Just so you know . . . I'm not on the pill or anything," I say softly.

"I've got condoms," he says, then smiles sheepishly. "Not on me, of
course. I'm not one of those *pendejos* who carries one around *just in case*."

Who better to get over the past than with someone I want to be
with . . . someone who I'm starting to fall in love with. I lean in and
whisper in his ear, "I'm nervous."

He reaches up and cups my face in his palm. "You need to trust me."

"I don't know if I can."

33

Luis

I'm not sure asking Nikki to come over on Sunday was the best idea, especially when Carlos decides to grill my girlfriend and embarrass the shit outta me.

"So, Nikki," Carlos says the second she walks in the house, "did you know Luis stares at a picture of you and some dog on his phone for like an hour before he goes to sleep? I swear he takes it in the can with him, too, but I don't know what the hell he's been doin' in there with it."

Carlos was never one to listen to directions. I told him this morning not to say stupid shit to Nikki. I should've known that wasn't gonna happen.

"Don't listen to him, Nik," I tell her.

"I second that," Kiara says, giving Carlos the evil eye. She whacks him in the stomach. "Don't embarrass them, Carlos."

"I think she should be flattered to know how much my little bro likes her," he says innocently.

"It is kind of a coincidence," Nikki says, unfazed. "Because I look at Luis's picture all the time, too." She looks at me and winks.

The entire house goes silent. Damn. I didn't know my *novia* could hold her own against Carlos.

She looks up at me adoringly. "Great minds think alike. Right, Luis?"

Damn straight. I wink at her and take her hand in mine. "Definitely."

Her eyes light up, and when the sunlight shines through the front window and hits them, I notice her brown eyes have golden specks inside.

Nikki tilts her head to the side and asks Carlos, "So, when are you and Kiara getting engaged? Luis told me you two have been dating a long time."

Go, Nikki! My girl can take the heat and dish it right back. That'll teach my brother to stick his nose where it doesn't belong.

Alex, who just came in from the kitchen, can't hold in his laughter. "She's got you there, bro."

"Yeah, Carlos?" Kiara chimes in. "When are we g-g-getting engaged?"

Carlos clears his throat. And moans in defeat. "Can we talk about this later?" he asks, then narrows his eyes mockingly at Nikki. "Warn me next time I get the urge to embarrass you and my brother."

Nikki gives him a thumbs-up. "Will do."

After we eat, Alex holds out *mi'amá*'s panty hose and says, "Competition time."

I stare at the hose. Alex will be long gone, back at his house, when *mi'amá* notices that two pairs of hose are completely cut off at the top of the leg. There's no doubt in my mind that she'll notice. It's not a matter of if, but when. And I'll be here to face the consequences.

The problem with my brothers, besides the obvious, is that we're competitive. It's not even normal sibling rivalry. If there's a competition, it's all-out war. The winner gets the right to brag about it forever, and the loser gets the right to be made fun of forever. It's kind of like a religious tradition.

The competitions in the past weren't fair because I'm younger than my brothers. But now we're about the same height and same strength, so any competition is going to be fierce.

"Let's head to the park," Alex says, then pulls out a tennis ball from the front closet. Paco seems way too excited to play.

Brittany puts a hand to her forehead. "He's been looking forward to this all week. I don't think there's any stopping him." She points to Alex. "I'm talking about my husband, not my son."

"I get a handicap because of my leg!" Carlos yells out, then yelps some kind of war cry he probably learned in the army but sounds ridiculous echoing through our house. If Reyes heard, he'll probably kick our front door down with his gun blazing thinking we're getting robbed.

"You're not gettin' a handicap," Alex tells him. "Your arm isn't damaged."

"I agree," I add.

"Man, you guys are brutal," Carlos says, although he knows full well that if either me or Alex had any injuries he wouldn't be giving us a handicap.

Nikki halts. "All right, I think Panty Discus needs to be explained. It sounds like a slam on women, to be honest." She puts her hands on her hips, and all I can think about is seeing those hips without any clothes covering them.

"It's not a slam on women," I tell her. "I wouldn't be surprised if one day it became an Olympic sport."

She laughs. "I don't think so."

We all head over to a huge, empty grassy area by the park.

"We're playin' in teams," Alex says. "Couples against couples."

"I'm not playing something that's named Panty Discus," Brittany exclaims. "I know you explained what it meant, but it still sounds dirty." She earmuffs Paco. "And I really don't want Paco saying it."

Carlos rolls his eyes. "Brit, get that stick out of your rich ass, please, and suck it up. You're playin'. And when my nephew is old enough, he'll not only be sayin' it, he'll be playin' it, too. It's a Fuentes tradition."

Brittany's mouth is open in shock. "Carlos, if I'm concerned about my son hearing Panty Discus," she says, whispering the offending words, "do you really think I want him to hear cuss words flying out of your mouth?"

"Can I at least spell them?" Carlos asks. I don't think he's kidding.

Alex gets in the middle of them. "That's fine. Brit, if you don't want to play, you don't have to. Paco can fill in for you, although to be honest, it'll probably kill my winnin' streak."

Brittany walks up to Alex and points her finger to his chest. "I'll do it, but only because I'm your wife and I love you."

Kiara watches Alex and Brittany with a longing gaze, then stares at my oblivious brother Carlos. Nikki was just joking with her back at the house, but I've got the feeling Kiara's been waiting for a ring from my brother. I don't know why he's been dragging his feet, because we all know it's gonna happen.

"I'm game," Kiara says with a sigh.

I look at Nikki. I can't wait to get this over with so I can be alone with her.

"How about you, Nik?" I ask.

"I'm game, too," she says, giving me look that gets my heart racing. "Just tell me what to do."

"What does the winner get?" Brittany asks.

"Braggin' rights," Carlos explains. "Which in this family is worth more than money." He turns to Kiara. "We better win, *mamacita*."

Alex sets up a stick as the starting line and shows everyone the homemade Panty Discus contraption—which is just a leg cut off of a pair of women's panty hose with a ball stuck in the toe end and a knot in the other end. "The object is to toss the Panty Discus as far as you can. Farthest combined toss wins."

"Oldest goes first," I tell him.

"Works for me." Alex stands at the starting line and starts twirling the ball over his head faster and faster before he releases it. It flies high and far in the air. When it lands, he's pretty cocky thinking that nobody can best him. He places a rock in its place. "Brit, your turn."

I watch as Brittany tries the same technique, twirling the ball over her head. He stands next to her, coaching, while Paco makes a game of trying to pat down my spiked hair. "Come on, Brit, I got full faith in you to pull this one out," Alex says to Brittany. "Twirl it faster now. Damn, girl, you look hot doin' that. Okay, release!"

She does, but the Panty Discus is released when the ball is aimed to the side and flies out of her hand, heading directly to her right and not straight ahead. It lands about fifteen feet to the side of the starting line.

"What. The. Hell. Was. That?" Alex asks, sucking in a breath.

Brittany huffs and cries out, "You said I looked hot and it *totally* threw me off. It's not my fault. I've never played this game before, Alex. Next time, shut up and let me toss it without your comments."

"*Chica*, that was embarrassin'. You need some intensive Panty Discus instruction." He playfully picks her up and carries her to where we're sitting. "When we get home—"

"My turn!" Carlos says, rubbing his hands together gleefully. "Watch and learn from the expert, people." He limps over to the starting line and circles one end of the hose over his head. "You takin' notes, Kiara?"

"I'm too busy w-w-watching your muscles flex," she says.

He wags his eyebrows at her, then whips the Panty Discus with all he's got and it lands a yard or so farther than Alex's toss. Carlos yelps out another war cry and kisses his newfound army muscles. "Army strong, suck'ahs!"

"You're *loco*," I tell him as he puts a stick to mark the place of his throw and hands the Panty Discus to Kiara.

Kiara imitates Carlos's helicopter-style move and does a pretty good job whipping the hose in front of her. It doesn't go as far as his, but at least it's straight. Carlos nods, impressed with her toss. "I think we've got it in the bag, Kiara," he tells her as he marks her spot.

My turn.

"Wait!" Nikki says before I step up to the starting line. She rushes up to me and crushes my mouth to hers. "Good luck."

"Mmm, I like good luck kisses. We should have Panty Discus tournaments all the time," I say.

She stands aside while I take a deep breath and channel all of my energy toward getting this thing past Carlos's marker. I twirl the hose around, then with all my might whip it in the air. It flies high, and I'm sure I got the height but fear I'm lacking the distance until it falls a few inches past Carlos's stick.

"No way!" Carlos says.

I kiss my muscles, mocking him. "Don't knock the swimmer, suck'ahs! Even in the off season we can kick butt."

I grab Nikki around the waist and pull her against me. "How was that?"

"Perfect."

"Your turn. Make me proud, *chica*."

Nikki walks up to the starting line, determination and focus outlined in her tense expression. She whips the ball around her head like a warrior with a war club, then releases the thing in the air with a loud grunt that echoes throughout the park.

It lands way farther than Kiara's. Adding up the combined distances, we win.

I point to Nikki. "That's my girl."

She jumps up and down, raising her hands in the air like we just won a trip to Hawaii. "We did it!"

As we're celebrating, a car drives up with a bunch of girls inside. The car stops and a girl gets out. She's got a huge grin on her face and is walking with a sway of her hips as she makes a direct beeline toward Carlos. "Carlos!" she says excitedly. "I can't believe it's you! My brother told me you were back, but . . . well, my friends and I were about to go to the city, but I made them make a detour. I had to check for myself to see if it was true."

It's Destiny, my brother's ex from high school.

My brother's eyes go wide with shock. "Holy s-h-i-t, Des. It's been a long time. How the h-e-l-l are ya?" He points to Paco. "Gotta watch the language around my nephew."

She laughs. "Hangin' in there. Going to school for nursing. What about you?"

"I'm in the army. Stationed in the Middle East, but I'm on leave."

"Wow." She makes a point of licking her lips as she checks him out. "*Tú eres guapo.*"

"You look great, too. The same as I remember."

"You still single?"

He holds up his left hand and points to his ring finger. "Yep. Still a bachelor."

"Awesome." One of her friends calls to her. "I got to go, but it was great seeing you." She pulls out a card from her purse. "Call me some-time. My number's on the back. I'd love to catch up."

"Cool," he says, shoving the card in his back pocket.

We all watch as my brother's ex-girlfriend wraps her arms around him and hugs him tight. There are a few kinds of hugs. A short, impersonal "obligatory" hug. A medium-length "it's good to see you" hug, and then there's the kind of hug that Destiny is currently giving my brother. It's a lingering, "I want to be more than friends" hug/squeeze combo.

I look over at Kiara, standing beside Brittany, absolutely aware of the kind of hug Destiny is giving my brother.

"Really, call me," she calls out as she goes back to her friends.

When Carlos finally turns around and faces us, he must see the look of shock on our faces. I think nobody wants to talk first, because we don't know what to say.

Kiara finally does the talking.

She holds up her left hand and shows off the "no ring" finger. "*Still a bachelor!*" she says sarcastically, mimicking him. "Are you *kidding* me?"

"What?" he says, clueless. "It's the truth. What do you want me to do, lie to her?"

"No, I want you to press your bodies together and grind against each other like you were doing."

"I didn't grind against her. It was an innocent hug good-bye."

"I-I-Innocent? Honey, that hug was anything *but* innocent."

"Kiara, you're overreactin'. You want to argue, is that what this is all about? 'Cause I'm leavin' soon and we won't be seein' each other for at least six more months. The last thing I need is you creatin' drama."

"No, I don't want to argue. And I'm not creating drama, Carlos. *You* are." Kiara's nostrils flare in fury, and I notice her eyes getting watery. But she doesn't lash out at him, or start bawling. Instead she just says, "Maybe you should get back with Destiny. I think she'd like that."

"Is that what you want?"

"It seems like that's what *you* want. Why don't you take out that card and call her?"

"Maybe I will," he yells, pissed off now.

"Good. While you're at it, why don't you ask her to marry you. You obviously don't want to marry me," she says, then walks back to our house.

"Carlos, I love you, but you can be the biggest idiot sometimes," Brittany pipes in, then follows after Kiara.

Nikki steps back, says, "I'm gonna go with the girls," and jogs away from us.

Alex and I both look at Carlos.

Carlos holds up his hands. "What?" he asks defensively, completely oblivious.

"You just dissed Kiara in front of Destiny," Alex says.

"I didn't dis her." He leans in and whispers, "I was makin' sure she didn't get a clue that I'm gonna propose to her."

"You could've at least introduced her as your girlfriend."

Carlos retrieves the discus and says, "Alex, the last thing she'd want to do is meet Destiny."

"He doesn't get it," I murmur.

Alex braces his arms on Carlos's shoulders. "Does Destiny think you have a girlfriend?"

"Why the hell would that matter?"

"Because, Carlos, she was flirtin' with you big-time."

"So what? Girls flirt with me all the time. That doesn't mean I cheat on Kiara. She knows I wouldn't fuck around on her."

"Other girls aren't your ex, dumbass," Alex says. "Now go apologize to Kiara, and fix this. Beg, if you have to."

"She thinks you don't want to marry her," I add.

"Shit," Carlos says. "I asked you all to look for *Mamá*'s jewelry box 'cause she said if we finally found it I could give Kiara the ring *Papá* gave her. It's at the jeweler bein' cleaned. I was gonna take her to Ravinia tomorrow and propose durin' intermission." He rubs the back of his neck and lets out a long, slow breath. "I gotta figure this out."

Back at the house, the girls are standing in the front yard. Kiara puts on a brave face, but it's obvious she's been crying.

"You told me you were over D-Destiny," Kiara tells Carlos. "But that's obviously not true. I'm g-g-going back to Colorado tonight. I'm tired of waiting around for s-s-something that's never going to happen."

"I was over Destiny the second you put those stupid cookie magnets in my locker in high school," Carlos tells her.

"I d-don't believe you."

"I wanted to make it special for you, but what the hell . . . I might as well do it now." Carlos takes a deep breath. "Marry me, Kiara," he blurts out in front of everyone.

"Why?" she asks, challenging him.

"Because I love you," he says, walking up to her and bending down on one knee while he takes her hand in his, "and I want to go to sleep with you every night and wake up seein' your face every mornin', I want you to be the mother of my children, I want to fix cars with you and eat your crappy tofu tacos that you think are Mexican. I want to climb mountains with you and be challenged by you, I want to argue with you just so we can have crazy hot makeup sex. Marry me, because without you I'd be six feet under . . . and because I love your family like they're my own . . . and because you're my best friend and I want to grow old with you." He starts tearing up, and it's shocking because I've never seen him cry. "Marry me, Kiara Westford, because when I got shot the only thing I was thinkin' about was comin' back here and makin' you my wife. Say yes, *chica*."

Kiara is crying now. "Yes!" she says.

We all give our congratulations and talk to a couple of neighbors across the street who witnessed the scene, but when I turn back around I notice that Nikki disappeared.

"Where's Nik?" I ask Brittany.

Brittany points to the house. "I asked her to go in your closet and get me one of your zippered hoodies. I'm freezing."

My closet? Oh, hell. I rush to my room and find Nikki searching for a hoodie hanging in my closet. If she sees the Glock . . .

"Hey," I say, standing in front of her. I start closing the doors, blocking her from my suit. Is it in the same spot as I left it? Did she find it? What the hell am I gonna say if she asks me about it? I could play dumb, but I've never been able to pull that off successfully.

"Hey," she says back. "Brittany told me to come in here and get a jacket for her."

"I'll get one," I say, steering her away from my closet.

Nikki looks at me, confused. "What's wrong?"

I've got a gun stashed in my closet. "Nothin'."

"You sure? You look agitated."

"I am." I want to bang my head against the wall, because she's onto me. "I wanted to tell you somethin'."

"What?"

Now I've got to come up with something on the fly. "I'm fallin' in love with you," I blurt out.

Oh, shit. Did that really come out of my mouth? I've never said that to a girl before, and promised myself that I'd never say it if I didn't mean it.

The scariest part is that I did.

34

Nikki

After Luis said the *L* word, I pretended that I heard Brittany calling my name and practically ran out of his room. I ignored the fact that he said it, and he hasn't brought it up again.

On Wednesday, I decide to go to work with him because we kind of need to talk about Sunday. I don't want to make a big deal about it, but I don't want to throw around the *L* word like Marco and I did.

Luis now works for his cousin. Enrique's Auto Body is located on the south side of Fairfield, on the corner of Washington Street and Main Street. It's on an intersection where gang members used to hang out. This particular part of Fairfield was famous for weekly drive-by shootings when I was in grade school. Even though there was a front-page article in the local newspaper a while back about the absence of gang activity in recent years, I get an eerie feeling just being here.

"This is it," Luis says when we pull up to one of the three parking spaces out front.

My eyes zero in on the old, random bullet hole marks on the side of the building as Luis leads me inside.

A guy with tattoos running up and down his arms is bent over a car's engine. He's wearing a dirty T-shirt and pants that need a good washing. "Hey, *ese*," the guy says.

Luis motions to me. "This is Nikki."

"*Encantado de conocerte, Nikki. Soy Enrique, el primo de Luis.*"

"She doesn't speak Spanish, Enrique," Luis tells him.

Enrique laughs. "Sorry. You look Mexican."

"Not all Mexicans speak Spanish," I counter.

"All the Mexicans I know do," he says. "Hell, a majority of Mexicans I know don't even speak English."

"My dad thought it was more important to perfect his English. We don't speak Spanish at home."

Enrique shakes his head, as if my dad's theory doesn't sit well with him. "To each his own."

Luis walks over and looks under the hood of the car Enrique was just working on. "Got a leaky gasket?" he asks Enrique.

"*Sí.* It needs a tune-up and—"

Enrique freezes when a girl walks in the shop. She looks like she's in her twenties, and she obviously knows Luis, because she runs up and gives him a big hug the second she sees him.

"You look like a man, Luis," she says, then rubs the stubble on his face. "The last time I saw you, this was peach fuzz."

Luis brushes her hand away. "Thanks for embarrassin' me in front of *mi novia*, Isa."

"Alex didn't tell me you had a girlfriend," she says. She looks surprised to see me standing a few feet away from him. "Oh, I didn't see you there. I'm Isabel, an old friend of Luis's brother."

I smile back. "Nice to meet you."

Enrique, who's been silent since Isa walked in, wipes his hands on his pants. I see him swallowing a few times, as if he's nervous. "Hi, Isa," he says with a big grin on his face. "I'm glad you're here. Really. I hardly ever see you."

"I've been busy working," she tells him.

"I know. I wish you came by more."

Isa bites her lip nervously. "My car has been revving when I press on the gas, as if it doesn't want to go. I thought you could check it out."

"Absolutely," Enrique says enthusiastically. "Give me your keys. I'll take a look at it right now. Luis, head out to the back lot. I lined up cars that need oil changes."

Luis tells me to wait for him while he changes into his work coveralls. I chat with Isabel for a few minutes, until Luis comes back.

"That's definitely a fashion statement," I joke, taking in his over-sized blue coveralls covering him from neck to ankle.

He points his thumb toward the back room. "You want to wear one? If you like 'em so much, I've got a spare in the back."

"No, thanks."

He pulls a toolbox off one of the shelves and motions for me to follow him. The sun is shining bright in the sky, and today it's warm, although with the fall Chicago weather, you never know what each day will be like. I sit on the ground in front of the car Luis is working on and lift my face to the sun.

"Is Enrique in a gang?" I ask so only he can hear. "I saw his tattoos."

"He's an OG—an Original Gangster . . . not too active anymore."

"What does that mean?"

He shrugs. "It means he's an old-timer, not a foot soldier. OGs like Enrique only get called on when there's somethin' big goin' down. He stays pretty much to himself, but . . . you know . . . loyalty runs deep."

"He likes Isabel," I tell him.

"I know." He sits on one of those rolling dollies and pulls out tools from the toolbox. "But he said she's turned him down every time he asks her out. She's kind of hopelessly pining for the guy she was in love with in high school."

A pang of regret that I spent so much time hopelessly mourning my doomed relationship with Marco settles inside me. It was a waste, and I can never get that time back. "Was it a bad breakup?"

He stills. "They didn't actually break up. He died."

"That's so awful."

Luis doesn't look at me. "He was Alex's best friend."

"How did he die?"

"He got shot."

Questions start swirling through my head. "By a rival gang?"

"No. By his own gang." He looks sad as he sits on the wooden dolly and stares at the ground.

"I don't get it, Luis. Why would someone even join a gang?"

"Some people don't have a choice," he says before lying down on the dolly and rolling his upper body under the car.

I tap his leg.

He slides back out and looks up at me.

"There's always a choice. You didn't join a gang even though your brothers did." I lean down and kiss him. "You didn't take the easy way out. I love you for that."

He raises an eyebrow when the *L* word escapes from my lips.

Oops. That was not supposed to happen.

"I didn't mean *love* as in the 'I love you' kind of way," I'm quick to point out, then slap my hand over my face to hide my embarrassment.

He sits up and gently nudges my hand down. "Don't worry, *mi chava*," he says, then winks at me. "I know what you meant. Listen, you don't know what my brothers went through. They did what they needed to do. Don't judge them. You don't know what it's like to be us . . . to be poor and live in the middle of a street war. You never had to live with drive-bys and watchin' your best friend die in your arms. It sucks."

"You're right, I can't imagine what it's like. I'm just glad you're not a part of it."

He nods, then spends the rest of the time working while I watch.

"Can I help you?" I ask. "I feel bad just sitting here while you're working."

His hand appears from under one of the cars. "Hand me the oil filter wrench."

I look at the tools laid out. Umm . . . they all look the same to me. I look back at his waiting hand. "You stumped me."

I hear him laugh. "Sorry. It's the thing that looks like a claw with red rubber handles."

Considering there's only one thing with red rubber handles, I have a pretty good idea which one it is. I pick it up and place it in his waiting hand.

When he's finished, he slides back out. "You remind me of my sister-in-law. She knows shit about cars, except how to put the key in the ignition."

I raise my hand. "I know how to do that."

"Please tell me your dad at least taught you how to change a tire."

"I don't have to know how to change a tire." I reach into my purse and pull out the handy card I always carry with me for those types of emergencies. "My dad got me a Triple-A membership for that."

He rolls his eyes. "You should know how to change a tire. Remind me to teach you one day."

We spend the rest of the time talking. It's scary. The more I know about Luis, the more I like him. We're so totally different, but I *get* him.

We never run out of stuff to talk about, and even when there's a lull in the conversation it's not awkward.

"Would you ever consider applyin' to Purdue?" he asks me when he's underneath the fourth car in line for an oil change.

He already told me that's his first choice of schools. "I don't know. It wasn't on my top ten list. Why?"

"I thought maybe, you know, if you and I were still . . ." His voice drops off. "Forget it, Nik. I think I've breathed in too many oil fumes."

If we're still together by the end of the year, it would be great if we could go to the same college. I feel so close to Luis right now, and we're growing closer every day. I have to remind myself not to get sucked in.

I need to tell him how I feel.

I tap on his knee. "I think we're getting too serious."

"You're a pessimist," he says, rolling out from under the car again. "Have some faith." He pulls me down to him and caresses my back. I can feel the warmth of his hands penetrate through my shirt. "I have dirty hands," he says. "Your shirt is probably ruined."

The sound of footsteps coming toward us makes us part.

"What's up, man," Marco says. He's standing with a huge scary-looking guy.

I clutch Luis's bicep tightly.

"You gonna introduce me to your friend?" the scary guys asks.

I can feel Luis's bicep flex. "Nikki, this is Chuy. He's a buddy of mine."

Chuy puts his cigar in the side of his mouth and stares at me long and hard. It makes me feel like he's assessing my value. "You go to Fairfield High?"

"Yes."

"I've never seen you around before."

"She lives on the other side of town," Marco chimes in. "Right, Nik?"

I nod.

"Listen, guys," Luis says. I sense that he's deliberately taking the focus off of me. "If you're lookin' for Enrique, last I saw he was in the garage."

"I'm not lookin' for Enrique," Chuy says. "I was lookin' for you, Fuentes. I've got a task for you."

I feel my heart stop beating as I realize what's happening.

Luis has been recruited into the LB.

35

Luis

Nikki's shocked face when Chuy said he was looking for me says she knows what Chuy's visit is all about. She picks up her backpack and purse off the ground. "I need to go home. Now."

"What are you in a hurry for?" Chuy asks. "You have a problem with me talkin' with your boyfriend?"

"No, she doesn't. Let's talk inside," I tell him. Damn. The last thing I want is Nikki to start asking questions again.

Chuy takes his time as he disappears into the shop. Marco falls in line behind him.

I turn to Nikki. "I'll be right back," I tell her. "It's not what you think."

She's looking at me as if I'm a stranger, not her boyfriend. "I want to go home."

"I'll take you in a minute. Just . . . stay here," I say. "Please."

I walk inside, anxious to get rid of Chuy and Marco. "Where did Chuy go?" I ask Enrique. Isa is still here, talking to him as he works on her car.

"In my office," Enrique says. He can't say anything against Chuy because of his unwavering loyalty and honor he pledged to the Latino Blood a long time ago.

Chuy is sitting at Enrique's desk, like it's his own. Marco is standing next to him like a bodyguard.

I close the door just in case Nikki decides she wants to listen in on our conversation. "All right, what's goin' down?"

Chuy taps his ash right on Enrique's desk. "This guy owes me five Gs. I need you and Marco to collect it. Tonight."

He reaches into his back pocket and pulls out a piece of paper. I scan the address. Augusta Lane. "That's deep in Fremont 5 territory," I tell him.

"Yep."

All I can think about is the look of betrayal on Nikki's face as I left her by the car outside. "I can't go into F5 territory without gettin' my head blown off," I blurt out.

"Yes, you can. And yes, you will." He gestures to the door. "That honey of yours out there looks real nice. I could use a hot chick like that to sell for me over at DePaul. The college boys love to buy from pretty girls. Ain't that right, Marco?"

Marco nods. "That's right. Mariana's makin' a killin' over there."

This is bullshit. "Nikki's off limits," I say, loud and clear so there's no mistaking that she's never to be thought of as an asset to the LB. I'll be damned if I drag Nikki into the LB.

"It's time I let you in on a little secret," Chuy says, sitting up now. "There's a safety-deposit box at Chicago Community Bank with your name on it. Once you turn eighteen, you have access to it. I've got the key." He pulls out a shiny silver key from his pocket and slides it over to me. "After your birthday you're gonna get me whatever's in that box. You come back from the F5 tonight and show me that you can handle the heat. Loyalty, Luis. You have to earn it, then you reap the benefits."

I pick up the key and put it in my back pocket. "Who put it in my name?"

"That's not important. What's important is you provin' your loyalty." He lets out a stream of smoke. "You do this, and you'll see more money than you ever dreamed of, kid."

Marco follows Chuy out of the office. I step in front of him before he reaches the door. "What do you have to do with this, Marco?" I ask him.

"I just follow rules."

"That's what you want to be, a follower?"

"I've got no other choice, and neither do you. This is big, Luis. I know it. Chuy knows it. It's about time you get with the program." He pushes past me. "The sooner you break it off with Nikki, the better. She'll just complicate things. I'll meet you at the warehouse in an hour."

After he leaves, I scan the piece of paper with the address on it once more. My nerves are about to snap.

Nikki is waiting for me in the garage, talking to Isa. I don't want to lie to her any more than I already have, but I don't want to risk losing her.

"Hey," I say as I walk up to her.

"Take me home, Luis," she orders. "I should have known not to trust you."

36

Nikki

Trust. He begged for my trust, when all along he was affiliating himself with the Latino Blood . . . with Marco. My heart isn't melting. It's breaking.

I storm outside and straddle the back of his motorcycle.

"Let me explain," Luis says. I shake my head, unwilling to listen. My suspicions were right all along. "It's not what you think."

Love. Is it just a word boys use to manipulate girls?

"I don't want to listen to anything you have to say," I tell him. "If you won't take me home, I'll walk."

I start to get off the bike. He curses under his breath, then says, "You don't have to walk. I'll take you home."

I get on the bike again and grab the back instead of holding on to him. If I touch him, I could lose my nerve and let him explain away why everything points to him being a Latino Blood. I'm afraid I'll believe him, because I want to believe him. *It's not what you think*, he'd said.

He pulls up to my driveway. "Nik," he says as I hop off and head for the door. "Nik!"

I stop, but don't turn around.

"You come from this rich family and live in this rich neighborhood. I don't. Guys like Marco and Chuy . . . they're my people."

"I'm your people, too," I murmur softly.

"Not in the same way." I feel his hands on my shoulders. "I'm not a Latino Blood, Nikki." He turns me around and holds out his arms. "See, I'm not marked. I'm not gonna say I'm not hangin' with the Blood, but I'm not one of them."

"I don't want you hanging with them."

"That's like me tellin' you not to hang with Kendall."

He's right, even if I don't want him to be. The Latino Blood has a presence on the south side of Fairfield where he lives.

"I don't know, Luis," I say, stepping away from him so I can think clearly. "I have a feeling you're not telling me the whole truth. I need you, and I'm afraid you're already a Blood."

"I'm just hangin' with them, that's all."

"I've been told that before. By Marco. We all know how that turned out."

"Nikki, I'm not Marco. I'm not in the Blood. And I'm not gonna leave you."

I look into his eyes and all I see is sincerity. No deceit. "You better not be selling drugs, or we're through."

"I won't sell drugs," he says. "I promise."

37

Luis

Boxcar Alley is in the crappiest neighborhood in the western suburbs of Chicago. The houses are set behind the backdrop of a boxcar graveyard, ripe for dirty drug deals and homeless crackheads.

Without time to spare, I take the gun from my closet and drive back to Enrique's. He'll give me advice without blabbing to the rest of my family. He's kept to the Latino Blood's Code of Silence even when other guys blew it off.

I told Nikki I wouldn't do drug deals. I hate lying to her. If doing drug deals are a way to gain Chuy's trust and protect my family, what choice do I have? I don't want to do Chuy's dirty work any more than she wants me to, but I have to. I was being honest when I said I wasn't a Latino Blood. While Chuy might consider me one, I'm not. I'm just playing his game so I can find out what the LB has planned. I've got to be strategic or this isn't gonna work.

Enrique looks at me from across his desk. "Damn, cuz. Boxcar Alley's a rough place to be. That's enemy territory."

"Marco's goin' with me," I tell him. "For backup."

"Want me to go with you? Problem is they know me, and if a couple of Fremont 5 OGs catch sight of me, it's gonna get rough."

"I don't need them retaliatin' against this place, or you."

"All right. You just watch your back at all times, Luis. Take my Mustang. At least you'll have a chance to get away if the Fremont 5 *pendejos* start trouble. Most of their young bucks got shitty aim." He pats the back of my shirt. "You strapped?"

I nod. "You and I both know I ain't gonna use it."

"Don't accidentally shoot yourself." He looks me straight in the eye and says, "If it's you or them, let it be them."

I meet Marco at the warehouse. We speed all the way to Boxcar Alley, through towns that are worse off than mine. I slipped on a black hoodie and sunglasses, so hopefully nobody will notice that I don't belong in this 'hood.

Marco's obviously been here before, because after we park he says to follow him. We pass a liquor store with a drunk out front talking to himself. Guys walking down the street heading toward us are definitely out looking for some action or a fight. We duck into a drugstore and stay out of their line of vision until they pass. I'm confident we could make a good showing in a fight against three or four guys, but when it comes to ten against two, I wouldn't bet on us.

We weave through the streets behind the boxcars. I only lift my head when I have to. Marco struts right up to the house as if he collects in F5 territory every day.

"Don't you want to check the place out first?" I ask him. "Or have a plan?"

Marco waves his hand, dismissing my concern. "Nah, it's cool."

A guy answers the door. "What do you want?" he asks roughly.

"Money. And if you don't give it to us, today will be your biggest fuckin' nightmare," Marco barks through gritted teeth. His eyes are open wide, like he's one crazy motherfucker. I think it's just an act until Marco pulls out a gun and points it right at the guy's head. "Give up five Gs or get your head blown off. Which is it?"

"Yo, Marco," I say. "Cool it, would ya?"

"It's cool. Stay out here and keep watch. Don't let anyone in the house."

The guy holds his hands up and backs into the house as Marco walks inside. I don't know what the hell to do. Marco is obviously on a power trip. Shit. If he starts shootin' people . . . I start thinking of my life behind bars.

This wasn't supposed to be how it went down. I was supposed to come back to Fairfield, graduate, go to college, then apply to NASA's space program—the chain of events on the timeline of my life. I had every aspect of my life perfectly planned out.

As it looks now, the only place I deserve to go is jail. I look up at the darkened sky. I'm about to lose everything . . . including Nikki.

A few minutes later, when I'm about to knock on the door and tell Marco I'm done with Chuy's bullshit orders, he steps out.

"Did you get the cash?" I ask him.

"Yeah."

"So it's all cool?"

"Umm . . . I think we should bounce, like fast."

We hurry through the maze that's Boxcar Alley. I look back and realize a bunch of guys are on our tail. They're waving guns, and we're trying to lose them in the overcrowded graveyard of old railroad cars.

It's not working.

We duck behind one of the boxcars. Marco peeks his head out, and a bullet flies past his head.

"We need to get out of here. We're screwed if we stay in one place," he says.

I've never been in a shootout, but I've witnessed them. I pull out my gun, but keep it at my side, partially hidden. Marco does the same.

"Our car is right there. See it?" I say, my adrenaline pumping at full speed.

He nods.

"We're gonna run toward it, and drive away without lookin' back," I tell him.

"Got it."

"If they shoot, start unloadin' at the rail cars to scare 'em. Hopefully they'll take cover at least until we can get to the car."

There's no time to strategize a plan B, because the guys are about to surround us. If we don't move now, we're fucked.

"Now!" I yell, and we both book it toward Enrique's Mustang.

My pulse races as a shot rings out. Then another. And another. I jump into the car and look over at Marco. He sticks his gun out of the front window and unloads the chamber as I start the car.

I screech away, knowing that we barely made it out alive.

"Put the guns in the glove compartment," I tell him, handing mine over to him. I check the rearview mirror for cops, but don't see any.

The sound of our heavy breathing fills the car.

"That was close," Marco says, leaning his head back on the seat. A second later he says, "Holy shit. Luis?"

"What?"

"Dude, you got shot."

I look over at my bicep. Blood is rushing down my arm and staining the seat of the car, so I strip my hoodie off and tell Marco to tie the sleeve around my arm. "I'm fine," I tell him. "It's a scratch."

"Scratches don't gush blood, Luis. You sure you're okay?"

I can just imagine *mi'amá's* face when she sees I'm bleeding. "I'll go to Enrique's and spend the night. He'll know what to do."

"You're lucky you made it out alive," Enrique says when I show up to his place a half hour later. "Your arm . . ."

"I kinda ran into a Fremont 5 bullet," I tell him.

He nods. "Your ma is gonna shit twice, then she's gonna kill you. Chuy's one sonofabitch, sendin' you kids into F5 territory."

"Tell me about it."

I take a shower in Enrique's apartment above the garage. The bullet exited but left a two-inch gash, and now that I'm sitting down looking at the fleshy wound, it hurts like a bitch. It won't be hard to hide, even with a bandage. I'll just wear a hoodie and long-sleeve shirts until it heals.

"Where did Marco run off to?" Enrique asks me after he closes up the garage and meets me in the apartment.

"The warehouse." I put on a shirt Enrique lends me after he calls *mi'amá* and tells her I'll be bunking at his place tonight. "What do you know about me bein' blessed in?" I ask my cousin as he takes a beer out of his fridge.

"I don't know anythin' about that," he says as he gives me an intense stare. "And if I did, I probably wouldn't be able to tell ya. *¿Comprende?*"

He knows something. I nod. It's no use trying to get any info out of him. If he was sworn to secrecy, he'll go to the grave with it.

The Latino Blood Code of Silence.

It's one code I haven't broken yet, but intend to crack sooner rather than later.

38

Nikki

Two weeks after Luis promises me that he's not in the LB, it's his eighteenth birthday. I know my parents are at some dinner party in the city, and my brother is at some gaming tournament in Wisconsin, so I invite Luis over for a private birthday dinner.

I'm not a chef, but I do know how to follow a recipe. I got a Mexican cookbook from the bookstore. We don't have authentic Mexican food often, and most of the recipes are foreign to me. Other than breakfast, my parents usually order takeout or eat at Brickstone. If Mom does cook, it's pretty much a simple pasta dish or something from the meat market specially prepackaged and marinated so all we have to do is throw the stuff in the oven.

Luis arrives at six, right on time, with a bunch of yellow daffodils in his hand. The stems are wrapped together with a big yellow ribbon. "Hey," he says.

"Hey," I say back.

He scans my skinny black dress that hugs every one of my curves. "Damn, Nik. You look amazin'." He looks down at his jeans and cringes. "Sorry I didn't get more dressed up."

"I don't need you dressed up. You look like a stud just the way you are." I take the flowers. "You didn't have to bring me flowers. It's your birthday, not mine."

"I wanted to bring you somethin'," he says. When I put the flowers to my nose to smell them, Luis looks nervous. "I didn't know if you'd like 'em. Carlos told me to bring you red roses, but I thought you'd like yellow. They remind me of you. They brighten a room . . . just like you."

I reach out and touch the stubble on his face, wondering how I ever thought he was the least bit similar to Marco. His tender gaze pierces my heart. "I love them. Come on in. I made you dinner," I say proudly.

"What's that?" he asks as his eyes settle on the wrapped box I set on the table.

"Your birthday present."

"You didn't have to get me anythin'."

"I know. I wanted to. Go on, open it." When he does, I hold my breath.

He pulls out what looks like a twisted black iron rock, but I know it's not *just* a rock. He rolls it around in his hand, studying it. Does he know what it is? Hopefully he doesn't think it's a cheap paperweight.

"It's a meteorite," I explain quickly. "From Argentina. Inside the box are the authentication papers, explaining where and how it was found."

He looks at me over the meteorite with a stunned expression on his face. "I know what it is. I've seen them in museums. And in books. But I've never held one. Or owned one." He examines all sides in awe, feeling each curve and crevice with his fingertips. "I can't believe this was in space. It's so cool . . . surreal."

"It's yours," I say.

"I don't know what to say. It must've cost you a fortune. I just . . .

wow. I'd beg you to return it and get your money back, but I don't want to part with it."

I kiss him on his cheek. "It's okay. I didn't need that college fund, anyway." He cocks an eyebrow, and I smile mischievously. "I'm just kidding. I had money saved up from babysitting and birthdays." With my forefinger, I run a path down the front of his shirt. "Besides, you're worth it."

"That's debatable, *mi chava*." He stills my hand. "It's the coolest gift anyone's ever given me."

"Good. Mission accomplished."

"Not yet." He puts the meteorite gently back in the box and kisses me passionately until I'm wanting more and my insides are melting. I'm breathless and never want to stop. Knowing that we're alone, and I have another gift planned for him, makes me want to skip dinner altogether. "Thanks for the gift," he says against my lips.

"My pleasure." Flustered now, I step away from him and gesture to the dining room, where everything is set up. "I made an authentic Mexican meal."

"Recipes passed down from your *abuelita*?"

"Not really. Try a cookbook I bought yesterday at the mall."

He laughs. "Next time you want to make an authentic Mexican meal, call me first. *Mi'amá* taught me and my brothers to cook when we were kids."

After serving him a plate of chicken enchiladas and guacamole, I realized that I should have followed the recipe and mixed the avocado by hand instead of blending it in a mixer. It was like soup, and did not taste good at all. I made a flan for dessert, but it fell into chunky gelatinous pieces as I served it to him.

"You did an awesome job," he says as he fishes for the slippery flan eluding his spoon.

"You're lying. It sucked. Face reality, Luis. I should have ordered takeout. If you were Mrs. Peterson, you'd give me a D minus on this meal."

He laughs. "An A plus for effort. The tortilla chips were awesome."

"That's because I bought them ready-made at the Mexican grocery in Wheeling," I say.

When we're done, he helps me clear the table and put the dishes in the dishwasher. Afterward, I see him leaning against the kitchen counter watching me. "You have a plan for the rest of the night, or are we gonna wing it?"

I take his hand and weave his fingers through mine. "I have another birthday present for you."

"What is it?"

I lean close to his ear and whisper, "Me." He swallows, hard. I watch as the muscle in his jaw twitches. "Want to go upstairs . . . to my bedroom?"

He nods slowly. "I didn't think you could top that meteorite gift, but you just did."

I take his hand and lead him to my room. My heart is racing the entire time, because I've prepared myself for this. I tell myself it's okay, because I want this as much as Luis. I'm in control here. I just have to keep myself in check and not let my emotions run wild.

Luis walks around my room, studying the pictures on my wall. Most of them are of me and my friends. Some are dogs from the shelter. He stops when his eyes focus on the one of me and him at Alex and Brittany's wedding two summers ago. We both had no clue the photographer had caught the moment on camera.

He points to it. "How did you get this?"

"Brittany brought it over when she had dinner at my house one night."

He points to the expression on my face. "You were so pissed. Look at me, with that stupid-ass cocky grin. I thought I was the shit back then." He shakes his head, then scans the rest of the pictures.

While his back is turned to me, I reach around and slowly unzip my dress. "You *are* the shit, Luis," I say in a teasing voice.

"Nah, I'm—"

He stops midsentence as he looks at me and it registers that I'm unzipping my dress. My mouth is dry as I slide the straps down my shoulders slowly until the material falls to the floor in a pool at my feet.

His eyes never leave me. Mine never leave him.

"What were you saying?" I ask.

"I forgot." His gaze travels down the length of my body. I dressed in pink lace panties and a matching bra, prepared for us to be together tonight. "*Mi chava* . . ." He takes a step toward me. "I didn't think you could look more beautiful than when you opened the door tonight. But you do."

I hold my breath in anticipation and longing as his fingers skim lightly over my shoulders before gently slipping my bra straps aside.

This is okay, I tell myself. I can enjoy this and stay as emotionally detached as I want. His lips replace his fingers. He kisses one shoulder, then brushes his warm lips across my neck and kisses the other one.

I grab on to him for support because his warm breath brushing over my skin makes me dizzy. I want him here with me, I want him close . . . but this is sex. It *has* to be just sex.

I grab him over his pants, then unzip his jeans.

"Easy, girl," he says, amused.

He puts an arm around me, holding me steady, as he bends down to kiss me. It's not just any kiss. His lips move slowly over mine, brushing against them before his tongue reaches out. I feel his hot breath mingle with mine as our tongues glide over each other's in a slow rhythm that makes my skin hot and sweaty. His hands move slowly up and down the curve of my back in the same rhythm as our kiss.

Truth is, being with Luis makes me want to ditch all of my self-awareness and give in to every temptation.

He pulls his shirt over his head, then tosses it aside. He's got a big scab on his arm. "What happened?" I ask, tracing around it.

"Just got a cut workin' at the garage," he says, dismissing it.

"What were you doing?"

He hesitates long enough for me to question whether he's about to tell me the truth.

"It's not important." He kisses me again, trying to make me forget about his mystery wound. It works for the moment.

We strip naked and move to the bed. Instead of jumping each other's bones, he takes his sweet time running his hands over every inch of my body as if he's going to memorize it for a painting later.

I follow his lead, skimming my palm across his hot skin in a slow, torturous pattern until he's panting. I lean over him and use my lips and tongue, exploring every inch. He grabs the sheets so hard his knuckles turn white. It makes me feel like I have the power, not the other way around.

Until it's his turn to explore. I try to stay calm. But it's hard. I brace myself for it to happen any minute now. He gently pushes the hair out of my face as he gazes into my eyes. "I'm livin' my fantasy," he says.

"What fantasy is that?" I ask.

"Bein' alone with the girl I love. I love you, Nikki. You know that, right?"

Umm . . . "Yes. Me too," I say dumbly, trying to block the rush of emotions threatening to surface.

His thumb traces my lips and I swear his eyes are getting all glassy. "I've never felt this way about another girl before," he whispers.

No.

I don't want to keep hearing words of love.

Luis is dangerous and has the ability to suck me in if I let him. I can't let that happen. He's got secrets. I've got secrets. We can't share them, but we can share our bodies.

"Let's have sex," I blurt out. I reach over and open my side-table drawer. I pull out a condom from the box I bought over the weekend and hand it to him. "Here."

Lo único que quiero es hacerte el amor, mi vida." I look at him with a blank stare. I think he forgot that Spanish came out of his mouth automatically. "I want to make love to you, Nikki. More than anythin'. But you said—"

"Forget what I said. Let's do it." He leans in to kiss me again, but I put a hand on his chest and nudge him away. "Put the condom on."

"Now?"

"Yeah, now."

He seems a little frustrated that I'm rushing this, but he rips open the package and puts on the condom. If we do this fast, and I'm able to keep myself free of emotion, it'll be fine. Tonight will wipe the bad memories of me and Marco away.

He's poised above me now, his hands braced on either side of my head. I gaze up at his light brown skin slick against mine. "Come on," I say, urging him along.

His lips are inches away from mine. "I got to be honest, Nik. This isn't how I imagined it."

"It's fine. Let's just do it. Hurry up."

I squeeze my eyes shut. I can't look at him. Not now, when I'm determined to stay emotionless. He hesitates, then swears under his breath and pushes himself off me.

Cold air rushes under the blanket as he sits on the edge of the bed. "What's wrong?" I ask. "Why'd you stop?"

He pulls off the condom and tosses it in the trash. "This ain't workin' for me."

"Why not?"

He looks back at me, pissed. "Shit, Nik, you're actin' as though this is a one-night stand between strangers. I'm trying to make love to you and your eyes are shut so damn tight it looked like you were wishin' I was someone else."

"I'm not . . . I wasn't."

"Forget it." He grabs his boxers and puts them on. "Next time your boyfriend tells you he loves you, you might want to acknowledge it with more than a *yeah, me too.*"

"I don't want you to love me," I snap.

"Too late, *mi chava.*"

I sit up. "I can't do the love thing, Luis."

"So you just want a fuck partner, is that it?" he snaps, then shoves his legs into his pants. "It would've been cool of you to let me know we were just gonna screw so I didn't make a fool of myself pourin' out my feelings."

"You didn't make a fool out of yourself. Don't be mad. I just don't want to get hurt again. I won't repeat what I did with—"

"Marco," he says, finishing my sentence. "I'm fuckin' sick and tired of it always comin' back to you and Marco. You still in love with him?"

"I'm not . . . I don't. You have no clue what I went through." I can't get the words out.

"Tell me, then. Tell me, so you can finally move on."

"I can't."

He grabs his shirt off the floor and looks at me with a grave expression on his face. "Do you love me?"

I clutch my blanket to my chest and give him the only answer I can. "No."

39

Luis

I want to destroy something, anything. I left Nikki's house tonight knowing one thing—it's over. I was an idiot to think she feels the same way about me that I feel about her. I wanted to believe she was holding back because she was scared . . . but in reality she was just using me to get over someone else.

Instead of going home, I drive to the LB warehouse. On the way, I notice a car in the rearview mirror that I've seen a couple of times before. Am I being tailed? I speed through busier parts of town and lose them. At the warehouse, Marco is sitting with a bunch of guys. Some are drinking beer, some are smoking dope. It's the scene *mi'amá* wanted to shelter me from, probably because she knew I'd be drawn to it at some point.

I've reached that point.

"Hey, *amigo*," Marco says. I can tell by his bloodshot eyes that he's completely wasted. "I thought you were goin' out with your *novia* tonight."

"She's not my *novia* anymore." I grab a beer and chug it. It's cheap stuff, but I'm guessing it'll do the job.

"Congratulations. You finally dumped the bitch." He holds up his own can of beer in a congratulatory salute. "On to bigger and better."

"Right." I crush the first can in my hand and reach for another. Then another. By the time I'm on my fifth beer, I'm feeling damn good. Like I don't give a shit about anyone, especially Nikki.

I need to tell her tonight was a mistake, and it'll never happen again. I won't give her the satisfaction of letting her think she hurt me. I pull out my cell and call her.

"Hey, Nik," I say when she answers. "I'm with Marco." I put my arm around my homie and say, "We were just tradin' stories about you. Ain't that right, *amigo*?"

Marco laughs. I know she can hear him. I'm being a complete *pendejo* and I'm making this up as I go along, but in my drunken state I don't have a filter. She might as well have stabbed me in the heart.

"I'm hanging up," she warns.

"No!" I yell into the receiver. "I need to say one more thing."

"What?" she asks.

Time to be the asshole she thinks I am.

I concentrate on not slurring my words, but I don't know if I'm successful. "I'm done with you."

She hangs up on me. My words hurt her. I know I'm gonna regret that call in the morning, but right now I'm flying high and don't give a rat's ass.

I stumble over to the cooler and grab another beer. By the time I finish it, I'm seeing double and I'm completely unable to think . . . about anything. I don't even remember what I said to Nikki, or even if I really called her or if I just thought that I called her.

"Hey, Luis," Mariana says, coming up to me. "You're wasted."

"Tell me somethin' I don't know."

"Is there trouble in paradise?"

I shake my head and hold up the beer can. "This is my paradise."

"I know what will get your mind off of Nikki."

"What?"

"Me." She kisses me, and I'm too weak and too stupid drunk to think about pushing her away. She's not what I want. She knows it, but she doesn't care. I could close my eyes and pretend she's Nikki . . . that would really prove I'm an asshole.

Mariana leads me to a room off to the side. I sit on an old, beaten-up couch and she straddles me, but my body won't cooperate—as if it knows what it wants and Mariana's not it. "I'm in love with her," I say, stopping Mariana before this goes any further.

"Why?" Mariana asks, annoyed.

"She's my angel."

Mariana slides off me and heads for the door. "You don't know what you're missin', Luis."

Yeah, I do. I've had one-night stands before . . . they're all the same. With Nikki it matters . . . which is why tonight hurts so fucking bad.

"Sorry," I tell Mariana.

She doesn't answer. Instead, she walks out and slams the door behind her.

In the early morning, I wake up and realize that I fell asleep at the warehouse. Everyone is gone except for the few LBs that call this shithole their home.

My head is spinning even before I manage to lift myself into a sitting position. I wonder if I look as shitty as I feel. Glancing down at the empty cans of beer beside me makes my stomach churn. I'm gonna puke.

I stumble outside and hurl until there's nothin' left. I'm so weak I can hardly stand.

"Rough night?" Chuy asks, coming up beside me.

"*Sí*."

"I used to get fucked up like that when I was your age. Fun times, huh?"

"I'm not havin' fun right now," I tell him as another wave of nausea hits me.

He laughs as I puke my guts out again. "You still got that key I gave you?"

"I haven't had a chance to go to the bank," I tell him. "Besides, I think I'm bein' followed."

He laughs cynically. "I'm havin' you followed, Luis. You're valuable to me, and the Blood."

I've got to watch my back even closer now, dammit.

Chuy pats my back, hard enough to rattle my sensitive stomach. "All right, *amigo*. You get one more week and then I've got to put the pressure on. Consider this a warning. Go home," he orders. "Alex and Carlos are there, but don't tell them you were here."

"How do you know where they are?"

"Haven't you realized it by now, Luis?" Chuy says. "I've got eyes and ears everywhere. Hell, even when I was in the can I knew your every move. When you were in Colorado, I had my guys track you."

"Why me?"

"When you're ready to know, I'll tell ya. Now get your sorry ass out of here."

I walk through the door of my house, but can't make it to the bathroom so I run back outside to puke in the bushes. I ignore the stares from my family as I stumble through the house and head straight for my bedroom. Sleep. All I need is sleep. I fall facedown onto my mattress.

"Luis!" *mi'amá* says from the doorway. She's pissed, and I'm not in the mood to hear her yell at me. "Where were you? I've been calling you all night, without an answer. What's the use in having a cell phone if you refuse to answer it for your own mother?" She narrows her eyes at me. "What's wrong with you? Are you on drugs, Luis?"

Out of the corner of my eye I think I just saw her cross herself. If she starts lighting the memorial candles and begins praying to *Papá*, I'm seriously going to lose it.

"I was drunk," I tell her. "And now I'm hungover. Answerin' your call would've killed the buzz, so I ignored it."

I hear her suck in a shocked breath, then I feel something whack me in the back of my head. Her shoe.

"Isn't that child abuse?" I ask her.

"It would be, if you were a child. You're eighteen, Luis. You're a man now. Act like it!"

She slams the door shut. The sound is like a jackhammer banging against my skull, which I'm sure is exactly what she intended. *Mi'amá* isn't subtle, that's for damn sure.

The room is finally a sanctuary, and I close my eyes. My peace is short-lived, though, because I hear the door creak as someone opens it.

"You gonna hit me with your other shoe?" I mumble against the pillow.

"Nah," Alex's voice echoes through my head. "*Mi'amá* told Carlos and me to come in here to make sure you're not dead, which is pretty much what she thought when you didn't answer your cell last night."

Alex and Carlos—the tag team from hell. They're the last people I need shit from right now. If they decide to trail me, too, I'll have an entire entourage.

"I'm fine."

"Then sit up and talk to us."

"Okay, in that case I'm not fine. Go away." I moan. "Unless you want me to puke all over you."

"What happened with you and Nikki last night?" Alex asks.

"*Nada*. We're history."

Carlos chuckles. "Yeah, right. Believe me, I've been in the same condition you're in, bro. Gettin' shitfaced over a girl isn't a solution. Talk to her and work it out."

"I'm not talkin' about it."

I open one eye and see Alex crouching beside the bed. "I'm not lettin' you fuck up like we did."

"Face the facts, Alex. I'm already a fuckup, and I don't intend to change that fact anytime soon."

40

Everything has changed in the blink of an eye. Luis, me . . . us. I spent the rest of Saturday night crying in bed, wondering how everything spiraled out of control. Luis's call in the middle of the night didn't help. God, how my heart raced when I saw his number come up. I hoped he would tell me that he'd wait for me to open my heart to him, that it didn't matter how long it took. If he really loved me . . . Oh, it doesn't matter. He said it was over.

The problem is that the feelings I had for him, and still have for him, are so intense they scare me. I wanted to make love to him, body and soul, but my fear made me pull away. In the end, all I could give him was my body. It wasn't good enough.

On Monday I try my hardest to avoid seeing Luis at school, but every time I open my eyes I spot him either at his locker or walking down the hall with friends. He makes no eye contact with me, even in chemistry when we're facing each other across the lab tables.

"Are you coming to watch the soccer game with me after school?" Kendall asks me after chemistry on Tuesday.

"No. Definitely not," I tell her.

She stops and gives me one of her pity looks. "Why won't you tell me what happened Saturday night?"

"Luis and I broke up."

"I know that part. Want to share why?"

"When I'm ready. I'm just not ready now."

She sighs. "All right. I'm here for you."

"You're always here for me. It's time you get another best friend who doesn't carry around so much baggage."

"Not gonna happen." She gives me a warm smile. "You're my inspiration."

"For what? A drama queen?"

"No. Do you realize how many dogs you've helped rescue? You're the girl that doesn't give up on the underdog."

"I feel like I'm the underdog."

"Then you know never to give up on yourself. You're stronger than you think you are, Nikki."

Every minute of every day I'm tempted to text *hey* to Luis. Or call him, just to hear his voice.

On Wednesday, Mariana and Luis are talking at his locker. They sit next to each other at lunch. In chemistry, he makes a joke and she laughs so hard I think her lungs are going to burst.

On Thursday after school, I'm thankful I'm scheduled to work at the shelter. Being with the dogs will help me get my mind off of Luis.

I check in at the front desk, then head back to the cages. My heart skips a beat when Granny's cage is empty and the pink identification card is missing from the slot on her cage door.

Did she die in the middle of the night, all alone and scared? Or is she so skinny from not eating they had to take her to the vet? I rush over to Sue in complete panic mode.

"What happened to Granny?" I ask her.

"She was adopted." The phone rings. "I thought you knew about it," she says before she answers the call.

How would I know? I didn't do the paperwork on her. I open the adoption log book and scan the approved applications. When I read the name Granny on top of the latest application my heart swells with happiness that she finally has a home.

Until I look at the bottom of the page at the name of the person who adopted her. Luis Fuentes.

I gasp. "He didn't."

"Your friend came in right before we closed last night and adopted her," one of the other volunteers tells me.

Luis knew I wanted her. How dare he come and snatch her. He took Granny just to spite me. Oh, how could I ever have thought I wanted to be with someone who'd adopt a dog just for revenge?

My mind is in a rage as I spend my assigned time cleaning out cages and walking the dogs. After I clock out, I get in my car and race to Luis's house.

I knock on the door.

No answer.

I pound on the door.

Still no answer.

I put my ear to the door and hear the television, so I know someone's got to be home.

I shimmy through the space between the bushes and the front window. I eye Luis sitting on the couch with Granny in his lap, then knock on the glass to get his attention. He looks at me, and I give him the universal sign language for "open the damn door" by pointing to it.

By the time I shimmy back to the front stoop, he's opened the door.

"I puked in those bushes a few days ago. You might want to be careful where you step."

Eww. I'm careful not to step in anything unidentifiable, but since the bushes are in the way, it's no use. "I can't believe you stole my dog."

"I wouldn't steal a dog, Nik. How cruel do you think I am?"

"I meant Granny, and you know it."

"How can I steal a dog I officially adopted at a shelter?"

I narrow my eyes at him. "You knew I wanted her."

"Yeah, so? You know the sayin' . . . you snooze, you lose. You want to hear it in Spanish?"

He's doing his best to upset me and it's working. "No. You didn't even want a dog."

"I do now. Granny and I are bondin'." He crosses his fingers. "We're like this."

"This whole adopting thing isn't really about Granny. This is about *us*."

"There is no 'us' anymore, remember?"

His words sting. "So you steal the *one* dog at the shelter you know I have a special attachment to just to piss me off and rub it in?"

"Oh, please. You were smotherin' the poor thing. I didn't get her for some retaliation against you. There were a few burglaries in the neighborhood and we need a good watchdog."

"She's *blind*, Luis!" I yell. "She can't watch anything. I don't even think she can bark. Granny's got one foot in the grave."

He pretends like my words are an insult to him and his dog. "Shh, don't let her hear you say that."

"You're kidding, right?"

He shrugs. "Listen, the lady at the shelter approved my application.

You got a problem with it, talk to the shelter. I don't give a shit what you think anymore."

If I were a cartoon, a big great gust of steam would be coming out of my ears right now. "What about Saturday night, Luis? You told me you loved me."

"Isn't that what guys are supposed to say before they screw their girlfriend? I thought it was a prerequisite."

"You don't mean that."

"What do you want me to say, that I want to get back with you just so you could think of another guy while we're in bed together? No, thanks."

Granny waddles to the front door. Luis reaches down and picks her up. Seeing him holding her so gently in his arms shows off the warm and caring side he's trying to hide from me.

"You don't know what I think about, Luis. And don't tell me you weren't keeping secrets from me. You were obviously doing something shady for that Chuy guy. I know he wasn't recruiting you to join the Boy Scouts. I chose to ignore all the warning signs and trust you. You lied to me, didn't you? You keep more secrets than the Pentagon."

"I lie to everyone. It's no big deal."

"It's a big deal to me." I point to his arm. "That didn't happen in the garage. You were in a knife fight."

"Wrong. Try gunfight." He puts Granny on the grass so she can waddle around and he holds his hands up. "Okay, fine. You got me. You're lookin' at the newest Latino Blood recruit, baby. I've been dealin' drugs and gangbangin' with Marco behind your back. That's my secret. What's yours?"

I swallow and prepare myself to reveal the truth. It doesn't matter anymore, so why are tears running down my face? I wish I could hold them back, but I can't. I'm angry, I'm hurt, I'm sad . . . He's just like Marco. I tried to deny it, but the truth slaps me in the face.

"I was pregnant with Marco's baby the day he broke up with me." Luis steps back, shock written all over his face. "I lost the baby right after we left Alex's wedding and I almost died. This thing coming between us wasn't about me and Marco!" I yell, getting riled up now. "It was about *trust*. And in the back of my head I knew you were lying to me about the Blood. Don't blame me for holding back, Luis. I was almost ready to let go and try to trust again. It took me a while, and I wasn't really good at it, but at least I was trying, which is more than I can say for you. It was *you* who was holding back all along." I pull the meteorite out of my purse. "Maybe I couldn't say it yet, but I tried to show you how much I cared." Tears stream down my cheeks as I chuck the meteorite into the street.

I expect him to go running after it, but he doesn't. His eyes are fixed on me.

"Why didn't you tell me?" he says softly. He reaches out to me.

I whack his hand away. "Don't you dare touch me ever again!"

41

Luis

A week later, as I hop on my motorcycle in the library parking lot after working on my essay for Purdue's application, a car that I've noticed trailing me for the past two weeks stops in front of me and blocks my path.

A guy steps out of the car. I've seen him at the warehouse a couple of times, but I've never talked to him. He's an OG. "Chuy wants to talk to you."

"Later," I tell them.

"No, you don't get it." A big guy steps out of the back. "He wants to talk to you now."

I leave the motorcycle in the parking lot and get in the backseat. I've been avoiding this meeting. The key Chuy gave me has been like a weight on my conscience.

Chuy is sitting in the backseat, waiting for me. We're driven randomly through town.

I take the key out of my wallet. "I can't do it. I thought I could, but I can't." The way Nikki looked at me with complete and utter hatred when I tried to console her after she told me she'd been pregnant with Marco's baby made me realize it was really over for good. She hated Marco, hated the LB, and now she put me in the same category because I've betrayed her, just like Marco. The entire week I've tried to feel him out to see if he knows about the pregnancy, but he hasn't taken the bait. Either he doesn't know about it, or he's determined to keep it a secret.

"I know you feel a pull toward the LB," Chuy says. "But you don't know why."

I stay silent. Every word he just spoke is the truth. I won't admit it because I'm ashamed of it.

"No need to hide your true feelings. *Tu papá* wanted you to be in the Blood, Luis. He made sure you were watched over and protected. He brought you to the warehouse a week after you were born, to be blessed in with LB written on your forehead in his own blood . . . a full-fledged Latino Blood."

No fucking way. "My father died before I was born," I say. "Alex told me he was there, he saw our *papá* get shot . . . what you're sayin' doesn't make sense, unless—"

"Your father wasn't a Fuentes," Chuy says, interrupting my confusion. He pulls a picture out of his suit pocket and hands it to me. "I was there."

I look at the picture of Hector Martinez with a huge grin on his face as he holds a baby in the air like a king presenting his newborn baby to the people. The prince. In the middle of the baby's forehead, written in blood, are the letters *LB*—Latino Blood.

"That's you," Chuy says. "And your *papá*. Your *real papá*."

As soon as the words leave Chuy's mouth, a feeling of dread washes over me. It can't be true. But there have been signs. I've never seen my birth certificate. When Alex was shot Carlos donated blood, but *mi familia* never even approached me to do the same. It always rubbed me raw. Were they worried that I'd find out Alex and I weren't a match, or that I'd somehow find out we were only half brothers? Chuy said I was blessed into the Latino Blood, but *mi papá* died before I was born. I couldn't have been blessed in, unless my father was a member of the LB at the time.

I need answers, and I need them now. Did *mi'amá* shield me from the gang life because she didn't want me finding out the truth?

I used to know where my loyalties lie. Now I'm not so sure.

"Drive me back to the library," I say to the dude driving. "I need to get out of here."

The guy looks to Chuy for direction. Chuy nods his approval. Even when they drop me off by the library and let me out of the car, I feel trapped. He knows where to find me, how to lure me back with threats I can't ignore. I left the picture in Chuy's car, hoping to leave the image of Hector proudly holding that baby—me—behind.

I find myself driving to Alex's apartment. I knock on the door, hoping he's home. I need answers, and he's the one person who can give them to me. Alex comes to the door. "Luis, what's wrong?" he says.

"Are you my brother?" I ask plain and simple.

"Of course I'm your brother," he says, confused.

"Let me be more specific, then. Am I your *half* brother?"

He doesn't answer. He stares at me, with those Latino Blood tattoos on his own chest and arms mocking me.

"Fuck you, Alex!"

"What's going on?" Brittany says, coming into view with Paco in her arms. "Luis, you look sick. I hope you didn't catch the flu from Paco. Are you okay?"

"Weese!" Paco yells, clapping and excited to see me.

"No, I'm not okay." I look at Alex with contempt. "Does Brit know?"

Alex nods slowly.

"Do I know what?" Brittany says innocently as she wraps Paco tight in a blanket. "What's going on between you two?"

"Alex was just confirmin' that I'm not his brother," I say.

Alex stands in front of me, face-to-face. "You *are* my brother, dammit."

"Yeah, half. What's the other half, huh? Tell me."

"I don't know what you heard, but—"

"Hector Martinez is my father, isn't he?"

I glance at Alex's shoulder where Hector shot him not long after he killed Paco.

"Isn't he?" I say again.

"Sí, Luis," Alex says, defeated. "Hector Martinez was your father."

Brittany puts a comforting hand on my shoulder, but I shrug it off.

"Does Carlos know, or am I not only the black sheep of the family, but also the last to know who my own *fuckin'* father is."

Alex doesn't want to tell me. He'd rather keep me ignorant and innocent, but that's all in the past. I'm not a kid anymore. Far from it.

"Tell me!" I scream at him. My entire body is tense and I suppress a vicious rage that's bubbling inside me.

"Calm down."

"Don't tell me to calm down. Don't say another word to me except the absolute truth."

"Okay." Alex brushes his fingers through his hair. "He suspects. He brought it up once about ten years ago, and I shut him down. I told him never to bring it up again, and he hasn't."

"Well, hooray for Fuentes family secrets." It feels like I've got a lump the size of a basketball in my throat as I ask, "Did he rape our mother? Am I the result of a rape?"

"No."

"She cheated?"

"Not exactly. Why don't I take you home and you can ask her yourself."

"I don't have a home, Alex."

"Don't be stupid, Luis. Your home is wherever your family is. *Mamá* did things she thought would keep us safe."

"So she whored herself out. Nice."

Alex pushes me, his eyes blazing mad. "Don't talk about *mi'amá* like that. She did what needed to be done, period. Don't judge her when you don't know what went down."

All this time I've been so stupid. The evidence was right in front of my face and I never even put the pieces together. I had this ridiculous delusion that I was the golden child, because I was in my mother's stomach when my supposed father was shot and killed—the last gift my father gave her was me.

But in reality I've never been the golden child. I've been the black sheep . . . I've called myself a Fuentes and I never was one.

I step back. "*Adios,* bro."

"What's that supposed to mean?"

"It means I'm out. For good."

"You're not goin' anywhere."

"You have no hold over me, Alex. Hell, we don't even share the same father." I think of all the times I felt bad for Carlos because he seemed the odd one out. He didn't have the brains or even temper that Alex and I were born with.

Joke's on me. I don't even have the same blood.

"You think your DNA matters?" he asks. "It doesn't. You were my brother as soon as you came out of *Mamá*'s stomach and I held you when you were less than an hour old. You were my brother when *Mamá* worked and I wiped your ass and changed your diapers. And you'll be my brother until I take my last breath! *¿Comprende?*"

"You denied me my history . . . my heritage!"

"I denied you nothing, Luis. Your biological father was . . ." He hesitates.

"Go ahead and say it. Come on, Alex, don't hold back now."

"Hector Martinez was a manipulative asshole who threatened people with their lives so they did what he wanted. He was a murderer and drug lord. We did you a favor by not tellin' you that half your genes were from a man without scruples or a conscience."

"You better be careful, Alex." I push him back, ready for a brawl. "That's my blood you're talkin' about."

My words must sting, because Alex pounds his chest. "Wake up, Luis. You're lookin' at your blood. *I'm* your blood."

I regard him with disgust. "All I see in front of me is an ex–Latino Blood. A traitor to my people."

"That's bullshit."

"Watch your back, bro. You never know who's family . . . and who's the enemy."

I storm away from him, blocking out Alex's demands to come back, mixed with Brittany's pleas not to leave. She says we can work it out.

I'm done working things out.

Chuy was right. Being a Latino Blood is my destiny, my birthright. I told myself I wanted to get close to Chuy to gain insider info about the LB. I was lying to myself. All along I wanted to be in it, be a part of the drug deals and danger. I walk into the LB warehouse with one thing on my mind—living up to my father's legacy.

Chuy is sitting in his makeshift office talking to some OGs. One look at me and Chuy sends everyone else out of the room—except a guy named Tiny, who isn't tiny.

"I'll go to the bank and see what's in the safety-deposit box," I say. "But I've got conditions."

His ever-present cigar is hanging from his mouth. He takes it out and blows smoke in the air. I watch as it lingers above his head before disappearing into the smoke-filled room. "Conditions?"

"Sí. First, you never threaten Alex's family, Carlos, or mi'amá again. Second, you initiate me like everyone else." No more straddling the line. I've chosen my side, and I don't want anyone mistaking me for something that I'm not and was never intended to be.

"Glad you've come around, Fuentes."

"Don't call me that," I say roughly. "I'm not a Fuentes and you know it, so stop the bullshit. You agree to my terms or not?"

We stare each other down. "Sure. Hector predicted you'd be a fighter," he says proudly, reminding me of the picture of Hector holding me when I was a newborn. He nods to Tiny to get the other OGs back in the room. "Luis here wants to solidify his place in the LB family, boys," he calls out as they pile back in. "Problem is, Luis, you've already been blessed in. No need for an initiation."

"I want it. Jump me in like a new recruit."

He laughs. "What, you *want us* to kick the shit outta you?"

"I want to be initiated like Alex. I'm not takin' the easy way out. I can handle it." I'll show them I don't need to be protected from the truth. I can just hear Hector Martinez from the grave egging me on, challenging me to prove to all these guys that I'm as tough as he was.

He cocks an eyebrow. "You can handle it, huh?"

"I'm my father's son," I say stoically. "Bring it."

"*Mi placer*," he says, amused. "Yo, Rico!" he yells. "Round up some others and give Luis here a Latino Blood thirteen-second welcome. I'm gonna join in, too." He cracks his knuckles one by one. "I'm gonna enjoy this."

42

Kendall thinks I'm a survivor, but right now I don't feel like one. All I feel like doing is going over to Luis's house so he can hold me and tell me everything is okay between us.

I'm dreaming. It's not okay between us and never will be.

"Dad," I say, sitting down with him as he watches a soccer match on television. "How come you and Mom never took us to Mexico?"

He shrugs. "We travel a lot, Nikki. You went to Brazil with us two years ago. And Argentina when I spoke at the conference there. You practically gobbled up all the gelato in Italy."

"But why not Mexico?"

He blows out a long, slow breath. "I guess if we went, I'd feel like I had to show you where I grew up. I don't want to look back, Nikki. Your mother doesn't want to, either."

"A lot of the Mexican kids at school have parents who don't even speak English."

"On the south side," he says.

"Yeah."

"We're trying to raise you and your brother to not have the we/them mentality, and the resentment between the *haves* and *have-nots*, which I'm afraid is rampant on the south side. Your mother and I discussed it a lot before you were born."

"It's like we're white. I don't eat Mexican food and none of the kids I grew up with were Mexican."

"We're not trying to be white, Nikki. We assimilated. Is that so horrible?"

"I feel like in the process of wanting to fit in so bad, you and Mom have neglected to make us proud of our heritage. I love being American. But when I look at the kids on the south side . . . like the Fuentes family . . . I'm jealous."

"What's there to be jealous about, honey? You have everything you need, and most things you want. We're living the American dream. I know the mentality of most Mexican families on the south side of Fairfield: work like a dog, send money to relatives back in Mexico, and don't have high expectations because they'll never be met. Most Mexican kids on the south side of Fairfield aren't expected to go to college. After high school they're expected to help their parents provide for the family, and protect what they call *the 'hood*. That's not our mentality."

"I know." I want to tell him what's been nagging me for the past two months, ever since I was with Luis on Derek's boat. "I want you to tell me about your childhood, Dad. Not now, but when you and Mom are ready. It's really important to me. Being Mexican is important to me."

"Does this have anything to do with you spending so much time with Luis?"

"Maybe. We broke up, and I miss his family and being surrounded by people who showed off being Mexican like it was a badge of honor. I know it's stupid, but I really liked that." I also miss Luis so much,

I ache for him and have cried myself to sleep every night since his birthday.

"If you want to go to Mexico, I'll talk to your mother. We have no plans this summer, with you going to college in the fall." He pats my knee. "I think you're right. We need to look back sometimes and realize the past taught us to appreciate our future."

It's true. I need to go back to my own past, so I can heal and look forward to the future. Marco is the key.

I leave the room and walk outside to call Marco. When he doesn't answer, I text him.

Me: can we talk?

Marco: Can't. I'm helping Luis get jumped in ☺

43

Luis

Chuy is standing in front of me, in the middle of a circle of about fifteen guys. My cousin Enrique isn't here, but Marco is. And a couple of other guys from school. He's also rounded up some of the guys who were around when Alex was in the Blood.

"Here's what's gonna happen, Luis," Chuy explains. "*Mis vatos* and I are gonna take you in the back room and kick the shit out of you for thirteen seconds. When it's over, you're in."

"Can I fight back?" I ask.

"No. If you even attempt to, our punches will be harder," he says, not missing a beat. "This is to break you down before we build you back up bigger, stronger, and tougher. Like a stallion, *ese*. When we're done, you're a Latino Blood."

"Let's get it over with."

"Damn, you *are* like Hector. That crazy motherfucker was as impatient as you are," Chuy says.

All of them lead me to a room without any windows. I notice dried blood stains on the floor. I should be scared, but I'm not. Marco catches my attention. He's excited, like my jumping in will raise his position in the Blood.

A few of the OGs stand behind me, probably making sure I don't get last-minute jitters and escape.

"You ready?" Chuy asks.

I nod. A deep rage simmers inside me, desperate to be unleashed. I don't know how much longer I can hold it back.

Chuy grabs my chin, his fingers digging into my skin. "Your face reminds me of Alex," he says. "I enjoyed bringin' him to his knees when he jumped out. What sweet revenge this is gonna be."

I pull myself out of his grasp, but the second I'm free Chuy's iron-hard fist flies in my face. He must have a ring on, because something sharp slashed my cheek.

"One," he says, gloating over the obvious damage.

"Two," I hear him call out. The rest of the guys start closing in. I quickly shield my face with my hands and arms. It's hard keeping them up when, blow after blow, my body aches and wants to crumple to the ground.

"Three."

A blow to my side makes me want to cry out, but I don't. I hold it in. I can handle anything, even this. I want to fight back, but Chuy's words are in the back of my head. *Our punches will be harder.*

"Four."

Marco clocks me in the jaw when I move my hands for a split second. I taste blood, but don't have time to dwell on it as I struggle to stay upright. I'm waiting to hear the number thirteen. It'll be over at thirteen.

"Five."

One of the guys kicks the back of my knee hard. I stumble to the ground. I'm on my hands and knees now. I'm trying to stand, but can't. I get kicked hard in the stomach.

"Six."

I manage to stand up. Each blow feeds the restless fire inside me. *I can handle this. I can handle anything.*

"Seven."

I have my hands covering my head again, but I don't think it does any good. A kick to my back makes me wince. I'm losing energy fast.

"Eight."

Block it out, Luis. Block out the pain and think about something else. Think about Nikki, the girl who stole your heart and ran away with it.

"Nine."

These guys fight like pros, though. They fight as hard and rough as Alex and Carlos. If Nikki were here, would she care that I was being beaten?

"Ten."

I think it's almost done. I don't know. I'm trying to stay strong but the constant blows and kicks are threatening to break me down, just like Chuy warned. My body has been hit so hard, I think one of these guys must either be wearing steel-toe shoes or has been specially trained for kicking. No. I won't let them win. I'm in charge of my destiny, not them.

"Eleven."

Please let this be over soon. I feel my body going limp, and I can't hold in my rage any longer.

I don't hear the number twelve. Chuy has stopped counting. The bastard is just standing, prolonging the beating. The fact that with each blow I'm stepping into the LB and out of Nikki's life forever is too much to take.

Fuck this game Chuy's playing. I start swinging, ready to bring down anyone who dares to get near me.

"Shit," I hear someone yell after I punch him.

I bring two more down while some OGs are trying to pin me to the ground. Chuy is standing off to the side, enjoying this. He's got a cocky grin on his face that needs to be wiped off, right now.

I deck two more guys and squirm out of the grasp of the OGs and go after Chuy. I want nothing more right now than to unleash my fury on him. He swings at me, but I'm faster. My fist connects with the side of his jaw. He flies back, and I get brief satisfaction while four of the OGs grab my hands and twist them behind my back.

Chuy is bleeding out of the side of his mouth. He doesn't bother wiping it off . . . instead he licks it like a bloodsucking vampire. I may not get out of this alive, but at this point I don't give a shit.

"We have a little miscommunication, *pequeña mierda*. You seem to think you're runnin' this show. Maybe you forgot that I'm the boss here. Not you. You think you could replace me?"

"Yeah," I mumble.

He punches me in the gut and I double over, but the guys holding my arms like a damn vise straighten me back up.

"Wrong answer. I'll ask again. You think you could replace me?"

I take a deep breath, force myself to ignore the piercing pain my body is in, and look up. "Yeah," I say.

He punches my face, this time harder—if that was even possible. My head reels in pain.

"Wrong answer. I'll ask again. You think you could replace me?"

I try to open my eyes wider, but I can't. I do the best I can, though, through the haze. "Yeah."

He punches me in the gut again. He might have broken a rib, 'cause I felt something crack.

"Wrong answer. I'll ask again. You think you could replace me?"

It's done. I lost Nikki. I lost NASA. I lost everyone else. The only thing I have left is my father's legacy as a hardass who never backed down until he was dead and buried. I'll hang on to that legacy for as long as I can.

"*Sí.*"

"Delgado, get me an electric shaver," Chuy orders. "And a screwdriver . . . a sharp one."

"Why?" Marco asks.

"Just do it, you stupid little fuck. If you don't want to end up like this *pendejo*, do it."

Chuy's next blow to my head is the last thing I remember before I black out.

When I come to, I'm lying on the cement floor.

"*¡Felicitaciones!*" Chuy says as he crouches beside me. I catch sight of the gold rings on his fingers. "You're one of us now."

I just want to lie back down right here on the floor and sleep until my body stops screaming out in pain.

44

Nikki

Marco finally answers my call after an hour of me trying nonstop.

"Where's Luis?" I ask him.

"I dropped him off at home a few minutes ago," Marco's voice echoes through the receiver. He chuckles, the sound mocking me. "He's in bad shape, but he'll survive. He's one tough motherfucker. Didn't know he had so much fight in him, but Chuy brought him to his knees."

My heart slams in my chest. "You could have stopped it."

"You're delusional. Luis wanted it . . . he asked for it. Get your head out of your ass and face the fact, Nik. You don't have a hold on him anymore. The LB does."

"Why did you pick the LB over me, Marco? Tell me the truth."

"Money, status, brotherhood. You and I would've never lasted, and I knew it. You were a temporary distraction from my goals."

A temporary distraction. The truth definitely hurts, but it's a dull ache instead of real pain. I'm over him, over us, over what happened as a result of our relationship.

"I was pregnant the day we broke up," I tell him, then look at the picture of me and Luis dancing at Alex and Brittany's wedding, still up on my wall. Somehow seeing Luis's goofy grin as he tried to get me to smile gives me the hope and the strength to get through this conversation. "I've carried guilt about not telling you for over two years. I had a miscarriage, and our breakup—combined with losing our baby—messed me up for a long time."

I stop talking and wait for his reaction. I don't know what I want him to say, or what I expect him to say.

"How do you know the kid was mine?" he says in a cocky tone.

He knew I was his first and he was mine. There was nobody else. His question is so insulting he doesn't deserve an answer.

I hang up on him, then call Kendall. "Luis got jumped into the Latino Blood tonight," I tell her. "I'm going to his house to make sure he's okay."

"I'm coming with you," she says. I hear Derek's muffled voice as she tells him what's going on. "Derek's coming, too. We'll be at your house in five minutes."

"Hurry," I tell her.

I knock on Luis's front door, but there's no answer. The door is slightly open, so we walk in.

"Luis?" I call out.

No one responds. I go to his room, knowing that he's here . . . feeling his presence somewhere in the house.

"I'll check the bedrooms," Derek says. "You two stay by the front door. If you need to get out of here fast, just go."

Derek opens the door to Luis's bedroom. I squeeze Kendall's arm, scared of what he'll find . . . if anything.

"What the hell happened to you, dude?" Derek asks.

"Why are you here?" I hear Luis answer.

"He's here," I whisper to Kendall.

"Nikki wanted to make sure you were okay." Derek waves me over. "I'll, uh, be right outside the door if you need anything . . . like a hospital."

I gasp when I see Luis sitting on his bed with his back against the wall. His head is resting in his hands. There's blood all over his face. His head is shaved, and his completely bloodied shirt is in shreds on the floor.

Granny is sitting beside him, her head on his thigh. She knows he's hurting.

I rush over to him, afraid to touch his face for fear I'll hurt him. "What did they do to you?" I ask softly, trying to hold back the flood of emotion threatening to rush out of me. I have to stay strong for Luis.

"Go away," he moans.

"I'm not leaving while you look like that," I whisper.

"I don't need you here, and I sure as hell don't *want* you here. We're done, remember? I'm not your charity case."

"Well, you look like one right now. Drop the ego and let me help you."

They shaved off his beautiful signature hair. Did they hold him down, or did he bow his head in submission and willingly have it shaved? Either way, they weren't gentle. He's got cuts all over his scalp.

"They shaved your head."

I didn't realize it before, but his spiked, boyish hair was a symbol of his innocence and individuality. Now he looks so tough . . . so Latino Blood. I lift his chin and urge him to look at me. When he does, I almost suck in a breath. His lips are busted up, his eyes are half closed because his lids are swollen . . . and he's got red, nasty cuts mixed with bruises all over his face, back, and chest.

When I look into his eyes, they've got an empty hollowness to them. It scares me. Will he change and become like Marco?

"What part of 'get away from me' don't you understand?" he asks.

When he cups his head in his hands, I catch a glimpse of the letters *L* and *B* gouged in his bicep.

"You need to go to a hospital," I tell him.

"I can't. They'll ask me what happened." He looks up at me. "I'm bound by a code of silence. You know what I need, Nik? Drugs. Illegal ones. Lots of 'em, actually. And make sure there's enough so I don't come out of it for a while."

"Stop talking stupid." I sit on the bed and take a long, hard look at him. "Here's what's going to happen. You're gonna let me clean you up. After that, you can tell me to leave."

"Didn't you hear me? Unless you have pain meds, I don't want you near me."

"Too bad."

Kendall and Derek help me wet some paper towels with hydrogen peroxide. I kneel in front of Luis and gently place one of the paper towels next to a cut by his eyebrow.

"What happened to the boy who said he loved me?" I ask.

"He died," he says dryly.

"I wanted to push you away," I tell him. "It's my defense mechanism."

"Congratulations, Nikki," he says. "You win."

He jerks his head away from me, but I make him face me while I clean off his chin and a nasty cut on his cheek. When I move to clean the wound on his bicep, the angry letters gouged out of his skin that'll leave permanent scars stare back at me.

He holds my wrist with his strong fingers and stills my hand, which is about to wipe off blood still oozing from the wound. "Don't help me," he says. "I *need* you to go."

"Why? We had a connection, Luis. I want to forget it but I can't."

His haunting eyes stare right through me. "Don't lie to yourself and think what we had was any different than what you had with Marco."

"I don't believe that," I say, shaking my head. "Maybe we don't have a chance for a future, but I know from the bottom of my heart that what we have goes way deeper than anything I had with Marco."

"You're wrong." He grabs my fist tighter, stopping me from touching him. "Yo, Derek!" he yells.

Derek sticks his head in the doorway. "Yeah?"

"Get her out of here, before I do somethin' stupid."

Derek touches my shoulder. "Nik . . . you need to let him go."

I swallow the basketball-sized lump in my throat. "I *love* you, Luis."

Luis squeezes his eyes shut. "Derek . . . get her out!"

I move away from him and take a deep breath. I can't get through to him. He's gone to the other side and left me behind.

45

Luis

Less than an hour after Nikki and company leave my house, I get a surprise visit from Alex and Carlos. Word obviously spread to them that I got jumped in, because they don't look surprised to see me all beat up.

"Go take a shower," Alex says, tossing me a towel. "You're filthy."

"Don't take too long," Carlos says, tapping me on the leg. "Because dinner'll be ready in forty-five minutes."

He picks up Granny, who hasn't left my side.

"I don't want dinner," I tell him. "And give me back my dog."

"You'll want to eat when you find out what I'm makin'."

I look up at my half brothers. I expect them to give me shit, but they don't. They're just . . . here.

"Your dog is depressed, just like you," Carlos says as he sets Granny on the floor.

I take a shower and let the hot water wash away the dried blood on my skin, but it won't erase the fact that I'm a full-fledged Latino Blood. Or the fact that I pushed Nikki away for good, which hurt way more than Chuy gouging the letters *LB* into my skin with the screwdriver.

I've lost her. It's a good thing, though. I'd just end up disappointing her, and I don't want to hurt her more than I already have.

When I step out of the bathroom, my brothers are sitting at the kitchen table. They're talking quietly, obviously discussing how they're going to deal with me. When I don't join them, they bring their plates to my room and lean against the wall while they chow down. The smell of beef and spices makes my mouth water, but I don't want to face them right now . . . or eat with them.

"What are you two doin'?" I ask.

Alex and Carlos look at eat other and shrug. "Eatin', bro," Alex says. "What does it look like we're doin'?"

I point to my bedroom door. "We have a kitchen, you know. Go eat in there."

"I'm cool," Carlos says. "What about you, Alex?"

Alex takes a forkful of *carne guisada*, which they both know is my favorite. "I'm cool, too," he says as he makes a big deal out of shoving the food in his mouth and moaning in pleasure as if he's in *carne guisada* heaven.

After dinner, Carlos lies down on a spare mattress on the floor in my room. "Aren't you stayin' at the hotel with Kiara?" I ask him.

"Not tonight. Or tomorrow. You fucked that plan up."

"Don't blame me," I tell him. "Go to the hotel. I want you to."

When I get my aching bones up to go to the bathroom, I notice Alex has camped out on the living room couch. "Go home to your wife and kid," I tell him.

"I'm stayin' here for the week. *Mi'amá* is stayin' with Brit and Paco, in case you were wonderin'."

"I don't need you and Carlos babysittin' me. I'm fine."

Once I get a bunch of Tylenol in me, I'll be fine.

He laughs as he scans my appearance. "Yeah, right. You look fine, bro. Go to bed and let your body start to repair itself."

"When's the lecture comin'?" I ask. I'm not stupid enough to think I'm off the hook from Alex and Carlos giving me shit.

"I'm not gonna lecture you," Alex says.

"I'm not, either," Carlos says.

"You do realize I'm an LB, right?" I say just to make sure we're all on the same page. "I didn't get mugged today . . . I got jumped in."

"Statin' the obvious, bro," Carlos says in a bored tone.

Alex picks up the remote and watches television. They're pretending like they don't care one bit that I'm part of the Latino Blood, but I'm not an idiot. They're playing me. But why?

"So you guys are cool with it?" I ask.

"I wouldn't go that far," Alex says. "But we get it."

"And we're gonna give you time to get out of it," Carlos says.

I hold my bruised ribs as I limp back to my room. "Come on, Granny," I say. My dog bumps her head into the wall and I want to tell her I feel her pain—literally.

"Oh, and by the way," Alex yells from the living room. "Enrique is givin' you a week off work."

I slowly lower myself onto my bed, trying to ignore every ache. I couldn't work even if I wanted to.

"Oh, one more thing," Alex calls out. "Your chemistry teacher is comin' to tutor you this week while you heal. You go to school lookin' like that and Aguirre'll call the cops."

"Please tell me you're jokin' about Peterson comin' here."

"No joke, bro. She's really lookin' forward to it," Alex says.

46

Nikki

Luis hasn't been back to school all week. I called Brittany, who told me that Alex and Carlos have been taking care of him. Alex says he's healing fast. Kendall, Derek, and Hunter invited me to play golf at Brickstone. I don't want to go, but I need to get my mind off of Luis.

I can't say how many times I've been tempted to go over to Luis's house. Six times I got in my car and started driving, but I always stopped myself before I crossed the railroad tracks to the south side.

"I'm glad you came," Hunter says as I set my golf clubs in the golf cart.

I give him a small smile. "Me too."

"Me three," Derek says, then nudges Kendall.

"Me four," she says, although she's less enthusiastic.

On the eighth hole, while Derek is coaching Kendall on how to do a chip shot to get her ball out of the sand trap, Hunter sits next to me in the golf cart. "Go to my homecoming with me," he says.

"Was that a question or a statement?" I ask him.

"Considering I don't want you to even contemplate saying no, I'd say it was a statement." He puts his arm around me. "You know I've always wanted to date you."

"Liar. You've wanted to add me to your trophy shelf."

"True. So how about it?"

I glance down at his green custom golf shoes with shiny gold designs on the tops. His initials are engraved in the gold. Luis wouldn't be caught dead in them. "I can't go to homecoming with you, Hunter."

"Is it because of my shoes?"

"No. It's because I'm in love with someone else."

"Does he know about it?"

"Yes. But he doesn't believe me."

When Marco and I broke up, and I saw him with Mariana, I didn't fight for him. I gave up and let the LB win. With Luis it's different. I realized that I'm not giving up on us, and I'm going to fight to get him back. I love him deeper than just my heart . . . I love him to the inner parts of my soul as if he's a part of me.

It's about time he knows it.

47

Luis

While Alex is out and Carlos is watching television, I sneak out my bedroom window with my backpack and head to the bank with the key to the safety-deposit box. I'm sure it's too much to hope I'll be back before they realize I'm gone. I have to know what's in the bank, so I can decide what to do. I sneak through back alleys to make sure I'm not followed.

At the bank, I give them my ID and sign a slip of paper declaring that I'm the owner of the box. Afterward, I'm directed to a locked vault. The bank employees leave me in the vault alone while I open the box and examine the contents.

Stacks of hundred-dollar bills stare back at me. I bet there's at least ten or fifteen thousand dollars here. My heart starts racing. I don't look up for fear there's a video camera watching my every move. Seeing this much money makes me nervous. What was it supposed to be used for? Why did Hector put my name on the box in the first place? I don't know if I'll ever get the answers.

There's also a piece of paper with a bunch of numbers on it and below them the letters CODEOFSILENCE—all caps, no spaces.

Under the money is another piece of paper, embossed and stamped as original—my birth certificate.

Luis Salvatore Martinez Fuentes.

I stare at the two last names . . . *mi'amá* acknowledged Hector as my father on my birth certificate. She gave me his last name, but never told me. On the bottom of the certificate, where it says father, Hector Martinez is listed—and the bastard signed the document.

Despite everything, I don't feel like a Martinez. It's not a part of me, and I won't adopt it as my own.

I jot the numbers down on my palm with a pen, fold the birth certificate into my pocket, then put the box back in its slot. Since I laid my eyes on the cash, I've been trying to convince myself to take it—it's mine, isn't it? *Mi'amá* needs it, Alex needs it . . . it could help Carlos and Kiara start their lives together.

But what if it's blood money, or drug money? Shit, I'm a Latino Blood with a damn conscience. Not a good combination.

I quickly fill my backpack with the cash, then take the bus to the local library, hoping I'm not being tracked. If Chuy knows I've been to the bank, then he knows I've seen what's in the box. Is he expecting me to just hand over the cash and give him the numbers on the paper? If I don't give them to him, will he kill me? If I do give them to him, what does he need me for, then? Best bet is that I'll be smoked either way.

If Nikki and I were together, she'd be in danger. I'm glad I gave her up, although it's killing me inside.

I can't tell Alex and Carlos what's goin' down. They're already involved more than they should be. I swear they haven't let me out of their sight for one minute since they came back home. If Carlos gets involved, and something goes wrong and he gets arrested, he'll most likely be dishonorably discharged from the army. Alex could lose his scholarship, his family . . . if he's in jail, he'll miss the birth of his second child.

I'll never let either of them get involved. I might be a Martinez, but I still feel like a Fuentes.

I look back and realize that I'm being tailed by a black Camaro. The guy driving looks suspiciously like the *pendejo* who opened the door in that house Marco and I went to in the F5 territory to collect the five Gs.

Luckily I know Fairfield like the back of my hand. I walk toward the police station, which is right behind the library. I walk inside the station lobby and wait while the car passes, then go behind the station and head to the back door of the library.

Once inside, I sign up for an hour of computer use. I Google the set of numbers I found in the safety deposit box, but nothing comes up. What would Hector do with the numbers? Probably not a phone number, but the number starts with double zeroes. I deduce that it's either some kind of code, a password, or an account number. A bank account, maybe. But what bank? There's probably thousands of banks. How the hell am I supposed to figure out which one? Or maybe it's not a bank account, and the numbers don't mean shit.

It's no use. My hour is up and I still don't have a clue what the numbers mean. I look behind me and see someone else waiting to use the computer. Damn. I need more time.

At home, I sneak back in through my window when I catch sight of Reyes smoking a cigarette on his back porch. He's shirtless and his back is to me. Plain as day I see a tattoo between his shoulder blades. F5.

Reyes is a gangbanger posing as a cop? Holy shit. What has he been doin', spying on me like the others? Was this all planned out? Chuy said he's been watching me all along, even when I was in Colorado. Could Chuy secretly be fuckin' with me?

I'm so fucking confused it feels like my head is about to explode. Not wanting Reyes to know I've seen him, I sneak around to the front of the house. When I walk through the door, Peterson is sitting at the kitchen table peering at me over her glasses.

"Weren't you supposed to give birth already?" I ask her.

She touches her protruding stomach. "Any day now. I'm on maternity leave, so you'll have a break from me for a few months. Don't be too broken up about it."

"I'm not."

"You almost missed our tutoring session," she says, then glances at her watch.

Considering my chances of surviving the next few weeks are slim, she doesn't need to waste her time. "Listen, Mrs. P., I know my brothers kind of coerced you to be here, but it's a waste of your time."

"I'm not giving up on you," she says, patting the chair next to her.

"I would."

"I didn't give up on Alex, and I'm not giving up on you. Alex had every reason to throw it all away but he didn't."

Alex never had the connection to the LB that I do.

"Show me your math homework," she orders in a no-nonsense voice.

"Not to be disrespectful, Mrs. P., but I'd bet I'm better in math than you." My brothers must have found my textbook and binders in my room and "helpfully" left them on the table for me. I pull out the math sheet I finished in five seconds.

"Mr. Gasper gave me a new worksheet. I made a copy of it. I bet I can finish the worksheet faster than you."

"How much?"

She pulls her wallet out, opens it, then slips a five-dollar bill out of the top. Attached to one side of her wallet are her checks . . . with a row of numbers at the bottom. The first two numbers are zeroes.

"What are those numbers?" I ask her, pointing to the bottom of the check.

"The bank routing number, and the bank account number. Why?"

I glance at my palm with the numbers written on it, and adrenaline pumps through my veins. That's it. The bank routing number, and bank account. "No reason. I've never had checks," I tell her.

Mrs. P. takes ten minutes to explain how checks work, and even pulls one of hers out of her wallet and makes me write one out.

"Sign your name here," she says, pointing to the bottom right corner. "This is a life skill that you should know, Luis."

"I've got other life skills," I tell her.

"Yeah, well, I don't consider cussing a life skill. Or fighting."

"I do. Necessary ones."

She shakes her head and sighs in frustration. "I will give you this important information about checks." She writes the word *VOID* in big bold letters on the front of the check she told me to practice on. "Let this be the last time you write your name on someone else's check. If you do, or forge someone's name on a check, it's a felony. You go to jail. Make good decisions, Luis. Focus on math and science and doing well in school. Those will help you. The fighting won't." She places Gasper's worksheet in front of me. "You ready for the challenge?"

I pick up a pencil. "You're on, Mrs. P. But I've got to warn you, I'm a numbers guy."

"Good," she says, patting me on the hand. "That skill will serve you well in college, and when you're up in space."

It's more likely I'll end up in hell before heaven or space.

48

I gave Derek a note to give to Luis. He texted me that he delivered it. Now I'm waiting. If he won't come to me, I'm going to him.

I debated what to wear, and now I'm second-guessing myself. What if he doesn't remember this dress, the one I wore the night I met him? What if he doesn't remember what room we were in when we first laid eyes on each other?

But the setup doesn't matter. What matters is that Luis knows I love him, and I'm not giving up on us trying to make this work.

I know he's a Latino Blood now, but if he realizes what we have is stronger than any bond he could have to a gang, everything will work out. I have to believe he really doesn't want to be in the LB and will find a way to get out.

I look at my cell phone. No call from Luis, no text, and it's nine o'clock. I told him in the letter to meet me here at nine. Every second that passes makes me nervous that he might not show, but I don't give up hope. Even at nine fifteen when there's no sign of him, I still have faith he'll come. I feel like that movie where the girl is standing on the pitcher's mound, waiting for the guy. When all hope is lost, the hero comes running onto the field and they live happily ever after.

Luis is my hero, even if he doesn't know it yet. He'll know tonight . . . if he shows up.

I check my clock again for the hundredth time. Nine thirty.

When I called the private grounds where Brittany and Alex got married, the lady on the phone told me I had to call their management office to inquire about a daily rental. To my surprise, Hunter answered the phone. Ends up his family owns the property, and he told me the house would be unoccupied for two days, so I could stay there for free. When I told him he might change his mind about letting me use the place because I was going to be with another guy, all he said was, "Lucky guy. I hope he's worth it."

"He is," I tell him.

At ten, I'm losing hope. I take the key out of my purse, ready to close the place up, when the door opens.

Luis is in the doorway. "Hey," he says.

"Hey."

"Derek gave me your note. Sorry I'm late. There was a little mishap with my dog."

"What happened to Granny?"

"She kind of wandered off, but I found her. Why did you want me to come here?"

"You haven't been at school." I step closer to him. "I missed you."

"You're wearin' the same dress you had on when we met."

"You remembered."

"How could I forget. I thought you were an angel from heaven."

"I'm still your angel, Luis."

"We can't do this." He looks around the room. "You pushed me away that night at your place . . . You were right."

"No. I was scared, Luis. The second I laid eyes on you, I knew you were dangerous . . . because I felt a connection."

"The same you felt with Marco," he says with a sad tone to his voice.

"No. Very different. Very, very different. You're a genius in chemistry class, Luis. Explain the electricity in the room right now. It's flowing between us . . . even you can't control it."

"It's lust."

"I think it's something else. Follow me," I say, then slide past him and head outside to the dance floor.

"You were a shitty dancer back then," he says, watching me as I play music I'd already set up from my portable iPod speakers.

I smile sheepishly. "I'm still a shitty dancer."

"I'm not who you think I am, or who *I* thought I was. I found out that my father was Hector Martinez, the head of the Latino Blood. I'm following in his footsteps."

I'm shocked, but everything makes more sense now. "Why follow in his footsteps?"

"Because I have to, Nik. It's my legacy. I was born a Latino Blood," he says. "And I'm gonna die one."

"Not tonight, you're not." I take his arms and put them around me as we sway to the music. I wrap my arms around his neck as a slow love song plays in the background. "I love you, Luis . . . unconditionally."

"Nik, don't do this," he whispers.

I hold him tighter. "I'm not holding back anymore. Luis, tell me you love me, too."

"I never stopped lovin' you, *mi chava*." I hear him curse under his breath. "But I can't drag you down with me. This can't happen between us, because you know I'll have to leave you."

I take his hand and lead him onto the beach, and into one of the many abandoned lifeguard stations. Flickering candles in glass containers surround the cramped space—candles I lit over an hour ago.

He stands against the wall, watching my every move.

"Last time we were alone together I held back," I tell him.

"I know. You didn't trust me, which was a smart move. You said you didn't love me."

"I lied." I run my fingers lightly over his shaved head and he closes his eyes. "You look so tough."

"I don't feel so tough." He opens his eyes. They sparkle with every flicker of the candlelight hitting them. He's got beautiful, mesmerizing eyes that pierce my soul. "You shouldn't love me. I don't deserve it."

I hold his face in my hands. "Luis, I admire the fact that you know what you want, and go for it even when the odds are stacked against you. You've taught me to be proud of my Mexican heritage. I am in awe of how smart you are, and that you push me away to protect me from the Latino Blood. I think it's adorable when you look up at the sky and instead of admiring it you want to go up there and explore it. I love you because you're the only person I want to make love to without any conditions and—and I love that you need me."

"I do need you, Nik. But I still don't deserve you."

Just knowing that he's here with me is enough. "We deserve each other, Luis . . . and I need you just as much as you need me. Hold me."

He steps closer, but hesitates. "If I do, *mi chava*, I can't promise I'll be able to let you go."

"Good."

He wraps his arms around me and I wrap mine around him. It's silent, except for the sound of our breathing and the gentle waves lapping against the shore. We stay standing, embracing each other, for what seems like forever. This is what it's supposed to be like.

"Want me to list all the reasons I love you?" he asks me. "I wrote a poem about it for English class . . . I called you my forever and always."

Hearing his words makes me smile, and I tell him what I'm feeling deep in my gut. "We're gonna make it."

"The odds are against us, Nik."

"Since when did bad odds ever stop you from your goal?" I ask, then lift his shirt up and kiss his abs. I follow the line of hair from his navel down until I reach the waistband of his jeans.

"Kiss me," he says, urging me up so we're face-to-face.

We start making out slowly, but as soon as he opens his mouth and his tongue slides against mine, it's no holds barred. Our bodies melt against each other and I feel his hardness through his jeans. I'm not holding back this time. I couldn't even if I wanted to . . . this is too intense.

"Your skin is so damn soft," he says as his hands reach under my dress and he pulls down my panties until I step out of them.

I push him against the wall. "Stay right there. Don't move," I order, then unzip his pants and ease down his boxers.

"Nik . . ." He groans as I touch him all over until I know he's about to lose control.

"Mmm . . ."

"I'm gonna . . ." He can't get out the rest of his sentence.

"Make love to me, Luis."

"I want to, baby, but I don't have a condom. I can't risk gettin' you—"

I put a finger over his beautiful lips. "It's okay. I'm on the pill now. I'm safe."

"Me too . . . I mean, you know, I don't have any STDs," he says.

"I'm ready then, and I'm not holding back this time. Do you want this as much I do?"

"More than you know." He kicks off his pants and boxers, then covers the floor with our clothes before he lowers me to the floor. "You really sure you're ready for this?" he asks, his face full of vulnerability and emotion.

I nod.

"I love you, *mi chava*," he whispers in my ear as we move together as one. "I'll always love you, no matter what happens, okay?" He brushes the hair off my face. His intense, soulful eyes pierce mine as we cling desperately to each other. He stills. "If I die tomorrow, move on. Promise me you'll move on."

Tears sting my eyes. "I won't let you die, Luis."

"Promise me, Nik. For me. Come on, if you love me . . ."

He knows his life is in grave danger. I can feel his tension, his pain . . . his sorrow.

I try to hold back tears, but they won't stop. I grab on to him, clutching him to me . . . feeling the love flow between us . . . a forever bond that defies explanation.

Afterward, we lie together and watch the moonlit waves way into the night. I don't want to sleep, but I curl into his warmth and my eyelids grow heavy.

"You can change your destiny, Luis," I say before I fall asleep. "If anyone can do it, you can."

I don't wake up until the sun shines through the wooden slats of the roof. Luis is writing something in candle wax on the wall beside me.

It's a heart with initials inside: *LF + NC.*

"Hey," I say.

He looks at me and smiles. "Hey. You sleep okay?"

"Real good. I like sleeping in your arms."

"Do your parents know you were with me?"

I shake my head. "No."

He sighs heavily. "They don't want you with someone like me. They're right, you know. I'm not innocent, Nikki. And I'm afraid that I'm in too deep to get out." He crouches beside me and gently touches my cheek with his fingers. "God, how I wanted last night to go on forever. But it can't."

"You're talking like this is the end."

"It might be. It involves a lot of money, and I'm in the middle of it. People have died for less money."

"I'm not letting you die," I tell him. I'll find some way to help him.

"I wish it was that simple." He squeezes his eyes shut. "I've got to go. I can't stall any longer."

I put on all my clothes and stand up. "I'm going with you, then. We're in this together."

He smiles. "I won't let you. You know that. I'm not puttin' you in danger. I can't call the cops, I can't tell my brothers . . . I'm on my own here."

Tears stream down my face as I reach up and kiss his cheeks, his eyelids, his warm lips. "I have complete faith in you and I love you no matter what. Remember that, okay?"

He nods. "You make me believe in the impossible."

We hold each other for a long time, until he tells me he's got to go. As I watch him drive away, I know what I need to do. He might not think I can help him, but I need to try. I drive over to Marco's house, hoping it's early enough that he's home.

He answers the door, surprised to see me. "What do you want?"

"I need you to help Luis."

"Chuy ordered everyone away from the warehouse when he meets with Luis. That usually means he wants no witnesses. I can't do anythin' to change it."

I grab his shirt when he starts to close the door on me. "You can't just sit back and let Luis get hurt."

He shrugs out of my hold. "It's not in my hands, Nik."

"So you're not going to help him?"

"I value my life, Nik. If I go against Chuy, I'm dead. I'm playin' both sides, waitin' for someone to go down. If the F5 are standin' at the end, I'm with them. If Chuy is on top, I'm with the LB."

I slap him. "You're nothing but a coward. How can you stand by, knowing that your friend's life is in danger?"

"It's simple. I'm lookin' out for number one, baby. Me."

49

Luis

Granny hadn't wandered off last night. I was late meeting Nikki because I was over at Derek's house. After he'd given me the letter from Nikki, I asked him if I could use the Internet at his house. It was a good thing my brothers didn't question me.

Within forty-five minutes, I'd had the answer I was looking for. The numbers I'd written on my hand and memorized were the bank routing and account number. The bank where Hector stashed the money is in the Grand Cayman Islands. The second I typed the password CODE-OFSILENCE and the amount was displayed on the screen, I almost fell off my chair.

Six million, three hundred thousand. *Dollars.*

I had to refresh the screen a bunch of times to make sure it was right. And then looked at the name on the account just to make sure I read it right. Luis Salvatore Martinez Fuentes.

Whether I give Chuy the money or refuse to, my life is in danger.

After I left Derek's house, I went to Nikki. I had no intention of making love to her last night. I went to her hoping to convince her that I'd given her up for good. I wanted to be an ass, to make it easier for her to move on and forget about me. I was going to tell her I was into Mariana, but the lie couldn't come out of my mouth.

Because I love the girl.

This morning I was tempted to ask her to run away with me and never look back. But I can't. I had to leave Nikki. Her mom thinks I'm not good enough. I don't want to prove her right.

I head for the LB warehouse, ready to face Chuy. I may not be the guy Nikki deserves, but I'm sure as hell not the guy Chuy wants me to be . . . I'm not Hector, and never will be.

I'm Luis Fuentes. Nikki had complete faith in me that I could fix this. I'm still skeptical, but I figure my odds are best if I take a chance on trusting the one person who might be the enemy. I pull out my cell and dial the number to Officer Reyes.

"This is Reyes," he answers.

I take a deep breath. "It's Luis Fuentes. I know you want to bust Chuy Soto, and I can help you. Before I do, I need to know if you want to ruin him because you're a cop, or because you're Fremont 5."

"What the hell are you talking about?" he asks. The tension in his voice carries through the line.

"Reyes, I know *mi'amá* trusts you. But I saw your F5 tattoos, and I have to know if you're playin' us. Are you just a cop as a cover, so you can provide inside info to your crew?"

"Luis, I'm not hiding anything from anyone. I used to be an F5 back in high school. I was in so fucking deep." He pauses, his voice flooding with anger. "Until my best friend got killed by a crackhead in a dirty alley in the city in a drug deal that went bad. His life was worth so much more than the payday the gang scored. That day I promised myself I'd find a way out . . . and when I did, I became a cop so I could stop other kids from making the same mistakes me and my friends did.

I've tried to bring down Soto, but he knows how to cover his tracks. Come to the station and you can tell me what you know."

I can't be sure he's telling me the truth, but my gut tells me to trust the guy. His story hits close to home. "I can't come to the station, 'cause something's goin' down right now," I tell him. "Just tape the conversation I'm about to have and you'll get all the dirt to put him away for a long time."

"Don't do anything stupid," Reyes starts to say, but I turn off the sound and stick the phone in my back pocket.

I've got a duffel full of cash. Nobody is guarding the warehouse door, so I walk right in.

"It's about time," Chuy says. "I was waiting for you. You managed to ditch my boys last night. Where were you?"

"If I thought that was any of your business, I wouldn't have ditched them." The last thing I'd do is let Chuy or Marco know I was with Nikki. The Blood and Nikki are two separate parts of my life, and I'll do everything in my power to keep it that way.

"You're a wiseass," Chuy says. "And you haven't proven that you can be trusted." He nods to the duffel. "Or have you?"

I toss the duffel to him. Just as he unzips the top and digs inside, my brothers barge into the room like a SWAT team.

Alex and Carlos are both here, ready to fight. Not a good idea. I've got this all figured out, and having them here is screwing everything up. If we get busted, or bullets go flying, I need my brothers out of here.

"Well, well . . . it's a Fuentes family reunion," Chuy says. "Nice of you to join us."

No, it wasn't. What the hell is going on? How did they know I'd be here, unless Reyes tipped them off? I turn to my brothers and say, "Alex, get the fuck out of here . . . and take Carlos with you. I don't need you guys here."

Carlos limps inside the room until he's standing next to me. "What, you think we were gonna let you meet with Chuy on your own? No way."

Shit. "This is not how this was supposed to go down."

Chuy pulls out a gun and points it at Alex. "Maybe it was," he says, unfazed. "This is my lucky day. I get to kill the entire Fuentes family."

"You forget that I have millions that I can turn over to the cops, or give to you," I tell him.

"I know," Chuy says. "That's why I'll kill you last, while you're watchin' your brothers die. Or you can save yourself and give me the info I need. I'm God in Fairfield. You don't believe me, just ask your cousin Enrique . . . Oh, yeah, you can't. I smoked him this mornin' when he wouldn't tell me where you were. Loyalty, guys. You're not loyal, you die. Period. Loyalty to the LB comes before loyalty to family."

No. Not Enrique. My stomach lurches.

With his free hand, Chuy pulls up a picture on his phone . . . of Enrique lying on the floor of his body shop with blood pooled around his head.

"Enrique didn't know where I was!" I yell. "He was the most loyal Blood you'd ever have, you *pendejo*."

Alex pulls out a gun and points it at Chuy. "Put the gun down or I'll kill you."

Chuy laughs. "You wouldn't, Alex. I know you. You haven't got it in you to kill someone. Besides, I've got a *chica* named Nikki who's beggin' for her life right about now."

What! I feel like he just punched me in the gut and the wind got knocked out of me. He could have stabbed me with a knife and it would hurt less. "You hurt Nikki and I swear I'll kill you with my own hands," I growl.

Chuy shrugs. "Put the gun down, Alex, or Luis's little girlfriend has a tragic accident. If I don't call my guys and let them know I've secured the money, she'll find herself in the Des Plaines river . . . tied to a big rock that sinks all the way to the bottom."

Alex slowly puts the gun down and kicks it over to him.

Chuy looks to Carlos. "You might as well give up yours, too."

A very pissed-off Carlos takes a gun from beneath his shirt and tosses it onto Chuy's desk.

"And what about yours?" Chuy asks me. "The one I gave you."

"I left it at home," I tell him.

"Prove it. Lift up your shirt and turn around real slow." After I do, he says, "Time to give me the numbers."

"Let my brothers go," I tell him. "This is between you and me."

"No," Chuy says. "This is between me and all of you. You're in this together as far as I'm concerned."

This is not happening. Despite all I've risked to keep them safe, I've managed to jeopardize my brothers' lives, and Nikki's. "If I give you the codes, you have to promise to let my brothers and Nikki go."

"I was bluffin' about Nikki." Chuy laughs. "I guess I should play more poker, huh? The first lesson in battle is knowin' the weakness of your enemies. Nikki is your weakness, Luis. You shouldn't have spilled the truth to Marco about how much you cared about the girl. I'll give you a hint . . . he's not really your friend. He got close to you because I told him to."

"I know *your* weakness," I tell him.

"What's that?"

"Money. You want it, and I have it. You hurt my brothers, you'll never see another cent."

Chuy holds up the gun and points it at Alex. "I'm gonna call your bluff."

I hold my breath as Alex holds his hand out, stopping me and Carlos from running in front of him. He knows we'll do it; we'll take a bullet and die for him.

Alex stands straight and tall, staring into the barrel of Chuy's gun.

A shot rings out. Shit. No! But wait, Alex is still standing. Even he looks surprised as he stares at Chuy with a red stain on his shirt that's growing bigger and bigger. Chuy was shot and clutches his shoulder as he collapses.

I look to Carlos, sure he had another gun stashed in his pants. But he's just looking at Chuy, stunned. He doesn't have a gun in his hand.

I look behind me. The shooter is standing in the doorway, the smoking gun shaking in her hand.

Nikki.

She drops the gun. She's hyperventilating as I pull her into my arms. "I couldn't let him hurt you . . . I had to . . . ," she cries out.

"He's still alive," Alex says, swiping the gun away from Chuy's hand.

I hear police sirens and pull Nikki close, telling her it'll be okay even though I'm shaking as hard as she is.

Reyes barges in, with his gun at the ready. The guy is sweating and breathes a sigh of relief as he eyes the scene. A few other officers surround Chuy and call for an ambulance.

"Shit, Luis. What the hell were you thinking?" Reyes yells after they stabilize Chuy and take him away on a stretcher. "You all could have been killed." He points aggressively at Alex. "I told you to give me the address to this place, then stay put. What the *fuck* are you doing here?"

Alex shrugs. "Listen, Reyes, once we realized what was goin' down, we weren't about to let our brother face Chuy on his own."

"He's our blood," Carlos explains, then pats me on the back. "The kind that matters."

"We need to find out if Enrique's okay," I say. "What if he . . ."

"I already sent a squad car to check out Enrique's Auto Body," Reyes says. He hesitates. "It's not good news."

I squeeze my eyes shut, wondering when the violence will ever stop. Sometimes I think Ben is right, that the fantasy world is better because reality sucks . . . but then I look at Nikki and I believe we can beat the odds.

Reyes makes us all go down to the police station to give our statements, and we're released to our parents after the district attorney is called in to listen to the taped phone conversation. No charges are filed against us, and the money in the duffel and the offshore account are handed over to the police. Nikki explained that the gun was Marco's . . . when they were together he'd shown her the place by the railroad tracks where the LB hid their guns. Marco had told Nikki that he was there when Enrique died and he knew what Chuy had planned at the warehouse. He was called into the station and charged as an accessory to murder.

"You're shakin'," I tell Nikki as I hold her two weeks later. We're sitting on the couch in her living room while her mother periodically checks in on us. She's not thrilled we're still together, but she's warming up to the idea slowly. Ben told us that we've inspired a new game he's working on . . . with us as the main characters.

"I'm so glad you're here," Nikki says, wrapping her arms around me and squeezing tight. "I have a secret that I haven't told you." She looks up at me, her expressive chocolate eyes a window to her Latina soul. I couldn't look away even if I wanted to. "I applied to Purdue a week ago."

"Really?" I ask, smiling for the first time since I left her at the beach.

"Yeah. Who else besides me is going to keep you out of trouble?"

This girl is my angel. From the first moment I laid eyes on her I remember thinking that God sent her down to earth just for me. She believed in me when I didn't even believe in myself. "Nik, I love you."

"I know," she says, then taps her heart with her fingers. "I feel it in here. I don't need the words to prove what you've already showed me. I'd do it all over, you know. The good and the bad . . . it was all worth it."

"I'd do it all over, too . . . but if that ever happens, hold back from kneeing me in the nuts. I'm sure our future children will appreciate it."

She leans away from me and her eyebrows shoot up. "Our future children? Luis, don't get ahead of yourself."

"Why not?" I ask her. "Doesn't the thought of marryin' me give you an adrenaline rush?"

"Yeah," she says, kissing me. "Yeah, it does. You once told me that I make you believe in the impossible. *You* make me believe in love, which I'd given up on. Thank you for proving to me it's not just a fairy tale."

50

Seven months after the shooting, three weeks until we graduate, I look at Luis across our chemistry table. Derek is talking to him, but he's not listening. I know this because he just gave me a wink/smile combo that reminds me of the first time we ever met. I knew the boy was cocky.

What I didn't know is that I'd fall in love with him.

"Nikki, are you paying attention?" Mrs. Peterson, now the mother of a little girl, says as she waves a hand in front of my eyes.

"To what?"

Luis laughs.

"What's so funny, Mr. Fuentes? We're working with acid. Paying attention is crucial. Please keep your relationship out of my classroom."

"Sorry, Mrs. P.," Luis mumbles as he focuses on the task at hand.

Mariana and I take a beaker and follow the instructions. "I can't believe you two are still together," she grumbles. "It's not gonna last, you know."

"I wouldn't bet against us, if I were you," I tell her as I take a dropper and put a small drop of acid on a piece of paper and examine what happens.

I feel Luis's eyes on me, so I look up. He licks his lips suggestively. I would roll my eyes, but instead decide to give him a wink/smile back and lick my own lips to throw him off balance.

"Dude!" Derek yells. "You just spilled acid on your arm!"

My eyes go wide as Luis sucks in a breath, then curses in Spanish as he rushes to the emergency shower in the back of the classroom. I run after him in a panic.

"Are you okay?" I ask.

He's under the shower, rinsing the acid off. "*Chica*, you distracted me."

"Sorry. I didn't mean to."

He smiles weakly. "Yeah, you did. I'll be fine."

I breathe a sigh of relief. "I could never forgive myself if you were permanently scarred."

Mrs. Peterson appears beside me. "Do I need to call an ambulance?" she asks, examining his arm and the red puffiness forming where the acid touched his skin.

"No," Luis says. "I'm okay now. It was just a drop."

"I'm banning you from this experiment and instead assigning you a twenty-five-page paper on acid." She points to me. "You too, young lady. And I'm changing your seats so you two are not facing each other. When are you two going to stop getting in trouble? Soon, I hope. It's a good thing I already had my baby or you would have just scared me enough to send me into labor."

She storms out of the room.

"Come here," Luis says, motioning for me to join him under the spray of the shower.

I step under the showerhead and in seconds I'm as soaked as he is. "What if Mrs. P. comes back here and catches us?" I ask as he bends his head down to kiss me. "You know about her zero tolerance policy. It's in the school policy manual, you know."

He kisses me while the water sprays us. "I've got insider knowledge about that zero tolerance policy," he says against my lips.

"What is it?" I whisper as I hear the final bell ring.

"She's bluffin'," he says. "She wants all of us to graduate."

I'm about to ask him where he got this insider knowledge when Mrs. Peterson appears in the doorway. "Are you two *still* in here?" she asks, rolling her eyes at the sight of us. She cocks an eyebrow. "You are seriously testing my patience. Luis, dry off with that towel on the rack and go to the nurse's office to have your arm checked out. Nikki . . ." She sighs. "What are you doing in here with him?"

"That's a really good question," I say.

"She was helping me," Luis says.

"With what?" Mrs. Peterson asks impatiently, then puts up a hand. "On second thought, don't answer that." She shakes a finger at Luis.

"You Fuentes boys are nothing but a pain in my rear. If you and your brothers ever have more children, make sure they go to another school."

"Fairfield is home," Luis tells her with a cocky grin. "And the best place to raise a family. I wouldn't be surprised if all of our kids went to Fairfield High. Admit it, Mrs. P. You know you'd love that."

"Yes, but . . ." Mrs. Peterson looks up at the ceiling and puts her palms together as if she's praying.

"No need to stress over it now," Luis tells her. "You've got about sixteen years before you'll have my nephew, Paco, in your class."

"What are the chances he'll be more interested in my chemistry class than girls?" she responds.

"Slim to none," Luis answers as he puts his arm around me. "He is a Fuentes, after all."

Epilogue

Luis and Nikki hadn't been prepared when the fertility doctor broke the news that Nikki was pregnant with triplets. They were even more shocked when they found out they were having three boys. Life has been eventful for them over the last eighteen years, with triplets who are distinctly different from one another.

Their son Enrique is so wrapped up in playing the violin and wanting to be the youngest member of the Chicago Symphony Orchestra that he doesn't have time to get in trouble. Then there's Juan, who is just like his uncle Ben. Juan is a gamer and an avid reader, preferring to live out his adventures in fantasy worlds created by game designers.

Luis and Nikki's biggest challenge right now is Luis, Jr.—or Junior, as everyone calls him. He is competitive and hot-tempered, which reminds Luis of Carlos. Junior is a charismatic and good-looking kid. When he walks into a room, heads turn—reminding Luis of Alex. Unfortunately, Junior is also too smart and cocky for his own good, which reminds Luis of himself at eighteen.

Junior is also an incredible athlete. At the age of five he begged his parents for hockey skates after watching the Chicago Blackhawks win the Stanley Cup. At the age of ten, he was playing goalie for the AAA travel hockey team. Now, in his senior year of high school, Junior's team has made it all the way to the state championships.

On the day of the championship game, Junior is nervous, more nervous than he'd been when his dad spent four months on the international space station two years ago. Junior wants to win this game badly. He knows college scouts will be attending, and he desperately hopes to play college hockey and eventually get drafted into the NHL.

Junior came to the rink early today so he can run drills before the other players take the ice. He sits on the locker room bench after stripping off his street clothes. This is going to be the biggest game of his hockey career. He knows it, and his family knows it. All of his uncles and cousins are coming to the game . . . even Uncle Carlos and Aunt Kiara have flown in with his cousins from Colorado to attend the game. It will be one hell of a night, ending with him either celebrating his ass off with a win or depressed as hell with a loss.

Junior reaches into his hockey bag to pull out his equipment just as a girl barges into the locker room—without knocking. If Junior were self-conscious or insecure, he'd probably have pulled out his jersey and held it over his briefs.

But he isn't.

The hot *mamacita* standing in the doorway has long, straight hair that falls in her face and thick, pouty lips that belong on a movie star. He bets she's a groupie of the Giants' first-string goalie, Dale Jacoby, who bragged about the number of girls he dated and screwed in the locker rooms of various rinks around the country. Junior had played on the same team with Jacoby when they were kids. Now they were opponents from rival high schools who were about to play against each other in the state championships.

Jacoby was in the news recently because he was handpicked by the Olympic hockey coach to try out for the US Olympic team. Junior wasn't jealous. At least that's what he told himself when he'd heard the news.

Obviously the bimbo standing in the doorway is thinking this is either the girls' bathroom or a place to meet Jacoby for a quickie before the game.

"Locker rooms are for players only," Junior tells the bimbo, annoyed.

"Duh," she says with attitude, walking farther into the room. Junior glances up and notices that she's carrying a hockey bag and has goalie pads slung across her shoulder.

"Can't Jacoby carry his own equipment?" Junior asks her.

The girl sets down the bag and pads in the middle of the room, right in front of his. "I'm sure he could, if he hadn't broken his leg at a party last night."

What? Jacoby broke his leg? Junior hadn't heard a word about it. He knew less than nothing about the Giants' new second-string goalie, who he'd never played against. "So who's playin' in his place?"

The girl unzips the bag and pulls out a neck guard and chest protector. "You're looking at her."

Junior can't help the laugh that escapes from his mouth. "You're a girl."

She quickly glances at the bulge in his briefs. "And you're a boy. Now that we've got that straight, I'll just let you know that I would use a girls' locker room, but they don't have one at this rink. And the other locker room is being cleaned for the next half hour . . . I guess there was a peeing contest in there when the Pee Wee league played this morning. They told me to dress in here. Just keep your eyes to yourself."

Junior looks at her, stunned. "Don't the Giants have a second-string goalie named Frankie Yates?"

"Ever hear of female hockey players?" she asks him, clearly annoyed. "Or have you lived in a cave your entire life? My name is Franchesca Yates . . . Frankie for short."

"I haven't lived in a cave, *chica*," Junior tells her. "I'm all for girl hockey players, especially ones as hot as you."

Her face scrunches up, like she's smelling something really bad. "Are you . . . hitting on me?"

She walks up to him then, standing toe to toe. She isn't as tall or muscular as he is, but she definitely stands straight and confident. He likes confidence in a girl, but this one needs to be brought down a peg. Part of playing hockey is psyching out your opponents before the game and talking trash during the game. It's tradition. Just because Frankie Yates is a girl doesn't mean she's exempt from the same treatment he'd give to Jacoby.

He'd just psych her out in a different way, because she's a girl.

"What do you say we get together after the game?" Junior tells her as he reaches out and fingers a strand of her hair. He knows he's affecting her just like he affects a lot of girls . . . he can tell by the way her breath hitches as his fingers accidentally brush against her cheek. "I can, you know, console you when you lose."

Before he has time to blink, the girl clocks him. Her fist lands solidly on his lip. She obviously has brothers who taught her how to fight.

"What the hell . . . ," he says, swiping his now busted lip with the back of his hand and seeing blood.

She backs away and shrugs. "Don't mess with me, Fuentes. And if you think you've got an easy win ahead of you, think again. I've seen you play before, and I wasn't that impressed."

"Well, I've never seen you play, so you're obviously not used to playin' with the big boys."

She laughs in a mocking tone. "I'm a transfer student from Minnesota, Fuentes. *Minnesota*. You know, that little state that breeds NHL players. Hockey is in our blood. I've played with girls who can skate circles around you, so it's you who'll need consoling tonight. I'm just guessing that getting beaten by a girl will crush that overblown ego of yours."

"Bring it," Junior says, then puts on his gear and walks out. Who the hell was she, anyway? He'd never even seen her play, so how good could she be?

Junior's dad and his uncles are standing outside the locker room, waiting for him.

"What happened to your lip?" his uncle Alex asks him. "It's bleedin'."

Uncle Carlos laughs. "I thought hockey players fought *on* the ice, not off of it."

Before Junior can answer, Yates walks out of the locker room in full gear. "Good luck, *Junior*. You'll need it," she says, then taps him on his equipment-padded butt with her goalie stick as she passes him.

Junior points to her. "Can you believe I have to play against that bitch?"

"What did you do to her?" his father asks him, eyeing his bloody lip.

"Nothin'." When his father obviously doesn't believe him, Junior adds, "Okay, I guess I was talkin' trash . . . and maybe I touched her hair."

"Guess she taught you a lesson, huh?" his father says.

A lesson. The last thing Junior wants is to be taught a lesson by the goalie of his rival team. Junior watches her long, blond ponytail sway back and forth against the name YATES on the back of her jersey as she struts down the corridor to the ice. He'd never thought it was possible to strut with hockey gear and skates on, but Yates sure as hell does it . . . and does it well.

After Luis and his brothers exchange knowing looks, they laugh.

Luis met Nikki when he was fifteen, fell in love with her when he was eighteen, and married her when he was twenty-three. The first time they'd met, she'd kneed him in the nuts. Eyeing his son's swollen lip and the intense reaction Junior had to the girl is a clue that there is something brewing beneath the surface that his son isn't even aware of yet.

Passionate, intense relationships are common in their family, and the older Fuenteses know it.

As soon as Junior takes the ice, Alex pats Luis on the shoulder. "You know what's about to happen, don't you?"

Luis nods.

"Look on the bright side," Carlos says. "She's got one hell of a right hook. With her on your team, your family is bound to win the annual Panty Discus tournament."

The three Fuentes brothers walk into the stands, proud fathers and husbands who dedicated their lives to their families.

They have no clue their mother, sitting next to their stepfather, Cesar, tears up every time her boys and their families get together. A long time ago she'd given up hope that her sons would live happily ever after. Their troubled, painful past has been behind them for a while now . . .

. . . and the future of the Fuentes family looks brighter than ever.

ACKNOWLEDGMENTS

Thank you to Emily Easton and the entire staff at Walker Books for Young Readers for letting me write about the three Fuentes brothers. *Perfect Chemistry*, *Rules of Attraction*, and *Chain Reaction* are the books of my heart and they mean the world to me.

A huge shout-out of thanks goes to my agent, Kristin Nelson, who kept me sane throughout the past nine months.

I want to express my sincere gratitude and thanks to Jose Ibarra and Josh Arroyo for letting me into your homes and your lives while I was doing research, and to Mia Searles, who introduced me to you both.

Marc Leavitt, a friend and detective in the gang homicide and sex crimes division in the Chicago Police Department, fitted me with a bulletproof vest and took me into the most dangerous neighborhoods in Chicago. It was an eye-opening experience that I'll never forget. Marc, you are the toughest guy I know and a true hero!

My good friend Ed Sanchez spent a lot of time with me going through the Spanish in this book. I take full credit for any mistakes I've made, as they are purely my own, but I hope I've made you proud!

As always, thank you to Ruth Kaufman, Karen Harris, and Erika Danou-Hasan for reading draft after draft and for listening to me cry and whine when Luis and Nikki didn't do what I wanted. Other friends and family that I need to thank for putting up with me are Marilyn Brant, Sara Daniel, Lisa Laing, Amy Kahn, Randi Sak, Marianne To, Jonathan Freed, Liane Freed, Michelle Movitz, Brandon Sak, Lori Cooper, Adina Adelman, Pam Adelman, Nanci Martinez, Kevin Martinez, Wendy Wilk, and Meko Miller.

A special shout-out to my amazing assistant, Melissa Hermann, who helps me in too many ways to mention. I owe you a spa day!

Alexander F. Rodriguez and Giancarlo Vidrio played Alex and Carlos in my book trailers . . . thank you both so much for making my heroes come to life!

I want to thank Moshe, Samantha, Brett, and Fran . . . I know this journey hasn't been an easy one and I appreciate your understanding while I've been working day and night on this book.

My fans are why I keep writing novels, and I love hearing from them. Keep the fan letters coming! Visit me on Facebook and on my website at www.simoneelkeles.net.

Find out how Carlos and Kiara first met in . . .

Kiara has always tried to keep the world at bay, so when Carlos is sent to live with her family, she's happy to keep her distance; Carlos is sure that Kiara thinks she's too good for him, which is fine, because he's not interested anyway, right?

But as the connection between them becomes undeniable, can they overcome their fears and realise that sometimes opposites really do attract?

Read all about Alex and Brittany's love story in . . .

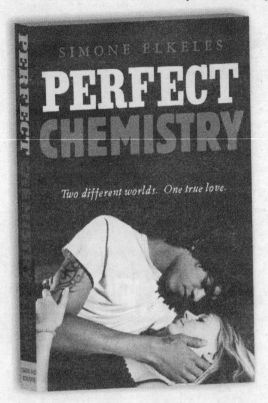

Brittany Ellis and Alex Fuentes couldn't be more different; she's the "perfect" cheerleader living a life of luxury and he's a gang member from the wrong side of town. But when they are forced together by a school project, sparks begin to fly and both Alex and Brittany realise that sometimes appearances can be deceptive.

Will their emerging feelings be enough to keep them together when the world is determined to tear them apart?